D0288602

THE
SECRET
ROOM

The Secret Room

BETH KANELL

The Secret Room

Published by Voyage, an imprint of Brigantine Media
211 North Ave., St. Johnsbury, Vermont 05819
Phone: 802-751-8802
Email: neil@brigantinemedia.com
Website: www.brigantinemedia.com

Cover and Book Design by Jacob L. Grant

ISBN 978-0-9826644-2-1

For Marion
a friend indeed

STARTING SCHOOL RIGHT after Labor Day weekend closed off the summer. All the months of open time vanished into a teacher's discussion question: "What did you do last summer?" And it didn't add up to a lot. At least, not for me. My family never goes on vacations. Summer on the farm is work time, and even though I walk in the woods, swim at the pond, and escape sometimes to the old treehouse that my brothers built at the edge of one of our fields, there's never much of anything to put into an essay. So the first weeks of school didn't really count.

Luckily, my life changed after a month of eighth grade. In the first week of October, really the start of autumn, I helped to measure the foundation of Thea Warwick's house.

It was a school assignment. Mrs. Labounty, who teaches math for all the middle schoolers, is really into hands-on learning, and every Friday she gives us a "project." Mostly they're things you do on your own, but sometimes she makes us work in groups, which as far as I'm concerned is about the worst thing a teacher can do. Leave me alone and I can always earn an A. But group and team projects—nobody wants to work with me really, so either I have to do the whole thing for the group and everyone gets an A from what I've done, which if you ask me is truly unfair, or else I stay quiet and let the group sink. Once last year I tried that, and the teacher gave everyone in the group a C, including me. And I am absolutely never a C student.

Anyway, I felt things might not be as bad as usual when Mrs. Labounty said, "Shawna Lee and Thea, you live close enough to do this one together." Thea's not so bad, really. New, and pretty smart, and thin of course. Everyone who moves here from out of state is thin, I've noticed. Last week Thea even stood in the lunch line with me, because we're the only two girls in grade eight who can do math in our heads, and it was square roots that week in class, which was especially cool because we both got it. So we practiced out loud while we waited in line.

Plus, Thea hasn't said anything about me being, well, fat.

So this afternoon, we needed to measure the foundation. The idea was to measure the outside of the house first, draw it, and then measure each of the rooms and map them. For extra credit, calculate the square footage taken up by the walls inside the house. Of course, that's the difference between what you get for the room sizes and what you get for the outside house size. I could write the equation, but who needed to? It was so simple. We didn't even discuss whether we'd do the extra credit part, we just knew, both of us, that because it was numbers, it would be fun.

The thing was, the numbers weren't coming out right. Not the extra credit part—that would come at the end. I mean, the numbers for the room sizes on the first floor weren't coming out to match the foundation we'd already drawn, which was the outside of the cellar walls. At least, we'd tried the best we could; a couple of rooms at Thea's house have been added on and in some places you can see where bits aren't original, sometimes even with cement blocks and stuff under them. We knew we should do the outside measurements over again and draw the add-ons more carefully. But because it was a rainy October day in Vermont, even at five o'clock the cold wet weather and dimness made measuring the outside again a real pain.

So we measured the inside of the cellar instead. Spiderwebs and dusty strings of spider silk made this very icky, frankly. I give Thea credit—she slapped any spiders she saw with the back of her notebook and kept hold of the measuring tape. I hate it when other girls scream and run and leave me looking like I'm not a real girl, just because I stand my ground and don't run away. That's not fair, either.

"Twenty-two feet, nine inches," Thea read off the tape, squinting in the light of a flashlight as she held the tape tight into the dim corner of the furnace area. "Mark it down for width." She put down the flashlight and reached up to twist her long, nearly black hair into a knot. She can do it without even an elastic.

I wrote down the numbers on my page. We could copy them over into her notebook, too, when we got upstairs. "Length?"

"Just a minute, let me climb up on the dresser so I can get around the water tank with the measuring tape." We'd need to get the length in five measurements and add them up. Thea's house used to be a stagecoach inn here in North Upton, and it's really, really long. The cellar is five rooms long. Really big rooms, honest.

I made a quick chart in my notebook. Room 1: twelve feet exactly. Room 2: ten feet four inches. We rounded off fractions of inches. Room 3 (half full of split wood for the living room woodstove): seventeen feet eight inches. Room 4: fifteen feet exactly. Room 5: ten feet six inches.

I changed all the feet into inches by multiplying by twelve, and added the total. "Seven hundred and seventy eight inches. What about the walls in between the rooms?"

Thea pushed her hair out of her eyes and squinted again, standing between rooms 4 and 5. "Five inches thick," she decided finally. "Each. So twenty inches for the four dividing walls."

"Umm. Wait a minute. Seven hundred and ninety-eight inches, then. Sixty-six feet and six inches. Six six six. Eeyou."

"What is it?"

"Oh, you know, in the Bible. The number of the Beast is supposed to be six six six." I could see from her face, though, she didn't know what I was talking about. That's the trouble with new people in town. My mother says none of them really know their Bible.

I told her I'd explain some other time. Bending over the notebook, I compared the numbers to the ones from the upstairs rooms, and groaned. "We're almost five feet off. We have to do it over."

I tugged the waistband of my jeans up in back and tucked my t-shirt back into the pants, pulling my sweatshirt down. Thea shook her head and pointed the flashlight down at my notebook page. "Add it again," she suggested. "On the paper. You watched me measure it, we can't be off by a whole five feet." But on paper, we were. When we measured the second time, the numbers came out exactly the same way, five feet wrong.

That's how we found the secret room, of course. The secret room at the north end of the cellar of the old North Upton Inn, with the boarded up entrance, the doorway so short we climbed into it with our heads bent down practically to our chests, and for a long moment I was afraid I'd be stuck in the doorway, my jeans dragging against the rough stonework and my sweatshirt getting absolutely filthy with more spiderwebs and dust.

I pushed on in, and in the beam from Thea's flashlight, we both saw the numbers and the letters on the wall at the same moment.

"A code," I breathed out, barely whispering.

"A code," Thea agreed. At that moment, we both knew what we'd do next. Look for clues, and solve the code. Of course.

SOLVING ANYTHING, FROM a math problem to a mystery, comes down to clues and evidence. Thea held the flashlight, while I copied the numbers and letters from the wall into my notebook. There were a lot of them. That's a good thing: A code where you only have a few letters or numbers on a piece of paper is much harder to solve than one where you're looking at lots of messages. When there's a lot that's been said, as long as it's in English, you can pick out groups that happen often and guess at what they might be. Like, in English anyway, there are really only two words that happen a lot that have just a single letter in them: *I*, and *a*. Thea and I made some guesses as we marked down what was on the wall. But time ran short—I could smell chicken cooking and knew supper must be almost ready. Thea had already invited me to stay, so we could do homework together for longer.

Thea's mother, Mrs. Warwick, called down the cellar stairs before we'd finished copying all of it. Quickly we agreed we'd come back later and get the rest of the code onto paper, and we propped the old boards so they blocked the opening into the secret space. Still, we had enough to start with, I was sure.

"Girls, come set the table," Mrs. Warwick warbled at us as we emerged into her kitchen, swiping bits of spider silk from our hair.

I didn't see Thea's brothers, but I could hear their voices along with a TV. They're younger than Thea: Thaddeus is ten, and Teddy's just three. Mrs. Warwick started to hand us plates, then pulled them back and sent us to wash our hands first. It was my first time there, so I just followed along. It turned out the Warwicks have two bathrooms, one downstairs that doesn't have a bathtub or shower, and the other one upstairs. Thea and I washed our hands downstairs, and as I looked down the hallway toward the TV sound, which was the news, I realized that was the room over our hidden room in the cellar.

"Do you think your father or your brothers heard us?" I asked Thea.

She frowned. "No way. The TV is way too loud, and anyway even if they did, it's no big deal. Dad said he won't mess with the wood much until Thanksgiving. And Mom's not going to let the boys go down to the cellar."

"Right."

Thea tugged off her smudged sweatshirt, dropping it into a laundry hamper, and I brushed off the dust from my own as best I could. My sweatshirt was just an ordinary one, green with a blue logo for North Upton School; Thea's, though, had a Hard Rock Café logo on it, and when she pulled it off, I noticed her T-shirt said University of Vermont—I wondered how she got it. A length of red string with a bead carved in the shape of a turtle hung at her throat. People from down-country wear necklaces and even earrings on ordinary days, not just for church, I've noticed. I told her, "I like that turtle."

"Thanks! I got it at Disney World. Come on, we better get back to help."

We laid out the silverware and carried the plates as Mrs. Warwick filled them with grilled chicken on top of some kind of salad, except for Thea's plate, where she put a handful of grated cheese. Thea is a vegetarian. I handed the boys their dishes and put my own down where Thea pointed. A white dressing coated the lettuce, and I could see black olives and what looked like bits of toast mixed into the salad. It looked pretty weird for supper, to me. I mean, where were the potatoes or macaroni? And the bread?

Oh. The bread arrived in a basket a moment later, and so did the boys, and Mr. Warwick. Aside from his bushy black eyebrows, he came as just a bigger size of Thaddeus, dark hair falling into his eyes and thin shoulders. Skinny. And glasses.

"So," Mr. Warwick said as he boosted Teddy up onto a higher chair and strapped him in, "what have you young women been doing this afternoon? Homework?"

"Just math," Thea told him. I nodded.

"Algebra? Geometry? Calculus?"

We looked at each other and grinned. I answered, "We don't do calculus until high school. I guess we're doing algebra and geometry at the same time—we're measuring the perimeters and areas of rooms in your house, and mapping the rooms too."

"Great! I'd like to see that when you finish. Barb," he said to his wife, "pass the bread down this way, please."

I looked at the salad on my plate, and wondered if maybe it was some kind of separate salad course, with the main course coming after. But if it was just salad, why was the chicken on top of it? I was baffled. Nobody else asked anything, they just ate it, with their forks, so that's what I did, too. It was good; warm chicken on top of salad, though, that was pretty strange, I thought. The little black olive rings scattered in the lettuce leaves tasted salty and good. When Mr. Warwick passed the bread, I took two slices and found the butter to spread on them.

"I don't have any homework," Thaddeus announced, sitting across the table from me. "I did mine at school. Can I watch TV, Mom?"

"Not tonight," Mrs. Warwick said. "It's a school night. Do you have something you can read?"

"Yeah, I guess." He looked disappointed for a minute, then

started to take his piece of bread apart and make little bread "pills" out of the soft inside.

I asked Thea, "Is that the rule for every school night? No TV?"

"Yeah. But sometimes we have videos on school nights, if there's time."

More weird stuff. What was Thea going to think if she came over to visit at my house, where the television never went off until bedtime? Not that I watched much of it when there was homework to do. Well, I decided, if I knew ahead of time that Thea was coming over, I could talk with Mom and Harry about keeping the TV off maybe for that evening. Big maybe. Getting to be friends with Thea Warwick wasn't going to be easy, I could tell.

When we all finished our salad, we passed the plates to Mrs. Warwick, who took them to the kitchen. She came back with dessert: carrot cake and chunks of apples and oranges in a big bowl that she put in the middle of the table. The cake was good, but it was hard to eat it as slowly as everyone else. I filled in with some apple slices to slow down.

Mrs. Warwick wiped Teddy's face and hands with a wet washcloth and let him run around. Then she turned to Thea and asked, "How was history today?"

"Better," Thea said. "The boys didn't goof off so much, now that we're done with the Boston Tea Party and all that. And next week we're doing the Civil War."

"Seems pretty fast, getting from the Revolution to the Civil War in a week or so," Mr. Warwick put in. "Any projects to go with all this?"

"Well," Thea started, and I said with her, "there's the History Fair."

We explained about the competition, how everyone had to do something about American history, from the Pilgrims to the end of the Civil War. "I think it's, like, a new program for our school," I added. "Some of the projects will go on to the state History Fair in March. So we're supposed to do research on our topics this fall, and then teach each other, in small groups, and that's going to be part of our grade, too."

Thea's parents made approving comments. Mr. Warwick said to Thea, "Why don't you look up some things about our house? I read in the town history that when our house was an inn, people met here to plan their politics. Maybe you can find something about the Civil War and our own inn."

"Cool!" Thea jumped right at it. She turned to me and said, "Have you picked a topic yet?"

"No," I admitted. "I was sort of thinking I might read that book, *Uncle Tom's Cabin*, and maybe write something on slavery, you know? But I haven't signed up for it yet."

"Wonderful, Shawna," Mrs. Warwick said. "And are you going to do a local angle for it, too? Like maybe the Underground Railroad?"

I didn't know what she was talking about. Actually, I guess I didn't really remember it from grade four history, the last time we'd done Vermont at school. But when she started to talk about it, even with Teddy running around making noise, it came back to me some. Mrs. Warwick told about white Americans who saw how bad slaves had it, how they helped them to escape from the Southern plantations, to escape all the way north to Canada. People from New England stood up for freedom, the way they always had. I don't know why it was called a railroad, though. It wasn't with trains at all.

Mr. Warwick, standing up from the table, nodded enthusiastically to his wife. "Probably even this village helped out," he commented. "Of course, by the time escaped slaves got this far north, I imagine they felt pretty safe. But I've read that some of the towns hid them from Boston slave hunters, and why not here, too?"

He headed out of the dining room, and Mrs. Warwick already was washing the dishes and calling out something about Thea taking Teddy upstairs for his bath. I didn't see him. I didn't know where Thaddeus had gone, either.

But that didn't matter. What mattered was Thea and me,

staring at each other and wondering, with Thea holding one finger to her lips in case I didn't know to keep quiet about it, and pointing with the other hand toward the far end of the house and down.

A hiding place? Could the secret room be a hiding place for escaped slaves?

I whispered, "Let's go work on the code."

She nodded, and together we ran upstairs to her bedroom, where she piled a bunch of big cushions on the floor, and we copied the code out of the notebook onto two separate pieces of paper so we could both have it.

This could be really big. This could be the History Fair project that would win first prize, not just at our school but for the state fair, too. And we had a real secret to work on. And best of all, as far as I was concerned, it looked like Thea's history project and my project would fit right into each other. We had more than just a math project here, for sure. This could be the start of a real best friend. For a moment I remembered how awful seventh grade had been, trying to be friends with Marsha Willson and always knowing she and her twin sister Merry were laughing about me behind my back. Then I pushed the memory away, and focused on Thea Warwick instead. A friend who liked math. And me.

I was so excited, I almost didn't feel hungry.

OUTSIDE, RAIN WHIPPED in sheets against the house. Through Thea's windows I could hear the wind, too. Her bedside lamp, sitting on the floor next to us, lit the pages enough to see clearly. Numbers. Letters. Mixed together.

I pulled a pencil stub out of my back pocket and started to circle similar clusters on the page. "These have got to be dates," I guessed. Thea agreed.

"But there are a lot of them," she pointed out. "So it's got to be more like a list than, you know, sentences and paragraphs."

"What about directions, or where somebody's going to go?" I imagined an escaped slave in the hiding space. "Wouldn't they want to tell people where to find them later? Like in Canada or something?"

"Can't be." Propped on her elbows, Thea shook her head emphatically. "I mean, I'm thinking about it, Shawna. They probably didn't even know really where Vermont was, even though they were here, and I don't think they'd know enough about Canada to code the places there. Think how lost we'd feel if we were in, like, Tennessee or something. But names, they'd want to put their names, right?"

Definitely. Names and dates. Up behind our farm, on the ridge, our family had a hunting camp—a cabin—and everyone's names were on the wall, with their birthdays, and how many deer they got and whether it was a buck. That's important for hunting season.

"Look for J," I suggested. "Like John, and Joseph, and Jeremiah. Bible names. If it was the old days, there were lots of Bible names."

Thea pounced. "Here. And here." She underlined each one and the letters that followed. "What about J, then this little n?"

An image of a cemetery stone flashed in my mind. "When you saw it on the wall, did the little n have a line under it?" I asked eagerly. "And was it sort of up, compared to the J?"

She looked blankly at me. "I don't know. You saw it too. Why, what would that mean?"

I drew for her what I was remembering: A J with a little n that had a line under it, pushing it up. And then a W with a little m. "John. William. See? That's how the old gravestones show it. To save the stone-cutting time, I bet, but maybe people did it even on paper back then."

Thea found five places where there was a J, then a little n. And one—I saw it first—a W with a little m.

Even while we marked them, even while we knew we were on the right track, it was like both of us realized at the same moment: It wasn't math at all, but some kind of list of complicated abbreviations.

"But we still have more numbers to figure out," I said, trying to look for the bright side. "Those can't all be dates. Maybe there's still a code in here somehow." Just a list of names and dates would definitely not be as interesting as something that included equations. But it would still mean figuring it all out.

So we circled and underlined, looking this time for what was left.

"All the numbers are under a hundred," Thea pointed out.

"Yeah." I started to write a list of the numbers on a separate sheet of paper.

"Are they prime numbers? Or squares?"

"Hmm. No, I don't think so. But—" a quick look back at our original page—"Thea, look how many of these are products of twelve. See?"

"You're right! Thirty-six; twelve; forty-eight." She wrinkled one of the pages as she grabbed it closer. "Shawna, look for products of six instead. That brings in lots of the other numbers, right?"

She was right. So maybe there was something hidden in the numbers after all.

I rolled over, head on a huge fluffy pillow, staring at the ceiling. What would be coded into products of six? "Eggs," I said out loud. "Dozens and half dozens. But you'd count those out in the barn."

Thea took another sheet of paper. "There are things we need to know," she announced. "I'm making a list."

Number 1: Check the little letters. Are they raised up and underlined like on the gravestones? "That would prove they're old, too," I mentioned. Thea nodded and wrote *Old* next to the question.

Number 2: Is it all one person's handwriting? "What do you mean?" I asked her.

"Well, if it's all one person, then somebody was making a list. Like maybe how many slaves were hiding there and how long. But if there are different handwritings, then maybe it's the escaped slaves leaving messages."

"Okay. Good."

Number 3: What years are the dates? "We have to prove these are from before the Civil War," I emphasized.

Number 4: Who could get easily to the cellar when this house was an inn?

We lay on the pillows, thinking about that and imagining. I asked Thea, "Does your father have a copy of the town history? We could start there, find out who was running the inn, and who the closest neighbors were."

"I think so. Let's go get the book."

"Wait a minute." I grabbed her arm, then pulled my hand

back quickly. Some people freak out if you touch them. "Sorry. I mean, let's think of more things first, before we go downstairs. Because it's almost eight o'clock and I'll have to go home. I think my mom and Harry have a copy of the history, too. We could both read it tonight."

"Yeah, that's good. Wait a minute—who's Harry again?"

"My mom's husband," I answered. "He came from New Hampshire."

"Oh yeah, right. I couldn't think for a minute if maybe that was your brother."

"Carl," I told her. "The brother who's on the farm is Carl. The other one's Emerson."

She rolled back onto her stomach, and wrote the names down. "Now I'll remember better." Thea tipped her head to one side. "We could work on this over at your house tomorrow," she offered. "I mean, it's Saturday."

"Maybe," I said cautiously. "After lunch, I guess." The afternoon would be good, because then Mom would make cookies or something. But I wasn't supposed to invite people for a meal without permission. And besides, sometimes Mom and Harry just wanted to unwind after working all day in the barn. I thought fast. "But we need to do more research in your basement first, don't we? To check the handwriting?"

"Sure. Okay, let's meet tomorrow after lunch here, while there's more light. Oh no, you know what?" Thea sat up in a hurry. "We have to finish the math project this weekend, too. We have to make the drawing and write it up."

"I'll do the drawing at my house," I offered. "I can take a copy of the measurements with me. You write out the equations for Mrs. Labounty. All right?"

"Good." And at the same moment, we both said, "But!"

We laughed together. We knew what we both were about to say: No secret room in the drawing or the math. We'd just make the north room larger by six feet in the drawing and the equations.

For now, this was our own secret.

It was five minutes to eight. I hurried to copy the measurements, and stuffed the paper into my backpack, tying the flap across to keep everything dry. "I've got to go. See you tomorrow."

Thea ran down the stairs with me, and stood at the kitchen door. Behind her I could hear her mother calling, and with a last quick wave, she shut the door and vanished inside the house.

EVEN THOUGH IT was all the way dark out now, and raining, the first part of the wet road had patches of light on it from the front windows at Thea's house. I managed to not step in any really big puddles for that part. Then there was a dark part, not too far, but enough so I felt my sneakers get really wet. I held the bookbag under my arms, curving my body over it as I hurried.

Part of our farm was exactly across the road from Thea's. Unfortunately, that was the part with the little vegetable stand and, behind it, the manure pit. I had to go through the dark around the littler barn to get to the house at the far end. I cut across the grass and the cold seeped to my feet and legs, with the water from the wet grass soaking my jeans and socks. Past the barn corner, the light from the back porch lit my way.

One of the cats stood up and meowed at me, stretching, then darted toward the back door and waited for me to open it. I stepped into the warm, dim kitchen and put my bookbag down so I could pull off my sneakers by the door.

Mom and Harry nodded to me from their twin recliner

chairs just inside the living room, where the blue light of the TV flickered. It sounded like a game show on, maybe *Wheel of Fortune*. Mom called out, "There's chocolate cake still, honey. Help yourself. And make sure you drink some milk, no soda." She always said milk was the healthiest drink. Since I was her "surprise" late-life baby, I guess she figured she had to take special care of me.

Harry said, "Did you kids get all your homework done?"

"Mostly," I called back to him. "I just have a little bit to finish." I was supposed to get homework done on Friday night if I could, because Saturday was always busy and Sunday was church, of course. But if there was a lot of reading, I could finish that on Sunday afternoon or evening. I'm good at planning how it all fits together.

I turned on the light over the kitchen table and pulled out my notebooks and the page of house measurements. On the side table past the sink, where the breadbox and the boxes of cereal huddled, I spotted the big cake holder with its rubbery Tupperware top. From the dish rack I pulled a cereal bowl, wide and deep, and cut a slice of cake. Then, thinking about how strange supper had been, I poured a glass of milk.

"Make sure the fridge shuts all the way," Mom called. She could tell what I was doing from the sounds in the kitchen, even when I was around the corner from her.

"Got it," I called back.

"Good girl." Somebody turned the TV sound up higher.

I pulled my papers toward the other end of the kitchen table, well away from the the angle of the TV, and dug for a ruler in the pencil-and-scissors jars by the phone. Then I settled down to draw Thea's house: outside dimensions, first floor, basement. It was hard to draw the walls with some thickness because of the proportions I was using: Thea's house, with the attached sheds and all, was nearly eighty feet long. The paper was eight and a half inches across, and eleven inches long. I turned it to draw the house along the longer direction of the page and tried a couple of numbers. If I made the drawing eight inches long, there would be ten feet of house to each inch. So a five-inch wall would be, how much, in the drawing? Five twelfths of one tenth of an inch. Ick.

I changed the proportions. Suppose the house uses ten inches across the length of the page. Then that's eight feet of house per inch of paper. One foot of house per one-eighth of an inch. A five-inch-thick wall would be about half a foot thick, or one-sixteenth inch of the page. I looked at the tiny divisions of the ruler and knew I couldn't really make the walls that thin on the paper.

Sighing, I stood up and scrounged in Mom's "everything drawer" close to the phone and found a roll of Scotch tape. It wasn't the clear "magic" kind, just the thick sticky stuff. So I'd have to use it in a way where I wouldn't need to mark on it, because you can't write in pen or in pencil on that thick old stuff. Okay, I could handle it.

I fastened two sheets of paper together, end to end, with a long strip of tape on the back, and two short bits on the front, near the edge. Then I started again on drawing Thea's house. This time, with two inches of paper for every eight feet of house, I could make the walls show up as having about half a foot of thickness.

Working slowly, and sharpening my pencil often, I got the first floor and outside dimensions drawn. I inked over them with a ballpoint pen. Another two pages taped together gave me the space for drawing the basement.

Mom's hand on my shoulder made me jump.

"Sorry, honey, I thought you heard me," she said with a little laugh. "Hey, that looks good. Is that the inn?"

"Yeah, where the Warwicks live," I said. "I'm almost done."

"Good. Harry and I are headed to bed. It's been a long day. Make sure you turn the lights out when you're done. And bed by ten, okay?"

"Okay."

Mom leaned over the table and put a finger on the first floor drawing. Her hands were rough from working with the cows and washing them so often, and the paper rasped as she touched it. "So that's the kitchen now?" I had labeled each room and marked the dimensions.

"Uh-hunh. It's pretty big."

"Used to be bigger," she said, surprising me. "Used to be a canning kitchen off the back, over here." She pointed to the rear of the house. "And the tavern was in here." The Warwick living room.

"You mean it was still an inn when you were a little girl?"

She smiled. "Even when I was a teenager. But the fire happened in the summer kitchen and part of the regular kitchen, and the inn closed up, long before I started dating your—" she coughed, "your father. So I can't say I ever did spend much time there. Not after I was married, anyway."

I found the page of measurement notes. "So Mom, what year was that fire anyway? How old were you then?"

She looked a little away from me, lost in her thoughts, and brushed one hand against her hair, pushing it back behind her shoulder. In the daytime she wore it in braids, pinned up, the gray and black braids circling her head and kept out of the way for baking or barn work. At night, when she sat with Harry, she took out the braids and brushed it all out. She looked just about exactly her age, I thought, forty-eight. I watched her remember and think.

"I guess I was twelve when the inn took fire," she finally said.

I did the math quickly: "Nineteen seventy-five?" I wrote down the fact, to share with Thea tomorrow. "And did you, umm, did you used to explore it or anything, when you were a little girl?"

"Not me! Whenever I got away from the kitchen or the barn, it was the mountain I explored," my mother emphasized. "Get me outdoors and give me a chance, and I was up that hill in a flash."

"Oh yeah. Well, thanks, Mom."

"Sure." She turned toward the stairs, and I heard Harry already on his way up. Then she looked at me again. "I might have some souvenirs from the inn days, still, in the attic," she mused.

"Really? Mom, could I have them? It's for a history project Thea and I are doing!"

"I thought you were doing math?"

"Yeah, tonight it's math. But then we're doing a history project on her house, too." Careful to skirt the secret part, I said, "About the old days and the inn, you know?"

"Sure," she repeated. She yawned, long and wide. "Remind me Sunday afternoon. I'll see what I can find. Is that soon enough?"

I stood up and hugged her for an answer, and she rubbed my head, then mumbled, " G'night, sweetie. God bless. See you in the morning. Brush your teeth before you go to bed."

Nearly nine o'clock. I listened to her slow, heavy footsteps on the stairs, then the shuffles and bumps of Mom and Harry upstairs. Good thing my mother didn't explore the inn in the old days. Still, she knew more about the Thea's house than I'd realized. I wondered what else she might know that she'd never told me.

Calling Thea to tell her we'd have stuff from my mother would be cool. Not until morning, though. It was too late, and besides, Mom might overhear something about our discovery. I didn't want to share it. I stacked my pages carefully, just as Midnight, our mostly black cat, jumped onto the table and purred against my shoulder. He sniffed at the cake crumbs left in the bowl, took one delicately on his paw, and licked it off. I'd better wash my dish. Mom didn't like coming down to dirty dishes at breakfast time.

From my bookbag I pulled out the reading assignment: *Johnny Tremain*. You could tell the teachers had all gotten together on the assignments—this one, even though it was for English class, was set during the Revolutionary War, just as we were covering the same thing in History class. I didn't like the book much, but at least it was easy to read. I settled back at the kitchen table, with another glass of milk, and resolved to get through the next three chapters before going to take my bath.

What would we read in English to go with the Civil War? The book list better include the Underground Railroad, I decided. Of course, *Uncle Tom's Cabin* was on the list; that was the adventure book Miss Calkins had said we could pick if we wanted credit for a Civil War novel. Maybe I should ask Miss Calkins for the whole list in advance.

Even though I was alone in the kitchen, I didn't feel lonely. I had a new friend—maybe even a best friend. Mom and Harry made a few more bumps upstairs, then settled down.

And from the cluttered front of the refrigerator, photos of my older brothers Emerson, twenty-six, and Carl, twenty-five, grinned across at me. Just past the refrigerator, over the sideboard, in a dusty frame, my sister Alice looked serious in her graduation cap and gown, the only college graduate in our family. I did the math: She'd be thirty in less than two years. Too old to really share things like sisters should, I thought. Still, I wondered what it would be like if she ever came home again to visit.

SATURDAY MORNING WAS cold. I woke up just before eight and knew I was being lazy—Mom and Harry always did the barn chores themselves on Saturday mornings to give Emerson a break. I didn't have to get up at five to do chores with them, but still, it wasn't fair if I just stayed in bed, not even doing homework or cooking or something.

So reluctantly, and already guilty about oversleeping, I shoved the blanket and quilt off me and pulled on yesterday's clothes from where I'd dropped them on the floor. Brr, they were cold. Jeans, t-shirt, sweatshirt. Bright sun above the curtain on the window lit some dusty spiderwebs caught on the jeans, and I brushed them off. Thinking of Thea's cellar and the hidden room made me smile.

In front of the wall mirror, I stopped for a moment to pull my brush through my hair. I leaned close to the mirror. "Shaw-nah," I purred at my image. Dark brown eyes fluttered back at me. I imagined some boy, not from the North Upton school but someone older, tall and moody and romantic, bending over to look into my eyes and saying he could look into them forever.

"Shawww–nahh," I stretched it out even further. At least I had a modern name, not like Alice or Emerson or Carl.

I sucked my cheeks in, as if I'd gone on a diet or been to some spa where they remade me. Cheekbones. I pushed against them to make the bones show more, and let my jaw drop just a bit, making my face longer. "That mysterious beauty with her dark deep eyes," went the scene as I let it flow over a page in a magazine.

"Shaww–NAH!" came from the kitchen instead. Mom's voice. "Are you up yet?"

"Coming," I yelled, grabbing a pair of socks and hurtling into the hallway. "Just have to go to the bathroom first!"

"Plug the coffee in! And bring another roll of paper towels out to the barn, would you?" she called as the door slammed shut again, leaving a wave of chilly air that hissed down the hall at toes level.

In the bathroom with the brighter light, I could see two zits starting to swell in the crease between my nose and my cheek, red and hard. Ick. In another day or so, they'd look disgusting. I scrubbed hard at them to convince them to disappear, brushed my teeth, and pulled on the socks.

In the kitchen I plugged in the coffeemaker—Mom had already filled it—and stretched to grab a roll of paper towels from the top shelf of the pantry cupboard. My stomach growled as I stuffed my feet into my barn boots, better than my sneakers, which were crumpled and stiff from getting wet the night before. "Don't go to work hungry," I could hear Mom's voice in my head, "always eat something before you go to the barn," so I grabbed the first thing I saw available, a big blueberry muffin with a crunchy sugared top, stripping the muffin paper off it with a quick twist and chewing as I hurried down the slippery porch steps. Yumm.

Yesterday's rain had left all the ground wet but the storm had vanished. A sharp wind and the blaze of blue sky with small clouds scudding across made this clearly a new weather day. Sun sparkled on the metal barn roof. I headed directly for the gray milkhouse door, partway open the way I knew it wasn't supposed to be. So I shoved it all the way shut behind me once I was inside.

I don't like the smell of the milkhouse: humid and thick with detergent smells and too much chlorine. And the rumbling refrigerator lines for the milk tank keep the little room itself hot and airless. But I love the smell of the barn. So I crossed the cement floor quickly to the inner door and moved with relief into the sawdust-and-cows aromas of the main barn.

Our barn is old, made so that every cow has a place to stand, with her head and neck caught in the dangling metal stanchions but her legs stamping and shuffling, tail swishing. You have to walk behind them and leave enough space so they won't kick, and so what comes out the back end into the gutter—cows poop and pee all the time—isn't going to splash you. That sounds gross, but it's under control: Our barn gets cleaned every day, morning and night, and the gutter-scraping chains carry the waste out into the manure pit. You've got to keep it clean if you want clean milk.

The stomping and complaining of forty cows filled the air. At the far end of the row the thump-pump of a milking machine clued me in on where Harry or Mom must be. I found them at side-by-side cows, each with a milking machine linked by one hose onto the steel vacuum pipe up above and its other hose connected to a low-hanging udder. The cows liked the feeling, the relief of having the milk pulled out of their swollen bags. Mom was just releasing the tit cups from her cow, a big black and white Holstein named Dora.

"Hand me the paper towels, honey," she called to me. "I'm out of them." I passed the roll to her, and she tore off a bunch that she stuffed in a back pocket, giving the rest of the roll to Harry. His cow was a coffee-colored Jersey, smaller and moving around a lot; he dodged her heavy hoof and slapped her backside, grunting at her to move back toward center.

"Thanks," Mom said as she slid the disinfectant dip onto and off each teat of her cow's udder and moved along to the last cow on the row. "And Shawna, you've got time to spread sawdust, haven't you? Harry had to give a couple of injections, so we're behind." She nodded toward the sawdust cart. The thick handle of a scoop shovel stuck out of the mound of grainy cedar sawdust.

Shoot. I didn't want to spend much time in the barn, really. But what could I say? Mom added, "There's a pair of gloves on the other side."

I shoved the cart along the walkway and around the end of the row. Sure enough, the other side of the row didn't have fresh sawdust yet, although most of the space behind the cows was scraped clean of the night's muck. So I dug the scoop into the cart and shoveled out a mound of sawdust, using a long steady swing to hurl it under the first cow's stomach and udder, and more under her rear end. Her tail swished toward me but I ducked and moved to the next animal.

Harry spoke to Mom from the other side of the row. "Aren't you going to tell her?"

"Tell me what?" I asked.

Mom laughed. "I'll tell you, but you can't go see until you finish the row, okay?"

"Okay—what?"

"Kittens! Four," and she bent under the cow and pulled on each teat to get the last bit of milk into the milking cups before detaching them. "They're over by the calves. In the old grain box."

That was enough to speed me down the aisle with my sawdust, dipping and throwing as fast as I could. It didn't really take long. I shoved the cart to one side of the big double doors, hung the scoop on the wall next to it, and bolted to the side part of the barn where half a dozen calves lay tethered. They all began to scramble to their feet and push at me as I came close—they wanted their bottles. I pushed them gently away from my legs, to get past them, and there, sure enough, was our biggest mama cat, the tortoiseshell one, curled inside the hay-filled box, with four tiny blind kittens nestled against her.

Carefully, so the mama cat wouldn't jump out, I touched the hot little head of one baby. Then I pulled back and just watched. Each one of them was a miracle, a breathing, sleepy ball of fur with perfect tiny legs and the stump of a tail. The mama cat glared at me, then licked the kitten that I'd touched.

Thea. Wouldn't she want to see the new kittens? This was better than showing her just a barn full of cows, for sure! I went back to where Harry and Mom were still milking.

"Can I do homework across at Thea's after lunch? And then bring her over later on to see the kittens?"

"Sure, honey," Mom said right away. "You can bring her here for lunch first if you want, there's plenty. And you can make some brownies for a snack for later, too. But you'll have to help me clean the house first, Shawna. Why don't you head into the kitchen and mix up some pancake batter, so we can all have breakfast together in half an hour or so. There's time for a break before the milk truck comes."

After breakfast, Harry went back to the barn to clean out the milking lines and do the paperwork for the milk truck. Meanwhile, my mother and I swept and vacuumed and threw laundry into the laundry room. It went quickly like that, teamwork. Emerson phoned from town to say he was dropping off groceries, so we cleared out the fridge some, too. Using a mix and an extra pack of chocolate chips, I put together the brownies and started them baking, while Mom folded clean clothes.

"Tell me again what you want to know about the inn," Mom suggested. "What's your project about?"

"History. Like, who owned it and what happened there."

She nodded. "You mean who owned it before the Warwicks?"

I shook my head. "Further back than that, because we need to know about it in the really old days, the Civil War and before." I tried to remember what years that would be. "I guess eighteen hundred, maybe, until, well, close to nineteen hundred." I knew that wasn't exactly right but it ought to cover the time.

My mother looked doubtful. "I think it was always the Dearborn place until recently. I don't know a lot about those days." She picked up an armful of jeans and shirts. "Couldn't you try the Historical Society? Down at the library?"

"Yes!" I jumped up and helped her with the rest of the pile of clothes. "That would be perfect! Can I go there now?"

The library was open Saturday mornings, but it closed at lunchtime. I needed to hurry. Luckily, Mom said she'd take the brownies out of the oven for me, if I'd just finish carrying the clean clothes to the bedrooms. I did, and tore out of the house.

Across the road, I knocked hard on the Warwicks' door, and soon Thea and I were racing down the road to the library end of the village school building. The librarian, Mrs. Toussaint, let us in, handed us her bulky green cloth-bound copy of the town history, and then, from a folder marked "1800s," pulled out a stack of old photographs. The fierce creases of her face softened as she spread the photos carefully on her desk and pushed her glasses up her nose.

"There!" Thea pointed to one of her house, with a sign attached that said "North Upton Inn." In the lower corner someone had inked the year: 1852.

Four people stood stiffly on the porch in the photo, and the three of us, Thea and Mrs. Toussaint and I, stared at the faces, wondering who they all were. Suddenly I noticed something even more important, so important I could hardly speak. I pointed, not quite touching the photo, which Mrs. Toussaint protected with a quick gesture of her hand. But we all saw the same thing there.

From an upstairs window, a face, blurred by movement, looked down toward the front lawn of the inn. Even though it was blurred, the short curly hair and the darkness of the face were unmistakably a black person. I took a long breath, and Thea grabbed my hand.

"They were there!" she choked out in a hoarse whisper.

Mrs. Toussaint clicked her tongue and pulled the photo back toward her. "Very observant of you both. I must say, I don't think I ever noticed that face," she mused, looking from Thea to me and back at the picture. "Of course, Barnet, over across the valley, had African-American people staying there in the Underground Railroad days. There's even an Underground Railroad hiding place there, or so people claim. But North Upton? We should seek out confirming details from the town records before we attempt any conclusions, of course. But now that I think about it more ... "

I stood completely still, waiting for Thea to let go of my hand, and waiting for Mrs. Toussaint's next words. She finally said them:

"I suppose you'll want to see the diary next, won't you?"

Thea's eyes were wide as she asked, "A girl's diary? A girl who lived there?"

"No-o," the librarian replied, smiling. "Not a girl's diary. It's the journal of Henry Dearborn. You know, the Dearborns who owned your house all those years. Sit down, both of you, and I'll take the journal out of the case. Are your hands clean?"

We held up our hands to show her, as she stepped across the room to a glass case on a long table. I wanted to crowd up next to her, but instead I perched on the edge of a chair next to the big library desk, and Thea sat next to me. In a moment, a leather-wrapped book about six inches across, with a big tag, tied on with string, lay in front of us on the desk.

"Journal of Henry E. Dearborn, North Upton, January 1850 to November 1873," I read aloud from the tag. "That's a lot of years to put into one book."

Mrs. Toussaint nodded. "Some years he hardly wrote in the book at all. And what he did write is small, so you'll want a magnifying glass." She handed one to Thea. "Don't get your fingers on the glass, use the handle, please. The pages in the second half are the records of his finances at the inn, you'll see—and I'll get you my copy of the town tax records, too, showing his property and the furnishings each year."

While the librarian pulled out more bound books, Thea and I paged carefully through Henry Dearborn's journal. There were no "Dear Diary" parts at all, nothing about how he felt or who he met. Instead, I saw short descriptions of how many guests stayed in a week, and stagecoach arrivals. The thin scraggly handwriting, bunched up to crowd a lot onto each page, looked like a secret code all by itself. And abbreviations in all the sentences made it even harder to read.

Thea read out loud, guessing at some of the words: "Monday, February 15, four inches snow, ten degrees, four a.m. Fourteen for lunch, two roller teams. Twenty-seven in shared rooms, one private room of three ladies." She looked up at Mrs. Toussaint. "Roller teams? What's that?"

"Snow rollers."

"Oh, I know about them," I said, while Mrs. Toussaint pulled out more pictures to show Thea. "Instead of plowing the roads, they rolled the snow flat, right?"

"For the sleighs to travel on, that's correct," the librarian agreed.

Thea looked quickly at the pictures, nodded, and said, "But how old was this Henry Dearborn when he was writing in this book?"

"He was born in eighteen-twenty," came Mrs. Toussaint's answer. "So he was—"

"Thirty when he started this one," Thea calculated quickly. "Then I bet there's an earlier one, too."

"But not with his writing in it. His father kept the earlier one. Samuel Dearborn."

The desk grew crowded with books and pictures, as each time Thea asked a question, Mrs. Toussaint pulled out something more to show. I didn't ask questions. I took notes instead, as fast as I could.

"We need the part before the Civil War," I reminded Thea.

Mrs. Toussaint overheard. "The Civil War began in eighteen sixty-one," she pointed out.

I borrowed the journal book from Thea and turned to the

pages in the back, the lists of numbers and abbreviations that told the business of the inn. And a moment later, I nudged Thea's elbow and, with a finger brushed across my lips to hint to her not to say anything out loud, I pointed to one list in particular: a list that looked an awful lot like what we'd copied down from the secret room in the basement of the Warwicks' house, that is, the Dearborn family's inn.

We looked at each other and just knew it together: This was it. This would let us solve the code from the secret room, for sure.

"Can we borrow this book?" Thea asked Mrs. Toussaint.

"No, dear—everything stays here at the Historical Society." Mrs. Toussaint nodded to emphasize her words, and her steel-rimmed glasses bounced where they hung from a ribbon against her chest. "Everything. So residents can all have access to it. But of course you can copy it down, just like Shawna is doing in her notebook, dear."

"She's Thea Warwick," I reminded Mrs. Toussaint. "It's about her house. Doesn't that make a difference?"

"Not from my point of view, dear. No matter whose house it is, we keep everything here, where we take proper care of it," the librarian announced firmly.

So that was that. I took notes like crazy, while Thea read lists and journal bits out loud to me for at least an hour more. My fingers started to cramp, and my stomach grumbled.

A big clock on Mrs. Toussaint's desk began to count out the time with a bell: Twelve rings. Noon. Mrs. Toussaint said, "Now girls, I'm afraid that's the end of today's open hours. You may come again next Saturday, and I'll keep these books and pictures set aside for you, so you can look at them right away when you come in. Will you both come back next Saturday?"

"Yes ma'am," I said right away, and we pulled our papers together, helped to stack the books, and stepped out of the back door of the schoolhouse, while the librarian finished locking up behind us.

"Come on," I told Thea, "it's time for lunch. We'd better go eat something. Hey, can we sort of change plans, can you come to my house for lunch?"

Right away, Thea said, "Yeah, sure. Just let me stop a moment to tell my mother, and I know she'll say yes."

"It's because I have something to show you," I said, thinking about the new kittens. "In the barn." I didn't say what, just grinned.

"Cool!"

We walked down the road together, talking about the journal and guessing about the coded lists, and I watched our feet scuff the yellow leaves together. Four shoes, two sets of feet, one friendship. No wonder the sunshine glowed so brightly in the red crowns of the autumn maples along our way.

MACARONI AND CHEESE. I could tell, as soon as Thea followed me into our kitchen. It smelled great.

Mom and Harry weren't home, though. A note on the table, next to some plates, said they'd gone to take groceries up to the camp. That's what we call the cabin up on the mountain where almost everyone in my family stays at some point during hunting season. Two more weeks until then. I explained to Thea.

"Wait a minute," she protested. "*Everyone* in your family goes hunting? You and your mom, too? I thought it was just men."

"Nope. And my mom's usually the one who gets the deer, even if nobody else does. She's wicked good in the woods." I added, "I hardly even go to deer camp on the weekends now, because of school. But when I was little, I used to stay for the whole two weeks." Something stopped me from telling Thea about my .22 rifle, though. Her arms crossed over her chest, she looked like she could only handle a little bit about hunting. Well, it was new to her, I could see.

I pulled out the pitcher of milk from the fridge and then used the big padded potholders to lift a foil-covered pan out of the oven. We dished up our own helpings, and I noticed Thea take just a small spoonful onto her plate.

"You can take more, it's okay," I said. "There's lots, and Mom won't mind."

"This is enough for me," she replied.

I decided she must be shy. Nobody would only eat that little bit of macaroni and cheese, with the top all crispy with breadcrumbs. That reminded me—she didn't eat any meat, so maybe she was afraid the food had something that wasn't vegetarian. "It's okay, there's no ham or anything in it this time," I assured her. Then I poured milk into two glasses.

Thea said, "Could I have some juice instead? Like apple cider or orange juice?"

"I guess." I went back to the fridge and brought out a plastic jug of cider. "Don't you like milk?"

"It's all right on cereal. But I'd rather have juice. You know, there's probably milk already in the macaroni and cheese. And cheese of course," she added.

What a weird thing to say! Of course there was milk and cheese in it. I didn't know why that made a difference in what somebody was going to drink. Everybody knows milk is good for you, right?

But this was my new friend and I didn't want her to feel bad about being fussy. So I poured her milk back into the pitcher and rinsed out her glass, so she could drink cider instead.

She looked around while we both ate. She spotted the photos on the fridge. "Are those your brothers?"

"Sure. That's Emerson, the older one. The other one is Carl."

Thea walked over to see better. "Carl's cute," she decided, and giggled when I made a face. She pointed up on the wall. "And is that your mom?"

I laughed. "No, that's my older sister, Alice! She lives in California. My mom's a lot older than that." Over on the TV was a picture from Mom and Harry's wedding, and I brought it over to the table. "Here's my mom, and her husband. From twelve years ago."

She was thinking about the numbers, I could tell. "So," she said casually, "Harry's not your father, though, right?"

"Right. My father died just before I was born. He had a heart attack. Harry was a neighbor who'd moved here from New Hampshire, and he helped Mom keep the farm going. And so after a while they just got married."

"Were they in love?"

What a question! I stared at Thea. "Um, I kind of think when people are older and get married, maybe it's not so much because they're in love. I mean, they were really already over that at their age, probably. You know?"

Thea nodded, but she didn't look convinced. It made me wonder. I'd never imagined Mom and Harry in love. They just always were together, so they got married, was what I figured. God said a man and a woman should help each other, and that meant they should get married. Right?

"Anyway," I said, "it worked out pretty well for everybody. And Harry's okay, he's got a good sense of humor and he works hard." I put our dishes in the dishpan. "Hey, let's go out to the barn, we've got new kittens!"

So out we ran. And it turned out Thea had been in barns before, didn't mind the smells, and loved kittens as much as I do. Besides, it was perfect to be just the two of us, scratching the youngest calves' noses, telling the mama cat what a good mother she was being, and watching the tiny babies pushing against each other to nurse from their mother's swollen rows of nipples.

With one thing and another, it was almost two o'clock when we got back to Thea's house, with our notes and a packet of my brownies, to finish our math homework together. We worked on it in her room, so her brothers wouldn't bother us. Then we pulled out the lists—the one from the basement of the inn, from the hidden room, and the ones we'd copied from Henry Dearborn's journal of the inn. And we began to de-code for real.

The first big breakthrough came when we matched part of the stage line schedule—clear enough from Mr. Dearborn's notes about arrivals—to the dates we could see in our list. It looked like the list from the secret room matched some of the arrivals for spring of eighteen hundred fifty-two. In fact, almost every time there was a stage arrival with more than a dozen or so people, there was something written in the secret room.

"So maybe it was easier to hide a runaway slave in a big group of travelers," I guessed.

"Yeah," Thea agreed. "Or it could be sometimes messages going back and forth, not always slaves, you know? Like, the people who were helping out could be taking messages on the stage with them."

"We need to know who was helping out," I decided. "We need more clues."

The secret room probably couldn't tell us names or anything, but even so, after a while we both itched to go back down there. We borrowed a broom and dustpan from Thea's mother, saying we wanted to clean up some in the basement. Down the stairs we went, flashlights in our pockets, because of course the ordinary cellar lights didn't shine into our hidden space at the end of the basement.

I liked sweeping the spiderwebs out of the little room, getting the dust out, too. Then I held the flashlight and Thea gently swept the walls, looking for more writing. We found another list by a pair of wooden shelves at the other end of the room. Thea climbed onto the bottom shelf to read it better.

When I saw how exactly she fitted between the shelves, kneeling there, I made a new guess: "Hey, maybe this was where they slept, you know? Like bunk beds. Maybe they spread out blankets on them." I climbed up next to her, and we tried both lying on the bottom shelf at once. It felt natural; yes, it must have been like that. "I bet three or four people could sleep on each shelf if they had to," I suggested. "There could be a whole family in here at a time."

"If a whole family could escape," Thea added doubtfully. We sat up, lighting our faces from underneath with the flashlights, laughing at each other's faces, and wiping spiderwebs off our clothes.

So when a deep, loud voice at the doorway suddenly said "Good God!" it made us both jump so hard that we banged our heads on the top shelf—the top bunk—and I dropped my flashlight on the floor, leaving Thea pointing hers in a moment of panic toward the figure blocking the light from the outer room. For a moment I couldn't even breathe—it felt like we'd been escaped slaves ourselves, discovered and trapped.

And then Thea said in a shaken and cross voice, "Dad! What are you doing here?"

Oh no. Our secret room wasn't our secret anymore.

THEA'S FATHER MOVED aside to let more light from the rest of the cellar into the small room, then stepped inside it. Just having one more person took up a lot of space—I backed as far as I could into the corner and felt on the floor for my flashlight. I found it and picked it up. It still worked. Shining it carefully at the floor, so it wouldn't get in anyone's eyes, I waited for Thea and her father to get back to talking. Caught in the tight space, I felt a wave of panic, and pushed it back, telling myself to just breathe, and it would pass.

Mr. Warwick said to Thea, "Your mother said you girls were playing house down here, so I thought I'd better check that the wood was stacked tight enough to not fall and hurt you."

"Dad!" Thea's voice rose in frustration. "How can you talk like that? We are way too old to play house. We were cleaning, that's all."

"In here?" He looked around, then reached to borrow her flashlight. "I never knew this space was over here. How did you girls find it?"

Thea explained about the math project again, and told her

father about the numbers not adding up. "And," she added in a loud strong voice, "Shawna and I are convinced this was a hiding place for fugitive slaves. On the Underground Railroad, Dad. Before the Civil War."

My heart sank. I guess it's hard to not tell your parents what you're thinking about, especially if you feel like you need to make a point. But now even the secrets of our secret room wouldn't be ours. I sighed.

Thea heard that and caught on right away. "Oh my god," she said to me, "I'm sorry, Shawna, I should have asked you first if you minded me telling my father. I'm really sorry."

"It's okay," I muttered. Mr. Warwick flashed his flashlight toward me for a moment, and I sucked in my stomach, standing as tall and responsible looking as I could in the little space. "It's just a school project, that's all."

From the excitement on Mr. Warwick's face, though, I started to suspect that things might be racing out of school project territory.

"I can't believe I never saw this space myself. Let me in all the way so I can look, would you?" he said eagerly. I took the hint and slipped around him to stand in the doorway myself, leaning to one side to let more light in. His wavy hair flopped over his glasses and was also getting spiderwebs in it, but he didn't seem to care. Catching sight of one of the lists of numbers and letters, he exclaimed, "You girls didn't write this, did you?"

"Dad! Of course not! Someone kept records here," Thea explained, and she pointed to the way the little raised letters on their lines stood for names. "Here's William, W with a little m." She turned to me. "That's Dad's real name—people used to call him Jim when he was a boy, but James is his middle name. Now everyone calls him Bill. It's a long story."

I nodded. Mr. Warwick was kneeling by the shelves now, shining the flashlight against each section of wall.

He scrambled back to his feet. "We'll bring in the state historian," he announced. "I'm sure there's an official one who can evaluate this. And someone from the college, of course. I can take photos right away to start documenting this. It's a good thing our digital camera has a big memory card."

With his long legs, he took the basement stairs two at a time, tugging at the railing. He carried Thea's flashlight with him. The light from mine flickered and went small. "The batteries are going," I said.

"Yeah."

We looked around the little space that wasn't ours anymore. Thea said again, "I'm sorry."

I blew out a puff of air. "That's okay. And—well, I bet we can still use it for part of our history project," I added lamely. I held my flashlight out to Thea. "Probably I should see if Mom and Harry are back yet. You take this. Your dad might want you to help him."

She clicked off the flashlight. "He won't. He'll be all over it now, with the camera and sending out e-mails and stuff. That's how he sees the world, in e-mails." She added glumly, "He's a software engineer, you know. A designer. He designs computer programs. That's how come we could move up here from Connecticut. He already designed a really big program for drawing house plans, you know? So now he can just design other programs that go with it and send them down to the office, and we can live here instead."

We headed slowly up the steps toward the kitchen, Thea in front. The kitchen, bright enough to make us blink after the basement, smelled of popcorn. "Hey Mom," Thea called down the hallway to the TV room, "can Shawna and I make some popcorn too?"

"Go ahead," Mrs. Warwick called back, "but make sure you clean up after yourselves."

"Okay, thanks."

Thea pulled a small machine out from the corner of the kitchen counter, where it had been mostly hidden by the overhanging cupboards. It wasn't like the popping kettle at our house; instead, it plugged into the wall. I watched her measure popcorn carefully, position a big bowl under the machine's spout, then switch it on.

We didn't try to talk while the machine growled and heated and began to spit popcorn out the side. I caught a popped kernel that bounced out. Thea caught another. She ate hers plain, so I did the same. In a few minutes the batch was done, and she silenced the machine.

Over the bowl of fresh white popcorn she sprinkled something that smelled funny. I asked, "Don't you use butter?"

"Nope. This is brewer's yeast. Mom says it's better for you, and it helps keep you from getting zits, too."

Thinking of the ones by my nose that hadn't popped yet, I felt embarrassed and wondered if they'd gotten big and white or red while we were doing things. But I couldn't check—there was no mirror in the kitchen. I excused myself and darted into the little bathroom down the hall; I pressed the two biggest zits until they bled a little, to clean them out, and then I held a tissue against them for a minute to make sure they'd stop bleeding. Dropping the tissue into the toilet, I pressed the flush lever and then turned on the sink water to wash my hands, in case somebody could hear the plumbing.

Back in the kitchen, Thea picked slowly at the popcorn with its golden dust of brewer's yeast. It didn't taste all that great, compared to butter and salt, but I kind of got used to it as we kept eating. If it could keep you from getting zits, I might as well eat it. Maybe that was why Thea looked so good. I'd tell Mom we should get some of this.

"So," Thea started.

I waited for her.

"So," she said again, "I guess we should tell Dad about the things we found out at the library."

"I guess." Then I remembered what Mom had said. "I forgot to tell you: My mother might have some things in the attic from when your house was an inn. She said she'd find them for me tomorrow."

"Cool! Shawna, listen." Thea lowered her voice. "Let's do our project anyway. We'll just kind of ignore Dad, unless maybe he gets us some things we can use. I mean, we could use his pictures, right?

"Right—sure." Because Thea looked really sorry, I tried to smile and cheer her up. "We'll probably end up with the best project in the whole school, if we have pictures and everything else. And we've got questions to answer still, like how many black people came here, and how long they had to hide downstairs."

She lifted a hand to high-five me, a couple of metal bracelets sliding down her arm. "Definitely! I'm glad we got this assignment together, Shawna Lee. We'll show them all."

Together we finished the popcorn, and then it really was time for me to go home.

"Tomorrow?" Thea asked.

"Late, though," I warned her. "I've got to go to church in the morning and then I'll get my mother to look in the attic. I'll come over when I can. You want me to call you first?"

"No, just come on over." As I headed back home, she waved from the doorway, then let it close with a bang.

THE SUNDAY MORNING alarm buzzed at five a.m., and I hit the snooze button. Soon, though, a clatter in the kitchen let me know that Mom was up and working. I dug through a pile of clothes in the corner and pulled out jeans and a sweatshirt.

Bang, went the kitchen door, extra loud. I sighed and padded down the stairs, and stuffed my feet into barn boots in the mudroom. It was still dark outside. Nobody should have to get up in the dark.

Out on the scrap of porch, I stood for a moment and stared into the darkness across the road. I couldn't see Thea's house from here, but I could see the empty field just past it. As my eyes adjusted, I realized there was a group of deer at the back of the field. It looked like two small ones and a large one—a pair of yearlings and the doe, probably. No antlers. One stood staring toward me. It must have heard the door. I clucked my tongue softly, as if I were calling a kitten or a calf. No, it couldn't hear that quiet a sound.

The pumps coming on in the milkhouse groaned and

rumbled. Harry had started to milk already. I saw the lights were all on.

When I looked back toward the field, the deer shapes had vanished, melted into the further darkness. Still, it was a good start to my day. It always feels magical to see the deer so close to the house. I slid my way carefully down the wet steps and onto the path to the barn. It was too cold, too dark.

Inside, the warmth of machines and cows and steam wrapped around me. I picked up a shovel for scraping manure from behind the cows, into the gutter where the chains of the gutter cleaner would later sweep it out of the barn and onto the heap behind the building. When I moved close enough to talk with my mother, who was wiping an udder with hot water before fastening the milking cups in place, I took up an old argument.

"Sunday is supposed to be the day of rest," I complained. "Nobody else in my class has to get up and work in the barn on Sunday."

"Lucky them," my mother said without sympathy. "And you know what Jesus said about animals on the Sabbath, anyway."

"I know, I know," I groaned. "Don't say it."

But she did anyway. It came from the time Jesus healed a woman on the Sabbath, and people complained. Mom quoted: "Doesn't each of you on the Sabbath untie his ox or donkey from the stall and lead it out to give water?"

She started to go on into the part about the woman being set free, being as important as an animal being taken out for water—but I slipped in my own Bible quote and she paused to let me say it: "He said to them, 'If any of you has a sheep and it falls into a pit on the Sabbath, will you not take hold of it and lift it out? How much more valuable is a man than a sheep! Therefore it is lawful to do good on the Sabbath.'"

"Good girl!" My mother seemed impressed.

"How much more valuable is a girl than a cow?" I improvised. "I should get to sleep in."

"Nope," Mom grinned. "Do good on the Sabbath. Clean those stalls, and then you can feed the calves. Jesus would have done it, wouldn't he?"

I gave in. "Probably. Probably he would have liked the calves a lot better than all those lepers pushing at him all the time!"

The milking machine chugged, and Mom's cow stamped a foot, then complained, stretching her neck to lick at the floor in front of her where the last of her pile of grain was out of reach. I moved it closer with a shove from my boot.

I saw the top of Harry's green John Deere hat across the barn, where he was milking the other row of cows. It reminded me to mention to my mother: "I saw some deer in the field across the road just now."

Sharply looking up, she asked me, "A buck?"

"No, just a big doe and a couple of youngsters."

It was important: You could only shoot the bucks. Hunting season had legal rules, as well as traditions. And Mom always planned her hunting carefully.

"It figures," she said. "But I've been tracking a big buck up on the ridge. Probably the smartest ones have already pulled back higher in the woods. Thank the early bow hunters for that."

In the sequence of deer seasons in the fall, bow and arrow season opened earliest. Rifle season, when Mom hunted, would start a couple of weeks into November. Mom said the bow hunters gave the deer a good scare, made them touchy about sounds and people in the woods. Made them harder to catch. She didn't really mind, she said; it was the challenge that she liked.

"Yeah, I guess," I agreed. I headed to the next stall and scraped the floor with a quick swing of my shovel, then moved again.

My mother called after me. "Shawna. Do you have your verse memorized for Bible class?"

"Yeah."

"Well?"

I tossed the words back toward her as I kept scraping, trying to get done as quickly as I could. "Jesus looked at him and said, 'How hard it is for the rich to enter the kingdom of God! Indeed, it is easier for a camel to go through the eye of a needle than for a rich man to enter the kingdom of God.'"

"Good girl," Mom said again. "And it means?"

"Rich people don't give enough to the poor," I told her. "So they're not really following Jesus, and they can't get into Heaven."

"Close enough." With a grunt, she swung the milking machine out of the stall and into the next. "Remember, Jesus said we always have the poor with us."

I wanted to tell her that I was the poor, and she could get into heaven sooner if she gave me more allowance, but I figured she wouldn't like too many jokes on the Sabbath, so I saved it up for another time. I rounded the end of the line of cows and moved over to Harry's row. Clean the stalls, spread the sawdust. Get more grain and hay out in front of the "girls." I had the easy jobs, really, because milking was heavier and messier and a lot more likely to include having some three-quarter-ton animal step on your foot or slap you in the face with a poop-caked tail. Ugh.

I finished my part of the barn chores and went over to check the new kittens. They slept in a bundle of brown and black fur, and I pulled them gently apart a bit, checking—they were all still alive. Good. Usually if a kitten didn't die on the first day or two after it was born, it was going to make it.

"Mom," I asked before leaving the barn, "did you remember where you put those old things from the inn? From the Warwicks' house?"

"We'll look for them later," she promised.

So I headed for the house, glad to be the first into the shower, to wash my hair and find some church clothes. Thank goodness it was cold out—Mom would let me wear my slacks without pushing me toward a dress.

After I'd washed up, I found my brown corduroys and a white shirt that wasn't too frilly, and rummaged in the closet for a sweater. My necklace with the silver fish—the code symbol for Jesus—waited on the dresser.

Darn! The corduroys must have shrunk or something. I tugged at the zipper, sucking my stomach in hard. I couldn't get the button at the top to fasten, so I added a belt. It would do. Switching to a longer sweater covered the belt and the tight zipper, too. Plus, it kept my breasts from looking big. Other girls at school mostly were just starting to have breasts. Mine, well, Mom had given me my first bra when I was ten. I thought about Thea. She was so thin—did she even wear a bra at all yet?

Bra sizes are really weird. First there's the measurement around your ribs, below your breasts. My measurement is thirty-four inches. Then you measured with a tape measure around the biggest part of your breasts and subtracted—the difference between the two numbers translated into a letter size for the bra cups, like A, B, C. My bra size is 34B. I guessed that Thea wouldn't be any bigger than 28A. For a moment, I felt sorry for her. Then kind of jealous instead. Maybe she liked being thin. Probably it came from being vegetarian. I could never be a vegetarian, for sure.

Thinking about letters and numbers took me back again to thinking about the coded list we'd found at the Warwicks' house. But it turned out what I should have been thinking about instead was what Mr. and Mrs. Warwick would do with the information we already had: the discovery of the hidden room in their basement.

When Mom and Harry and I got to church that morning, everyone was talking about it.

"Of course, they called me first," Mrs. Toussaint was telling Mr. and Mrs. Harris as they set out the coffee cups in the vestry. I put our coffee cake on the table and lingered to listen. Mrs. Toussaint said, "I've always suspected North Upton had a role in the Underground Railroad, as it is so close to Barnet, and of course the stage line came directly through here. You have to surmise that there were slaves sent up this way as they headed for Canada. But this is the first possible evidence for this village. If it holds up, of course."

"I never imagined," Mrs. Harris said, and cooed up at her

handsome husband, my history teacher. "Did you know all about this, dear?"

"Well, some," Mr. Harris hedged. It was easy to see he wanted to sound like he did know, but how could he? Thea and I had only just found the secret hiding place. He continued, "I teach the children about Vermont's role in the Civil War, of course. Why, nearly every village saw its young men enlist, to save the Union, you know."

"To free the slaves, you mean," his wife amended.

"No, dear," said Mr. Harris firmly. "Only the Quakers in Vermont really expected to tackle slavery by releasing all the slaves in all of the states. Vermonters who enlisted in the Army mostly did so to preserve the Union." He began to lecture about someone named Thaddeus Stevens from Danville, and Daniel Webster, who had had cousins up our way. I wanted to listen longer, but the church bell started to ring, so I hurried upstairs and sat next to my mother as Pastor Wilkins stood up in the pulpit and spread his arms wide in welcome.

I whispered to my mother, "Where's Harry?"

"He's coming," she said, and touched her finger to my lips. "Listen to Pastor."

"This is the day the Lord has made," came the clear firm voice from the front of the church. "Let us rejoice and be glad in it, and praise the Lord with hymn number two seven seven, 'Morning Has Broken.'" Mrs. Wilkins pounded out the opening chord from the piano at the side of the room, and we all stood up to sing. Harry arrived about halfway through, and my mother shared her hymn book with him, even though he never actually sings, just hums in the back of his throat.

But it wasn't until Pastor Wilkins announced his sermon topic that I realized Thea and I had totally lost control of our history project. Because Pastor Wilkins proclaimed from the pulpit, "Our text this morning will not be from Second Corinthians after all. We have reason to search God's word instead from Paul's letter to the Romans, chapter six, verses six and seven."

I knew those verses. I knew almost all of Romans five,

six, seven, and eight. Everybody who went to Pastor Wilkins's summer Bible School studied those. And I could see it was going to be slaves and freedom all season long in church now.

"For we know that our old self was crucified with him so that the body of sin might be done away with, that we should no longer be slaves to sin—because anyone who has died has been freed from sin."

Great, I thought with fresh resentment: Not only is our secret room not a secret any more. But the whole church—the whole town, for all I knew!—was talking about our prize discovery.

Of course, Thea's family wasn't there. Her parents didn't go to church. So I was baffled: How did they all find out so fast? And what would Thea say?

WHAT THEA WOULD say turned out to be, "My dad called at least a dozen people last night to tell them about the Underground Railroad hiding place in our house."

Spread out on the floor in Thea's room, we had two old photos of the North Upton Inn, one letter from 1926 on stationery that said the inn's name at the top, and a very worn out bed quilt my mother said came from one of the rented bed chambers.

And in spite of all this, which should have made us happy, we both wore rainy-day faces and kept saying to each other, "I can't believe they did this to us."

I didn't want to criticize Thea's father for telling people about the secret room. So I just said, "I still want to break the code, though. And I guess it can still be our project, I mean, the Underground Railroad part. We need to find more evidence of the people who were here."

"I guess." Thea scrambled sideways across the rug to reach the edge of the old quilt. She fingered the edges of a ragged part of the binding. She asked, "Did you ever go over to that place in Barnet that's on the Underground Railroad? Is it like our room?"

I shook my head. "I've never gone there. Maybe we could get one of our parents to take us over." I began to spread out ideas, out loud. "We could measure and photograph it and put the data next to the ones from the room that's here. And we could check the walls, see if there's any writing on them."

Thea nodded. "I like that idea. Compare and contrast, that's what my teacher in Connecticut called it. We had to write papers all the time that compared things."

"In seventh grade?"

"Even in sixth grade." She rolled over to look at me. "We had the same English teacher in sixth and seventh grade. She always said things like 'Think outside the box, boys and girls' and 'Be more imaginative with your examples.' Whatever that's supposed to mean."

I nodded. "I know. It's like Mr. Harris saying 'Don't take it for truth just because it's in your book.' I mean, isn't what's in books supposed to be true if you have the books in school?" That reminded me of what the history teacher had said in church. I told Thea how he'd been arguing about whether Vermonters joined the Civil War to free the slaves.

"Well, what else would they go to war for? Slaves, that's horrible. Whips and everything, and selling people's children." She shivered and made a face. "If I grew up black, I'd never forgive those days. I just know it. Wouldn't you feel like that, too?"

What can you say when somebody says something like that? For a moment, I couldn't think of anything at all. Finally I answered, "There's not a whole lot of black people in Vermont anyway."

"Yeah, I know. But there are in Connecticut. My old school had a lot of black kids. A lot of them were poor, but some of them, their parents were, like, teachers or doctors. You know."

"Did you ever have a black girl who was your best friend?"

"No, not really." Thea rubbed her face and looked tired all of a sudden. And I could tell that she wasn't thinking about the olden days and the Underground Railroad anymore. "Sometimes you think someone is your best friend and they're not really. I had this best friend in third grade, all the way until seventh grade. And then there was this boy we both liked. And it didn't ... I mean, I didn't ... well, just, I found out what she said about me to that boy. Nobody who is really a friend would say that, right?"

I was confused. But I could see it hurt, whatever it was Thea thought she'd just told me. I fumbled for the right words. "Friends have to believe in each other. You deserve to have really good friends, Thea. You really do."

"Thanks." She brushed a hand across her eyes and sniffed. She added, "Maybe things just changed too much. She didn't live all that close to where I did, you know? I mean, a best friend should live close to your house, right? That way you can do things together. Like your house and my house, that's good."

It really was good. Thea must mean I could be her best friend, right? I felt my face get red, and I had to say something to get her to stop embarrassing both of us. So I said, "Where's the code? I think we should work on it more."

That worked—Thea turned around to dig under the quilt and find our papers with the list and our guesses so far. Then she said, "Wait a minute. Quilts and codes. I think I have a book about quilts and codes. Something from when I was little."

She pulled open a cupboard and tugged out a box of picture books. "There are the ones I didn't want to hand down to Thaddeus and Teddy," she explained as she spilled them out onto an empty space on the rug. In a moment, she found what she wanted. "Look at this!"

The picture book had a farm on the front cover with a patchwork of fields, and sitting in the shade of a huge tree was a young black woman with braids in her hair, sewing something. "The Freedom Map of Cecily's Scraps," I read aloud. "What's it about?"

Thea thumbed open the pages and showed me the story. "It's actually about the Underground Railroad," she said. "And how people gave directions by designing codes in the patches they sewed onto their clothes, or even onto quilts. You know, like the Big Dipper."

That confused me completely. Thea explained: "The constellation, the Big Dipper. How it points to the north, and people could follow it at night and know they were heading toward freedom. Except the slaves called it the Drinking Gourd, and they had a song to teach each other, 'Follow the Drinking Gourd.'"

"Really?" We read the picture book together. It really was about the Underground Railroad. Or, at least, about how slaves could find out how to run away and who might get them going the right direction, which I guess was all the same thing.

Together, we stared at the old quilt on the floor next to us. It didn't look at all like the quilts in the book. For one thing, it hardly had any colors left in it. For another, it didn't have pictures on the quilt squares. Just triangles and diamonds—pretty good geometry, actually, but not exactly full of meaning.

A quiet knock came on Thea's bedroom door, and her mother was calling out, "Girls? I brought you up a snack."

Thea scrambled up and opened the door for her mom, who handed in a bowl of carrot and celery sticks with raisins sprinkled over them.

"Supper's at six, so you have another hour to do homework," said Mrs. Warwick. She looked around and said, "Where are your books?"

"Over here." Thea waved at our backpacks. "We were thinking about our history project, is all. Want to see these old pictures of our house?"

I picked up the two photographs that my mom had given us and pointed out the familiar features—the long porch, the many windows for the little upstairs room—and also the changes. "See, there weren't any trees in front back then. Probably so the stage could come close and drop off passengers."

"These are wonderful!" Mrs. Warwick exclaimed. "Let me borrow these for a minute—I'll have my husband scan them so we can have copies made. I'll be right back. You don't mind, do you, honey?"

What could I say? I nodded. "Sure, that's fine."

Leaving the door open, she headed back downstairs and I heard her calling out, "Bill? You've got to see these."

Thea looked as irritated as I was on the inside. "I can't believe it. She's as bad as he is. They're both just, like, constantly in our business here. Look, after you go home I'll talk to them. I'll tell them they have to stop doing this."

"That's all right." I shrugged. "It's your house. I mean, I understand. Don't sweat it."

I was glad to have the carrots and celery and raisins next to me. Putting a handful into my mouth helped me to not say anything else. You should always be nice to the person who is your best friend, I figured. Even if her parents are kind of, well, weird.

BRINGING THE FREEDOM map picture book to school seemed like a good idea when we finished talking Sunday afternoon and I went home for supper.

But on Monday morning, when Thea pulled it out of her backpack to show to Mr. Harris, a whole new kind of stress erupted. Who would have guessed a kids' book would make the history teacher go ballistic like that?

First of all, when he saw the cover, Mr. Harris practically snatched the book out of Thea's hands. She was sitting at her desk, in the last row. In history we sit in assigned seats by alphabet, but from my L seat, in the second row, I can see right across to Thea. Mr. Harris stormed up to her in a rush and grabbed the book.

"This!" He sputtered and said again, "This! This is exactly what I want you all to learn to question. Just *look* at this!"

Everyone stared. Some boys in the back laughed, and one of them said, "Does that count as a whole book on our book lists?"

But Mr. Harris wasn't listening. With his long, thin, white

fingers, he spread the book against his chest, facing the opened pages towards us as if we were little kids at story hour. "Look! What do you see?"

From the ripple of answers around him, he grabbed one: "That's right. An African American girl making a quilt, and according to the author of this book"—he sputtered again, then spat out the words, "according to this writer, a black slave in the mid-eighteen hundreds, before the Civil War, is passing along secret information about escaping to the north by sewing patches onto her clothes and onto a quilt to show escape routes and the right roads, all stitched into the fabric blocks. Now, think! Think, young ladies and young men. What's wrong with that idea?"

Met with silence, he posed a challenge: "Every one of you, pull out a blank piece of paper and a pencil. Now!" I scuffled in my backpack for my notebook and opened it to the blank pages near the middle. I already had a pencil out.

"Now," Mr. Harris repeated, "draw a map to get from this school to the grocery store in downtown St. Johnsbury. Use your rulers if you like. Show accurate mileage, directions, and make sure you have the directions of north, south, east, and west marked."

Everyone said, "That's too much! We can't!"

And banging the book on his own desk, Mr. Harris nodded with satisfaction. "And you are people who can already read, write, do basic mathematics, and study history and geography. Think—most black people held in slavery received none of those benefits." He calmed down a bit and went on: "And that ignores the fact that map reading, which more or less most people can do in today's American culture, is nevertheless a learned skill. Even making a map of the inside of a house is a learned skill, translating the spaces on paper into our own experience."

I knew Thea was embarrassed from the redness of her face; besides, I would have been crawling under my desk by now if it had been my book Mr. Harris was complaining about. But she spoke up anyway, waving her hand. "Excuse me, Mr. Harris. Isn't this book based on fact, though? So doesn't that mean that black people in the eighteen hundreds did understand that stuff after all?"

The teacher perched on his desk, ready to lecture, more relaxed, and my stomach eased up a bit. "Actually, this book is based on imagination. Lovely, kind, and very illustration-prone imagination." He finally slowed down and explained that teachers—or at least, teachers like him—dig into how true the history is when it gets written into stories, and he'd already been to a workshop about this one. "An accidental and well-meant coincidence of a quilt with stars in the pattern and the well-known song 'Follow the Drinking Gourd' led to this author imagining quilts as star charts and local maps. It was a lovely idea. But it came from the wrong kind of history: making it up, instead of investigating it."

Now James Ward, who sat right in front of Thea, put his hand up. "But Mr. Harris, how can you tell which books are investigating and which ones are imagining?"

Around me, other kids were agreeing and talking to each other. Mr. Harris shushed us all and went on. "James, that is exactly the question I hope you'll all be able to answer by June. And to move you toward those answers, I want each of you to go home today and actually investigate a piece of history. I want you to ask your parents about the day when you were born: what the weather was on that date, and where your parents were, and what the name of the doctor or hospital was. Bring the information to class tomorrow, and we'll explore how to confirm your parents' information. Now, please open your books to chapter four, and we'll go over the factors leading up to the Civil War." He nodded at the first row of seats, where Kim Amidon sat. "Please read aloud for everyone all of the chapter headings in this chapter, and we'll discuss whether they outline a believable premise."

Half an hour later, when the bell rang, Mr. Harris gave the picturebook back to Thea. He looked kind of embarrassed himself as he apologized, saying, "I hope you didn't feel on the spot, Thea. You couldn't have known what a controversial book this is, after all." She nodded, and the teacher asked with real curiosity, "Why did you bring this to class, Thea?"

"I guess I wondered whether it was true," she answered.

I pushed up next to her. "We both wondered," I said. "Because we're doing the Civil War for our history fair projects."

"Good choice." Mr. Harris nodded. "When you have an outline of what you'd like to cover specifically, bring it to me and we'll go over a reading list that makes sure you're using useful sources."

We swapped glances and Thea spoke first. "What if we're investigating real objects and places?" she asked. "Are those useful sources?"

I added, "Like a journal from the eighteen hundreds, and letters."

"Of course." He raised his eyebrows. "I presume you mean copies of a journal, copies of letters, not the originals. We'll go over your sources, and I'll find you some books to put your work into perspective. Remember, your outline is due the second week of November, and everyone's draft displays for the classroom are due December first, so don't try to handle too much at once. The history fair for finished projects will be in January, so we can polish our best ones for the state history fair next March. "

The seventh graders pressed into the room around us for their class, and Michael Willson slid his backpack onto Thea's desk, pushing hers toward the edge. She caught it and pulled the straps to shut it. "We better go."

Together we left the room, hurrying toward math class. Mrs. Labounty liked us, but she still wouldn't like it if we were late. And when we got into the classroom the only seats left were all the way up front, next to each other. "Sorry," we each mumbled as we scrunched into our chairs, pulling out the assignment we'd done together in Thea's house.

Behind me I could hear Maryellen Bryce whispering too loudly, "Maybe they have a baby book for math class, too!"

That Maryellen Bryce. I hoped she'd choke on her pen top. But I wouldn't give her the satisfaction of turning around to say so.

The rest of the school day was okay, I guess. I made it through the stupid dancercise routine in gym class, and when I got outside in the fresh air, I felt the stress drop away.

Thea and I turned to walk home, but her mother was in front of the school building in her minivan and beeped the horn at her. "Dentist!" Mrs. Warwick called out the car window.

"Oh yeah. I forgot," Thea told me. "I'll call you after supper. Maybe we can do math together."

"Okay. See you."

At home, the house was empty except for our oldest cat, Sissy, who rubbed up against my legs, almost tripping me. I poured some cat food pellets into her dish after I cuddled her some. Even old cats need attention. Midnight heard the pellets in the dish and ran down from the bedrooms. I made myself a peanut butter and strawberry jam sandwich and a glass of chocolate milk. Then I pulled out my assignment pad and looked at the choices: Math would be this evening with Thea. History would have to wait until Mom and Harry got home. Where were they, anyway?

I finally found a note by the phone: "We're up at the cabin. Turn on the oven to 350 at 4:30 and put the lasagna in. Home by 5:30. Carl's milking."

My big brother Carl. I could go out to the barn and hang around with him for a while.

But then again, maybe I'd better start *Uncle Tom's Cabin* for English class. I wondered if Mr. Harris would yell about this one, too, because obviously it was fiction. Turning the inch-thick paperback with its worn and curling covers in my hand, I saw a quote on the back: "So this is the little lady who made this big war." According to the back of the book, that part was fact: President Abraham Lincoln said it to the author, Harriet Beecher Stowe. I imagined myself in an old-fashioned dress with a big wide skirt, curtseying to the President, saying, "Pleased to meet you, sir." But if it was me doing it, it wouldn't be for some novel I'd written—it would be for an amazing math solution to a national emergency.

On the front of the book, a family of black people in ratty clothes leaned against a cabin that looked a lot like my mother's hunting cabin, her "camp."

After refilling my glass with plain milk and grabbing a couple of oatmeal cookies to take with me, I headed upstairs to start reading *Uncle Tom's Cabin*. After all, historical fiction that had been around this long had to have facts inside it, right? Especially if even President Lincoln read it. Maybe I could find out more about escaping slaves and where they hid—enough to get some mostly factual ideas about our not-so-secret room. That is, if Thea's father hadn't made it a hundred percent his own already. Groan.

LASAGNA IS AN excellent meal when there is enough garlic bread plus plenty of salad with Italian dressing. Mom and Harry were hungry from hiking around up on the ridge, even though they'd used the four-wheeler to get up there. Carl hadn't come in from the barn yet, so we set his portion back in the oven to stay warm. It was dark outside, but in the kitchen the golden light and Mom's laughter lit up the evening. She always cheered up around hunting season.

Personally, I believe the best dessert to go with lasagna is mint chocolate ice cream, because the mint helps fight the garlic in your stomach and keeps you from having garlic breath afterward. So I had an extra helping of mint chocolate ice cream afterward, so that if Thea came over to do math, she wouldn't be blown away by the garlic. And then, while I waited for Thea to call, I asked my mother for the details of the day I was born, like Mr. Harris had said to do. I got ready to take notes in my red history notebook. My mother washed the supper dishes as we talked, and Harry got a fire started in the woodstove, to take off the chill for the night. It smelled good.

"So Mom," I began, "this is for history class. I'm supposed to interview you about the day I was born."

My mother kept the hot water running into the rinse dishpan.

"What about it?"

"Well, let's start with the weather. May eleventh, nineteen ninety-eight," I prompted her. "I bet it wasn't snowing. So, was it raining? Or sunny? Was it a warm spring?"

"I don't remember," my mother said now. "It's too long ago, and I mix it all up with when your brothers were born."

"Come on," I protested. "They were both born in winter. And Alice was in the fall. I was your only spring baby. Maybe if you think about the rest of the day, you'll remember. What were you doing when you went into labor?"

Bang. Clash. Plates and bowls landed in the dish rack, clinking against each other. "You should ask Harry instead. He was the driver that day. Harry," she called out loudly, "come tell Shawna about the day she was born. She wants to know what kind of weather it was that day."

"Rain," bellowed Harry from the living room, over the TV news. "It was pouring rain. And it was still mud season. That's why your mother wanted me to drive."

"Besides the fact that she couldn't have been driving when she was in labor anyway," I added. "Did you drive her station wagon?"

I waited a moment and then repeated, "Did you drive her station wagon for her, Harry?"

"Nope. My truck. Helped her up onto the front seat and told her to hold on. Mud season, you know! Ruts in the driveway half as deep as the wheels on the truck. And that rain came down hard, and we slipped around a lot. I told her, cheer up, it would get the baby born sooner that way," Harry added. He came into the kitchen and stood next to me, reading my notes on the page. "Better write down the time. We left here at seven a.m. and we were at the hospital in St. Johnsbury at seven-thirty. Should have been sooner," he admitted, "but I slowed down around the curves by the river. Didn't want to deliver that baby myself, which I would have had to if we'd slid off the road, wouldn't I?"

I wrote more notes. "Were you scared, Mom?"

Harry answered instead. "Your mother was only scared of my driving, much more than of having the baby."

"Yeah, probably by your fourth baby, you don't worry all that much," I guessed.

Mom didn't answer, and when I looked up, I saw she was busy scrubbing the lasagna pan with a Brillo pad. Maybe she was embarrassed. I'd have to help her.

"So you were at the hospital in St. J," I prompted. "Who was your doctor?"

"We've always had Dr. Thompson for just about everything," she said. "But he was out of town, and—Harry, do you remember who delivered the baby?"

Harry snorted. "Mostly the nurses did the work. Some Chinese or Korean guy came in with the needle, but"—he cut off for a moment, looked at my mother's back, and ended quickly, "anyway, you were just about born already, Shawna, and just a few minutes later you were getting your first bath. Hated it then, too," he grinned, and poked me in the ribs.

The ringing of the phone saved him from having me sass back at him. I jumped for the receiver hanging on the wall. "Hello?"

"Shawna? It's Alice."

"Alice? Hi. Just a minute, I'll get Mom for you."

"No, stop," said my older sister's voice in my ear, as close as if California was next door. "I didn't call to talk to Mom this time. I called to talk to you."

I turned to tell my mother it was Alice but for me this time. I expected she'd be halfway across the kitchen already, to take the phone from me.

But she wasn't. She stood by the sink, still facing away from me, and Harry stood behind her, his big farmers' hands on her shoulders. Something in the room—the quilted pattern of ceiling light and table lamp, the steam-fogged window over the kitchen sink a black blankness against the cold night, the silence of my mother and Harry huddling away from me and toward that outward strangeness—something made me swallow hard before saying to my waiting sister, "Yeah? What did you want to talk about?"

Through the phone I heard two long breaths, in and out, and I said, "Alice? What is it? Are you okay?"

Alice said, "I was taking a cleansing breath. It centers you. Shawna, listen, I want to send you a costume for Halloween. From California. Do you know what you want to be this year?"

What was the big deal with centering? And why would Alice send me a costume? Always before, my mother had simply pulled out old clothes that could be cut or tied with sashes or painted. And we'd make a mask, from black paper or cloth or, once, from a grocery bag, with ears attached that stuck up, stiffened with coat-hanger wire. I knew it sounded stupid, but all I could think of to say to Alice was, "Why?"

"Because there are cool things out here. Because North Upton is like the end of the earth and Mom never gets good store-bought costumes. And just because I feel like getting you something. You know?"

"Look, Alice," I finally explained, "I don't think I'm going to wear a costume this year. I mean, I'm too old for that. I'm in eighth grade."

Another "cleansing breath" from California came at me.

"Alice? You still there?"

"I'm here. What, you don't want to wear a costume at all? When I was in eighth grade we had a costume party."

"Well, we're not going to this year. Maybe a dance or something, I'm not sure. But we've all grown out of costumes." I wanted to fill up the hollow phone line with something more, so I said quickly, "I'm doing a history project on the Civil War, Alice. I've got this friend Thea, across the road. She's new, and her house has maybe a room where the escaped slaves hid before the war, you know?"

"Where does she live? Which house?"

"The inn. Right across the road. Hey, Alice, you want to talk to Mom now? I was just interviewing her about the day I was born. Hey, do you remember that day? Were you in school or at home?"

Now a longer silence came from California.

"Alice?"

Quietly she said, "Okay, Shawna. Let me talk to Mom. Right now."

My mother came to take the phone, and I sat down again at the table. But the evening was ruined. Alice was so weird anyway—whatever she sent me for presents always looked too girly-girl, sort of, with pink ribbons or whatever. Maybe if I could get more family history from Mom and Harry, I could figure out more of why Alice was like that.

I looked at the clock and wished the phone call from Alice would end, so Thea could call me. Harry stood with his back against the sink, his arms folded, watching my mother, so I turned to look at her, too.

Braced against the refrigerator, my mother listened to my sister without words, just saying "Unh-hunh. Mmm." Then she said, "Not really. No, I don't think it's a good idea. No. She's thirteen."

They were talking about me. I listened harder but Alice's voice was so quiet that I couldn't tell what she was saying.

My mother said, "I'll think about it. We can talk about it when you get here. Okay, I love you too."

Without handing the phone to Harry for a turn to talk, she said goodbye and hung up. Harry stood there watching her until she finally met his gaze.

"Alice is coming home for Thanksgiving." She said it flatly, and I could hear no clue about what was going on.

Harry said only, "Then we'll figure it all out when she gets home."

"Figure what out?" I asked. "What did Alice say about me?"

"Never mind what, it's not your business," my mother said sharply. "Harry, would you help her finish her project? I have a headache."

Her slow steps headed toward the darkened living room, and she lowered herself into the recliner in front of the blue glow of the TV news, and Harry came across the room and peered down at my paper. "What else do you need to know?" he asked.

"Nothing else, I guess. Except—Harry," I lowered my voice, "was Mom okay about having me? I mean, was four children too many for her?" I was guessing in the dark of the strained evening and the strange conversation.

Harry patted my shoulder. "You're exactly what she wanted," he said quietly. "It's Alice that's the hard part tonight. Don't you worry."

At that moment the phone rang again, and I jumped for it. "Hello?" Finally, it was Thea—too late, though, to come over after all.

"Let's do our math on the phone instead," my friend suggested.

After a quick look to make sure that Harry was settling down next to my mother in front of the TV in the living room, I agreed. For the next half hour, we worked on areas, perimeters, and diagonals. When the assignment was done, I asked Thea, "What about our history project? Is your dad still asking questions about the room in the cellar?"

"Worse," she groaned dramatically. "He's bringing home somebody from the college tomorrow, to look at it, after school. You'd better be here with me, so we can listen to it all, together."

"I'll be there. See you in the morning."

"See you."

Just as I hung up, my brother Carl pushed his way into the kitchen, a cold blast of night air coming with him, plus the strong aroma of cows and milk and soap clinging to his oversize green barn jacket.

"All set," he told me. "Tell Harry I'll be here early tomorrow. The truck's coming for the calves."

I pointed toward the living room. "He heard you. Hey Carl,

do you want some supper? There's plenty of lasagna left."

"Nah. Thanks anyway, Princess. I'm headed for my own couch and a TV dinner and a beer."

He ducked his head to dodge the door frame, folding himself back out into the darkness, and I crossed the kitchen to flick on the yard light so he could walk back toward the other house more easily. I was glad he'd called me "Princess," the way he used to when I was a little girl.

At least there was someone in my family who still seemed normal for the night. I scooped a final half bowl of mint chocolate ice cream, and headed upstairs to read myself toward sleep.

IN THE MORNING it was cold enough to feel like Halloween, all right. The puddles had ice over them, and the mud ridges of the road bulged hard against my sneakers. I waited outside Thea's house, bouncing up and down to keep warm, my backpack bouncing too, and I tucked my hands into my armpits. Pushing my breath out experimentally, I watched it steam and swirl in front of me. When I heaved the air out from deeper in my lungs, there was more white steam. More moisture that way, I speculated. How many cubic inches of air inside a person's lungs?

The Warwicks' door banged and Thaddeus came backing out onto the steps, calling into the house, "Shawna's waiting for you, Thea. You're going to be late again!" He nodded at me, then started half running down the road. The warning bell rang from the school just as Thea came out of the house, one arm through the strap of her bookbag, the other buttoning her jacket. She wore a fluffy white hat at an angle that somehow made her blue wool jacket into a sailor's outfit.

I reached behind me and tugged down my Vermont green

sweatshirt to make sure it hadn't bunched up under my backpack straps. For a moment, I wished I had one of those jackets, too. Or at least a fluffy white hat.

"Ooh, Shawna, your hair's still wet," Thea said as she reached the road. "Let's walk fast so you won't catch cold." She added as we hurried together, "It looks good the way you've got it parted like that, the sideways sweep is good on you."

"Thanks," I said, and switched the subject, puffing a bit. "Hey, did you start that book for English? *Uncle Tom's Cabin*?"

"Nope. I re-organized my whole history notebook last night instead. Then I made a first draft outline for our project—you can work on it later. I figured I could read over the weekend. Did you start the book?"

I nodded. "It's weird, one moment it's an okay adventure with these slaves and slave-catchers and all, and the next, it's, like, women talking about clothes and houses and old-fashioned. But listen, this is important, I've just got to the part where a cousin from up North comes to visit in the South, and you won't believe this, she's from Vermont. Like, people from Vermont had relatives down South, and they argued with each other over slavery."

Thea got what I was saying, no question. We were almost at the school, and the last bell was ringing and we had to get into the rest of the line of kids going in, but she said really emphatically, "We have to read that book, then, fast. I'll start today."

Because we were almost late, there wasn't time to talk when we got to homeroom, and history and math and gym raced along. Finally in the lunch line, I caught up with Thea and asked, "What time is that college person coming to your house?"

"He's coming with my dad, like, after my dad's seminar up there. So, I guess about five o'clock. Can you come right after school, though, to finish the project outline?"

"Okay." I finished putting dishes on my tray, and fitted in a bowl of canned pears at the corner, so I'd have a balanced meal: two slices of pizza, salad with Thousand Island dressing, one of the little ice cream cups, the pears. And orange juice.

"I talked to my mom," Thea said as we pulled out chairs at the end of a long table. Maryellen Bryce was down the other end, so I half pointed at her and leaned across the table toward Thea, so we could keep our voices down. Thea went on, "She'll take us to Barnet on Saturday morning if we want. We just have to get permission to visit that place. That hiding place, you know?"

"Good. Listen, I'll do that part, getting permission. I'll call Mrs. Toussaint tonight and find out which house it's at and what the phone number is. Remember, we were supposed to be looking at her stuff again on Saturday, so I'd better tell her we're going to Barnet instead. "

Maryellen interrupted, calling down the table: "Hey look, it's the history girls. You got any sweet little picture books to study from today, Shawna Lee?"

"What's the matter, Maryellen, you need something closer to your own reading level?" I called back.

But the jab didn't stick. She just ignored me and leaned sideways against one of the seventh-grade boys and whispered something. He snorted into his milk and they both laughed. Nothing new. I twisted my chair to ignore her more.

Thea closed her mouth tight as she looked at them, turning mad and sad in the same moment. Then she shook her head and passed me two pages from her notebook. "The project outline," she explained. "Can you maybe fix any mistakes you see, or add stuff if you want, and give it back to me before health class? I can do a final copy while we watch the movie. I've seen it like a hundred times already anyway."

"Yeah, okay." I put the pages into my backpack quickly, so nobody else would see, and asked, "What movie?"

"They said in homeroom that Miss Pearl is absent, so they're showing that movie about the woman, Kitty Genovese, that got killed and nobody called the police the whole time it was happening. In Connecticut they show that movie, like, every grade from sixth grade on. It's supposed to be about peer pressure." She rolled her eyes.

I shook my head. "I never saw it. Is it any good?"

"No," Thea said firmly, "it's a downer, and—it's in black and white."

"Ugh."

The Willson twins sat down next to us, so there wasn't any privacy; besides, Merry and Marsha wanted to talk about the Halloween dance. Marsha had a pink plastic clipboard and a pen with a pink flower on the top end of it. It embarrassed me now, to think about how much I'd wanted Marsha to be my best friend last year. Compared to Thea, she had no style at all.

"We need you to bring brownies, Shawna," Marsha told me. "Three dozen. Can you handle that?"

I nodded and scribbled a note on the back of my hand. Marsha checked off my name and turned to Thea.

"Merry said maybe you had a lot of music CDs," Marsha said, her voice rising like it was a question as she tossed her streaked ponytail over a shoulder. "Because you lived down in Connecticut where the music stores are better. Do you?"

"Sure," Thea agreed. "How many do you want? I'll mark them all so you can give them back to me."

Merry cut in, "Can you lend us, like, twenty? So the DJ can choose? And do you have some Mariah Carey stuff?"

"Sure," Thea said again. "How about you come over to my house and pick out what you want?"

The twins flashed a look between them, and Marsha answered, "We could both come. Like, right after school. Today. Right?"

"All right." Lifting an eyebrow at me, Thea went on, "But it has to be right after, because Shawna and I have stuff we've got to do."

Whew! One minute the thought of the twins coming to Thea's house made me fiery mad, that she was inviting someone else over instead of me, and the next moment I felt cool and calm and relieved, because obviously what we were doing, Thea and me, was more important to her than the twins. Obviously.

Merry and Marsha drifted off, to push up against one of the boys and giggle, and I had barely enough time to finish my ice cream before the bell rang for English. No time for the pears after all—I dumped them and turned in my tray and dishes, diving back to my seat for my backpack.

In English class, I kept the history project outline under my page of notes, and added some parts about photos and letters to what Thea had written, correcting some of the names she had kind of wrong. Luckily I'm good at taking notes anyway. I did have to pay some attention, enough to put my hand up once with an answer. You have to speak up some or Miss Calkins gives you a zero for class participation.

Science class, routine stuff on units of measurement—and in health class, sure enough, that movie Thea had mentioned. She was right: It was really depressing. All about these neighbors knowing a murder happened, hours long, and never calling for help. Sick. Obviously a city thing. In North Upton, everybody would be there to rescue the person getting beat up. There is absolutely no privacy in this village, which of course is the whole problem with living here. But I guess maybe that's a good thing, sometimes.

Mostly I was just glad when I finally reached the important part of the day: the part that comes after school. I saw Thea walking ahead with the twins, but she turned to wave at me and pointed toward her house, so I hurried home to get rid of a bunch of books, find a quick snack, and tell Mom I'd be at Thea's until suppertime. I dodged around a truck parked in the driveway and called out "Hey, Mom," as I pushed open the door.

Mom wasn't in the kitchen, though—Emerson was.

As I stepped past a pile of barn clothes on the kitchen floor, I saw my "more older" brother at the kitchen table, unloading a big corrugated cardboard carton. I dropped my backpack and stepped across to punch his shoulder lightly as he looked up at me, a quick flash of smile interrupting his frown.

"Hey, it's the Princess," he drawled as he rumpled my hair. "How's tricks, Trix?"

"There's too much to tell you, I can't tell you all of it now." I snatched some gingersnaps from the cookie jar and wrapped them in a paper towel, then added two more in case Thea wanted some. I'd just have to keep them hidden until the twins had left her place. So I took out two more and ate them right away while Emerson laughed at me.

"What's the matter, no lunch today? Starving to death? Mom's not keeping a good enough eye on you, you better come stay with me instead."

"Yeah, right!" I punched his shoulder again, and he pretended it hurt. "Hey Emerson, what is all this?"

Stacks of hardware boxes in green and white, and of shotgun shells and rifle ammunition in red boxes and black and yellow ones, were lined up along the table next to the big box. Emerson shrugged. "Hunting season. Mom must be planning to take down a whole herd of deer. And the other boxes are screws and hooks and stuff, for the barn, I figure." He looked at the clock over the fridge. "Where is Mom, anyway?"

"Don't know. Maybe in the barn? Or up on the ridge." A quick glance out the back window confirmed the four-wheeler was gone. "Yeah, I bet she's up on the ridge with Harry, tracking or something. It's only three more weeks until deer season starts. Good thing, too, she needs to cheer up."

Emerson put the empty carrier box on the floor and gave me a quizzical look. "Mom getting moody with the shorter days? Nothing new, is it?"

"I guess. Hey, Emerson, did you know Alice is coming for Thanksgiving? Why does Mom get upset about Alice so much? You'd think she'd be happy, everyone together for the holiday, isn't that what everyone wants?"

"Alice is coming? No, I didn't know." One hand crept to finger the neat line of dark moustache on his upper lip, as my brother started to say something else, then paused, then began again. "Mom say why she's coming?"

"To have Thanksgiving with us, I guess. What else?"

Emerson shook his head. "Nope. Not Alice. After ten years away, she's just coming to have Thanksgiving dinner? There's got to be more to it. Alice is a sweetie, but never spent her money on anything without some kind of crazy mixed-up plan. You should know that, kiddo. That's just who she is."

I shrugged. I didn't like hearing Emerson talk like that. After all, Alice was my sister as well as his. I'd always wished she'd come home, and nobody would ever tell me why she didn't. Wouldn't it be good to have her here, even for just Thanksgiving weekend? "Maybe she just wants to see us," I objected. "To see me, even. It's been, like, forever since she saw me. I'm a teenager now." Even as I spoke up for her, though, I remembered how uncomfortable my mother had seemed when Alice called. What was going on?

Emerson thumped one fist gently on the kitchen table, enough to make his stacks of boxes rattle but not enough to topple them over. "So Alice is coming. Gonna have to pray on that, I guess. You pray too, Princess. And give Mom a hand, it's not easy on her."

I started to ask "Why?" but Emerson was already swinging through the door onto the porch.

"Gotta get back to the shop. Tell Mom I love her." And just like that, he started the truck in the driveway and was gone.

Nearly four o'clock! I scribbled a note, "At Thea's, back by 6," and dodged back out the door, backpack and all.

Across the road, Merry and Marsha Willson were coming out of Thea's house. I ran up the walkway. They kept saying thanks and how great the CDs were going to be for the dance. I asked, "Who's the DJ?"

One of those funny looks flashed from Marsha to Merry, twin looks, I guess, and Merry answered. "Our cousin Josh. He's bringing his own CDs too."

"Cool!" To Thea, I added, "He's at the high school, and he's in a band. He's all right." More than all right, he was hot, but I wasn't going to say that in front of the twins—or in front of anyone who might tell Mom I'd said it. My mother had standards for young ladies, even ones in blue jeans and sweatshirts. But Thea picked up what I meant anyway. I could tell by the twist of her smile and her bright eyes.

"Hey Shawna, come on in, we've got to get that outline done before my father gets home," she said, holding open the door. The Willson twins departed, and I ducked into the warmth and the family sounds of Thea's house, with her brothers talking and a clatter of dishes in the kitchen.

Upstairs in Thea's bedroom, we pulled out papers and pencils and I spread out my paper towel of gingersnaps, which were only a little broken from riding in my pocket. Thea said she'd have one later, and right away we focused on our project outline, making it sound as mature as we could. It was messy when we started, but Thea printed it over carefully onto a page we could show to her father and whoever:

1. Research: (A) Mrs. Toussaint's journal. (B) The town history. (C) Town clerk's office, deeds and taxes and anything else on the inn. (D) Field trip to Barnet to see and measure other hiding place—look for markings on wall (see 2).

2. Figuring: Work out code from Warwick cellar secret room. Check stagecoach schedules, records of deliveries to inn, dates from journal.

3. Written report: Show data, methods, results, conclusions, with at least two charts.

4. Photos and maps: Map of the Underground Railway. Photos of both hiding places. Copy Mrs. Toussaint's photos. Find photos of inn from old days.

5. Display for history fair: Get poster boards and construction paper and markers. Make a quiz for people to do when they come see the display. Costumes?

I was the one who put a question mark by Costumes. Thea thought we should dress up to emphasize our report, maybe like escaped slaves. Or the innkeeper or stagecoach driver. I sort of liked the idea, but I told Thea that at last year's science fair, which probably was like this history one would be, nobody had dressed up.

"The boys wore ties, and the girls put on Sunday clothes, not anything like costumes," I said. Thea shrugged. But she didn't want me to cross off the idea, so instead I just put the question mark. It was only supposed to be a proposal, after all. We could change it some as we went along.

Downstairs the dog started barking, loud and shrill. We ran down the stairs. Mr. Warwick and another man stood inside the door, stamping dirt off their shoes and hanging up jackets. "Girls," Mr. Warwick said, "this is Dr. Thomas from the college. He's a specialist in American history. I've told him all about your discovery. Why don't you get the big flashlights from the kitchen and meet us down in the cellar."

The college professor looked like an older version of Mr. Harris—tall, thin-faced, and wearing a tie and vest. He had a thick moustache, though, and kept wiping at it after blowing his nose. I smelled car exhaust and cigarette smoke as he nodded to us and pulled out a camera. "I've just been telling your father," he said to Thea, with another nod over at me. "The timing is terrific. We're having a Civil War history conference at the college in January, and I have a video crew lined up for this weekend, to shoot some local footage. If, of course, this is an Underground Railroad location, we'll include it."

Now Thea and I shared one of those looks that the twins were always doing. Conference? Video?

This was definitely not a secret room any more.

FOUR PEOPLE INSIDE the hidden room: Thea's father, the professor from the college, Thea, me. I could hardly breathe, and I tried to stay back in the corner, partway under one of the shelves to make more room.

Dr. Thomas shone his flashlight against the back wall first and pointed out strips of lighter wood, low on each wall. "Those held supports for another shelf," he announced. "Possibly a sleeping shelf like the ones at the end of the room. If, of course, this was a runaway slave hiding place."

Thea and I looked at each other and shared the thought: We hadn't noticed those before. We'd only really looked hard along the one wall, the wall with the two lists of code on it.

Mr. Warwick pointed out the numbers and letters to the professor. "We don't yet know what this means," he said. We? I cleared my throat to speak up, but Mr. Warwick went on. "Of course it could be a record of who stayed here and how long, or some way of letting other runaways know that family members had been here. Maybe a message for the ones coming in the next group. There could have been dozens, even hundreds, coming through here, seeing how we're so close to Canada."

I saw how the professor pulled back from Mr. Warwick, to disagree with him. "Hundreds, no. Probably not even dozens. My research suggests only about one dozen African Americans in all of Caledonia County in the decade before the Civil War."

"That's all?" Thea sounded as surprised as I felt. She added, "I mean, if people were hiding and helping in all the towns around here, in a whole ten years, how come there were just, like, so few?"

"Well, you know, this wasn't the shortest route to Canada then. Most of the fugitives were moved up by the Great Lakes, and then the Hudson River Valley was second, through Albany and along the far side of Lake Champlain. People collected money, of course, and sent it to help. But most of the Vermont effort was in Burlington. Even so," he smiled at Thea, "the advantage of only a dozen slaves to trace is that each Underground Railroad location in this region is very important." He turned to Thea's father. "Of course we'll have to examine the inn's records, as well as the town records, to try to confirm that this hiding place was used then. But in the meantime, I'll definitely send the video crew over here. We can fit you into the schedule on Sunday afternoon. There's a strong possibility you've got a genuine railroad station here, in spite of the low numbers."

He pulled out his camera and we all had to move out of the room so he could photograph the code and the corners and everything.

Teddy, the three-year-old brother, called out from the top of the stairs. "Daddy? I want to come down."

"No, Teddy, you stay upstairs." Mr. Warwick went up and called for his wife to take Teddy away from the stairs. I could smell tomato sauce and garlic. My stomach growled, but not very loudly. Thea leaned against the doorway of the hiding place. Then the snapping and beeping and flashing inside the little room slowed. A moment later, Dr. Thomas stepped out of the closed space, working his shoulders to uncurl them.

As Thea's dad came back down the cellar steps, the professor ignored us and spoke only to him. "You'll want to lock this, of course, to keep children away from it. The lettering on the wall is especially vulnerable to what children sometimes do. Above all, don't wash the walls or even sweep or dust. I can ask a team from the research center in Burlington to give you some advice on preservation, if you like."

"That sounds good," Mr. Warwick said. "I'll just fasten it shut for now, and I'll pick up a lock tomorrow."

Thea said, "But Dad, you have to give us a key, right? Shawna and I are still working on this, for our school project."

"We'll see," said her father. "You can always use my key. I don't think you need your own, sweetheart. Now, let's take Dr. Thomas upstairs, maybe he'd like a cup of coffee or some lemonade."

"No, no, that's all right, thanks anyway, I should be getting home myself." The professor zipped a cover around his camera and blew his nose again. "I'll need to check the crew schedule. Will you be available all afternoon Sunday? I'm not sure when they'll get here."

"Sure, any time is fine with me."

The men went up toward the kitchen, and Thea said, "We'll be up in a minute, Dad." She looked at me and held up a hand—wait until they close the door, she meant. I waited.

The door at the top of the stairs shut behind them, leaving us in the dimly lit cellar. I let my breath out—I didn't realized how much I'd been holding it—and I asked Thea, "What are we going to do?"

"Nothing, I guess," she said in a depressed tone. "Everyone's going to know about it now."

"But maybe they won't be as good as solving the code as we are, you know? And we have the letters and the map, too." I wanted Thea to cheer up. Even more, I wanted it to be important, what we were doing together. Urgently, I told her, "We've got to be the ones who figure it out first. We've *got* to be the first."

We linked pinkie fingers to make the commitment. Only the fact that it was suppertime kept us from running all the way up to Thea's room right away to work on the code some more.

"Come back after dinner," Thea urged. "We can do it. We can do it *first*."

Up the cellar stairs we went, and when I saw the Warwicks' kitchen clock, I realized I'd better get home—fast. Five after six. I waved to Mrs. Warwick, who was draining spaghetti and just called "Bye, honey," and I dodged around Teddy and saw the two men, still talking by the door. Mr. Warwick patted my shoulder as I slipped past him and out.

A little light hung in the western sky beyond the church. The safety light on our barn lit the road. Around the back of the barn it was dark, though, and cold. Hands pulled back inside my sweatshirt sleeves, I jumped up the porch steps, two at a time, and burst into the light and fragrance of the kitchen. "Sorry I'm late!"

My mother nodded and told me to set the table quickly, but she wasn't mad. So I kicked off my sneakers by the door and pulled out plates and forks and knives. Chicken tenders—I could almost taste them in the humid air, and I smelled boiled potatoes. Good.

"Just us three?"

"Four," my mother corrected. "Carl and Harry are milking together. We'll wait for them, and you can come mash these potatoes. I'm just putting on the peas." The timer gave a ding, and she bent to the oven and pulled out a pan of cornbread. There was some kind of cake already done, too, covered with a dish towel on a plate. She must really be in a good mood!

I asked, "Were you and Harry up on the ridge today?"

"No, Harry stayed down here. I went up on my own."

"See anything?"

"Mmm-hmm." She sat down abruptly on her chair, the one by the phone, and picked up one foot to rub it, in her lap. "My feet are killing me. I went out the old woods road past the river, kept finding signs for that big buck, and finally cut across enough littler stuff to figure out where the does are bedding down. I guess I know where to try to cut his trail now."

"Hey, that's great. So you'll be ready when deer season opens, right?"

Smiling, she switched feet. "If my feet last so long. One buck's not enough, but I guess there are a couple others I might know about, too."

I remembered Emerson and looked around. The stacks of boxes of rifle shells and the others of hardware—oh, there they were, by the hall. "Hey Mom, did you know Emerson came by earlier to drop off that stuff?"

"I figured." She stood up and rummaged in the fridge, handing me a plastic jug of milk and another of soda for the table. "Did you see him, honey?"

The rest of what Emerson had said came back to me. "Mom, Emerson says Alice must have some mixed-up reason for coming home for Thanksgiving. I mean, besides seeing us. But probably after so long away, she just wants to come home, doesn't she?"

For a moment my mother stood looking at me, measuring, and when she began to reply, I almost thought she'd tell me what she was really thinking. Obviously something had bothered her on the phone with Alice. But then the door from the porch slammed open as Carl came in, carrying another Tupperware pitcher of milk, and in the swoop of air and sound that came with him, the answer, if there was one, vanished. "Take off your boots," said my mother to Carl, who already had one off and the other halfway. "Hang up your jacket and go wash your hands. Shawna, come mash the potatoes, I've already got milk and butter in there."

In hardly any time at all, the four of us plus the food were all ready, and Harry closed his eyes to say grace. He folded his big hands together, with the stained yellow fingers twisted into each other. I shut my eyes.

"Lord, we just ask your blessing on this food, and on the hands that prepared it. And we just ask you to keep us safe and to keep giving us good work. And Lord, please bless this family and help us to be truly grateful. In Jesus's name, Amen."

"Amen," we all echoed, and we passed the dishes.

After a few minutes, Harry lifted an eyebrow my way and asked, "So how was school today?"

"All right, I guess."

"Homework?"

"Yeah, but not too much. I've already got the reading done, so it's just math and some history." I turned: "Hey, Mom? Have you heard from anybody else about the Warwicks' house? You know, about the room Thea and I found? This man from the college was there today taking pictures of it."

"Mmm. I didn't hear anything. You, Harry?" My mother took a second piece of cornbread and passed the dish toward Carl.

Harry nodded, swallowed some chicken, and wiped his hands on a napkin. "Sounds like you girls might have found one of those hiding places from the Civil War, that's what I heard. That right, Shawna?"

"I guess. Maybe. I mean, we don't really know for sure yet. But it would be cool, wouldn't it?"

Harry looked at my mother. "I never heard about anyone hiding Negroes here, Connie, did you?"

"Never did. And you'd think Gramps would have told some about it, but I never heard a thing. Now over in Barnet, I know they did it over there, at the Goodwillie House. You should ask Mrs. Toussaint, Shawna. Or maybe you did—what did she say?"

"She never heard of it either, but she has this old picture of the inn, and Thea and I think there's an African American face in one of the upstairs windows." I said "African American" really carefully, hoping Harry would pick up on it and not talk about "Negroes" like that.

"Is that so?" Harry was interested. "Well, then, I suppose if they were in the upstairs windows, maybe they were just staying at the inn like anybody else. Or working there, that could be, too." He leaned back in his chair, scraping its feet on the kitchen linoleum. "So maybe there wasn't so much hiding, just visiting."

I stared. What if Harry was right? But wasn't the secret room for hiding them? I needed to know more. A list began to form in my mind: *(a) Prove they were here. (Double-check Mrs. T's photo. Anything else on paper?) (b) Find evidence: hiding or just visiting at the inn? (c) How many people? Does the code tell us? Does anyone know for sure?*

Dessert was pound cake with berries, last summer's strawberries out of the freezer and topped with whipped cream, but I only had one and half bowls full, because I was in a hurry. "Mom, can I go over to Thea's again now? Just for a little while?"

"Not tonight," she answered firmly. "You've got homework, and so does she, I'm sure. And it's already past seven. You'll see her in the morning."

"Then can I call her?"

My mother looked at the clock, frowned at me, and said, "Just five minutes. Then homework! Wait a minute, young lady, the table gets cleared before you talk on the phone."

When I finally told Thea what Harry had said, it was as if she were right in the room with me. In her silence, I could picture her face, squinting and thinking.

At last she said, "We've got to find out more. More research, and more reading. Let's go see that library lady again before our Barnet trip Saturday. And maybe there's something in the books that we already have, too."

I rushed through math and the science study sheet, then dove into history, thumbing through the heavy text and then Mom and Harry's copy of the town history book, even looking things up from the index. But there was nothing that helped with what we needed to know.

So after my shower, I snuggled into bed with the book for English class again, *Uncle Tom's Cabin*. There had to be clues somewhere.

Clues: I leaned over the edge of the bed and dug through my backpack until I found the code from the walls of the hidden room. There was a pattern in the numbers and letters, but it slipped just beyond my thinking. As I fell asleep, I hoped I'd dream up the answer to it all.

14

AT FIRST I didn't know I was dreaming. It was dark, and I was in a truck: Harry's truck, driving it. My mother sat next to me, saying "Hurry, hurry!" I kept trying to steer around the curves in the dark road, and even though my feet didn't reach the gas pedal, the truck went faster and faster each time my mother cried, "Hurry!" So steering the truck took all my concentration. As I wrestled with the steering wheel and we swung sideways around another long curve of road, the truck lights lit up a pair of eyes in front of us, dark orange and staring right at me. I fumbled for the switch—somehow I knew there was a switch in the truck to make it rise in the air, over the animal on the road—but I couldn't find it, and with an awful lurch, we hit the enormous deer. Its body slid up the hood of the truck toward me, massive branched antlers off to one side, the eyes still staring at me although I knew it must be dying. I wanted to stop, but my mother kept saying, "Don't stop, we have to get there! Hurry!"

Suddenly, the deer was gone, and so was the truck, and I stood under bright white lights in a hospital. A nurse kept writing things on a white wall, with numbers and letters that moved into neat columns. Alice was there, arguing with my mother and trying to take a baby away from her. The baby was crying. I couldn't bear the crying. In the dream, I slipped between my mother and Alice and took the baby and cuddled it, and when Alice and my mother stopped yelling and turned to look at me instead, I asked them, "Where is the real mother? Is she hiding here? Where is she?"

Alice and my mother disappeared, and suddenly I knew it was a dream, but the baby's little mouth slipped warm and wet against my fingers, and I half woke up, and there really was something licking my other hand.

But a rough lick, not like a baby's tiny mouth. Wet and warm, but scratchy.

Glad to have company, I pulled Midnight under the covers and let him curl up in my arms while I rubbed his head and scratched behind his ears. I lay under his comforting warmth and the rumble of his purring, trying to remember the rest of the dream. The deer, I thought. I have to go back and make sure it's dead. I can't leave it there suffering.

In confusion, I fell back to sleep, and though I knew I had more dreams, all I remembered in the morning was that first one. Who dreams about hospitals and babies, anyway? It was weird.

But it made me realize something. There must have been a North Upton doctor from the old days. Doctors kept records of what they did. I didn't know why, but the dream made me sure that one more set of records, one more journal, would add enough to our letters and numbers to crack the secret code the rest of the way open.

Besides that, I had a hunch that we should go back to the list Thea and I had made, the one about the code. Too many things were happening this week, taking us away from our list of evidence and steps. It was time to concentrate and figure the rest of it out.

I scrambled into a sweatshirt and jeans. My mother would

call me for breakfast any minute. Giving my head a fierce shake, I pushed aside the other part of the dream: the part about my sister Alice. It was only, only a dream.

ALL DAY WEDNESDAY, kids at school talked about the Halloween dance, nine days away. I kept reading *Uncle Tom's Cabin* inside my other books, except in math class, when Thea and I drew our house diagrams onto the blackboard and showed how we got all our numbers. Mrs. Labounty liked our report for sure. Before we showed the part with the east end of the cellar, we changed the numbers back again to show where the secret room was—after all, the whole village knew about it now, so why not be truthful? "The truth will set you free," said St. Paul. I wondered whether people taught that to the slaves, while keeping them chained up and everything. God must not have been happy about that. Maybe part of why He let the Civil War last so long and kill so many people was to punish everyone involved in keeping slaves.

Anyway, mostly people asked about the room instead of about the math, which sort of spoiled the whole point of the report as far as I was concerned. And everyone just seemed to assume that people hid in the room. Nobody paid attention to what Thea and I said about the lack of evidence for that part.

After school, I met Thea in the schoolyard.

"We should go see Mrs. Toussaint," I reminded her. "I have to get the phone number for that place in Barnet. And we need to choose a different time to look at her books. Plus I think we should find out about doctors back then, and whether she has any diaries or books from them."

Thea wrinkled her nose in apology. "I can't," she told me. She pointed over my shoulder. "My mom's here. She says I have to ride with her to go grocery shopping—I didn't know until I saw our car." She made a funny face. "I'd rather go anywhere except grocery shopping! I'm sorry!"

I shrugged and smiled anyway. "That's okay. I'll do it. Call me when you get back!"

"Sure." She hurried across to the waiting minivan, where her brothers were bouncing in the back seat. A quick wave, and she was gone.

At the library building, I checked the door to the historical society room, but it was locked and the lights were out. So I went to the other end of the hall and entered the regular school library. Mrs. Toussaint stood by the large desk, putting things into her canvas carrier. There weren't any other kids in the room.

"Mrs. Toussaint? Could I talk to you for a minute?"

"A quick minute," she replied. "What is it, Shawna?"

"It's about Saturday. Thea and I can't come after all, because we've got a ride to Barnet for Saturday. Could I please have the phone number and name for who we call about seeing the hiding place over there?"

"Of course." She opened the phone book and copied a name and number onto a piece of paper for me. "That's fine, dear, and you may come back here on the next Saturday then." She reached to turn off the lights.

"Please—could you just tell me whether you have any diaries from doctors from those years? From before the Civil War, I mean."

She held the door open, gesturing for me to go back out into the hallway. "No, I'm afraid we don't. We have only one set of records from a doctor, one who served in the Second World War. I'm sorry, Shawna."

I followed her down the hall and out the main door. "Well, where would we look, Thea and me, if we wanted to know about babies being born and marriages and deaths, then?"

"The town reports," she said, then corrected herself. "No, the town reports only go back to eighteen eighty-five, I'm afraid. But the town clerk has a book of birth records with indexes that date to about seventeen ninety-two." Obviously Mrs. Toussaint liked numbers, if she could remember them like that.

"So can we see those when we come back?"

"No, they're not here, dear. They're at the town clerk's office in Upton. You know where the town hall is, don't you? Across from the park where the Upton fair is held." With a quick heave, she piled her bags into the back seat of a little red car parked at the side of the school. "Do you need a ride home?"

"No, thank you."

I pulled back against the wall to be out of the way as she backed the car out and drove out of the parking lot. The town clerk's office. One more place to go, one more thing to figure out.

A few seventh graders were hanging out by the swings, but other than that, the schoolyard was empty. I tugged my backpack straps over my shoulders and started home.

Already, the sun was low behind the ridge. Cool air pressed down from the hills, a taste of snow in it. Scuffing through the brown leaves along the side of the road, I passed our vegetable stand with the closed sign in the window, and by habit counted the windows in the inn—that is, the Warwicks' house. Nine windows in the main front of the house, each with twelve small panes of glass. Two narrow windows beside the front door, four panes of glass each. Four windows in the addition where the kitchen was, twelve panes in each one. I didn't count the garage windows, but stood for a moment multiplying and adding. One hundred and seventy-two panes of glass across the front, not counting the garage or the tool shed either. It was soothing to know something for sure.

In our kitchen I switched on the ceiling light, and found a plate of whoopie pies with an apple and empty glass, and a note propped next to them. "Taking Carl to town, bringing home pizzas. Harry's milking. Start homework!!"

The whoopie pies, still cool from the fridge, had that perfect mix of chocolate cake and creamy filling. While I ate my second one, I considered Alice's photo up on the wall, wondering if Emerson was right about her. And if he was: What was her plan? Why was she finally coming home this year for Thanksgiving? More important: Why wouldn't anyone tell me why she'd never come home before, in ten long years?

I licked my fingers and took a third whoopie pie, and decided I'd leave the fourth one on the plate. That proved I wasn't greedy.

Moving away from the table while I licked the cream off the edges of the whoopie pie in my hand, I walked along the row of other family photos: Grammy and Gramps, my mother's parents, who lived in Florida now; Harry's sister, Aunt Grace; a picture of Emerson and Carl and me, at camp, all wearing our orange vests for safety during hunting season.

The sideboard under the photos was bulky, heavy, dark, its two top drawers partly open with papers sticking out. Mom's Bibles lay in a stack, the big family Bible at the bottom, then two others, and her teaching Bible open at the top of the pile. Leviticus. Ugh. There were no good stories in that part. Me, I liked Judges and Kings, and the maps of all the invasions and battles.

I called the phone number for the Goodwillie House and the woman who answered said we could come visit on Saturday. Good! That was done. As I put the phone back, I looked again at the jumble of papers and things on the sideboard.

Beside the stack of Bibles sat an old breadbox. Flowers painted on the red tin sides dressed it up. The front of the breadbox lay flat open, because it was too full to shut the front anyway: jammed with old Town Reports sticking out, some crumpled and twisted. It looked totally disorganized. Thea's house seemed much more organized than ours. Well, I could tidy the breadbox at least.

I pulled out the Town Reports and began flattening them, sorting them by year. The cover of the year 2000 report showed our farm, in two photos a hundred years apart. You could see the little sign by the front door, "Century Farm." The state gives you that when your family has been farming at the same place for a hundred years.

Moving the reports into sequence, I thought about groups of five and how you could sort faster that way, instead of by decades. There were thirty-four reports in front of me, and it didn't take long to put them into sequence.

The one for the year when I was born wasn't in the pile, though.

I checked the breadbox again, and poked in the stack of papers at the other side of it. No Town Report for my year.

Kneeling, I looked under the sideboard, then behind it. Nope.

Maybe it was in one of the drawers. I set the stacked, sequenced Town Reports back in the breadbox, arranging them so I could see the place where mine was missing, and then I started taking papers out of the first drawer, flattening them, and making them into an organized pile. For a moment it seemed like I'd found the missing report, but it turned out to be a 4-H report instead. I began sorting the second drawer.

I found it. The front showed a photo of Mrs. Toussaint, with her dark tanned skin and sharp gaze, but the wrinkles on her face not so bad back then. Her glasses hung down in front of her and she stared out of the photo looking just as fierce as now, maybe more so. Under the photo it said "Reporter Jennie Toussaint retires: Fifty years of writing all the news that's fit to print." Wow, I didn't know she'd been a reporter. Somehow I'd always thought a reporter would speak with lots of slang and take risks. But Mrs. Toussaint spoke precisely and moved quietly. And if she'd worked fifty years by nineteen ninety-nine, and started work at, let's see, maybe eighteen at the earliest, then she was, gosh, eighty years old. That was seriously old.

I thumbed through the report, and found a long page about Mrs. Toussaint that said her family had come down from Canada in 1832 and helped start North Upton. I skipped past some of it, looking for the page with the births and deaths on it. I wanted to find my name.

But the page was missing—torn out.

Frustrated and confused, I closed the report and put it into the breadbox with the others. And when I heard tires in the driveway, I quickly pulled out my schoolbooks and spread them on the kitchen table, and opened a notebook and my history book. So when my mother beeped the horn and I ran to hold the door for her and the boxes of pizza, I could say truthfully, "Yes, I started my homework. I'll clear it out of the way so we can eat."

Pizza doesn't take long to eat if you're hungry. And when it smells so good, pepperoni and mushroom and cheese, and thick crust, I'm always hungry. I ate two pieces of pepperoni and mushroom pizza, and thinking about Thea, I tried the vegetable one too, with peppers and onions and sliced black olives. Mom noticed.

"I thought you only liked pepperoni pizza," she commented. "And you're not even taking the onions off. What's up?"

"This is okay, I guess," I admitted. "I might get used to it."

"Instead of pepperoni?"

I shook my head. "I still like pepperoni the best. But it's probably good for me to have more vegetables."

My mother tipped her head to one side. "Growing up means making your own decisions about what's good for you. And what God wants for you."

"Yeah." I didn't want to talk about God or Jesus or this week's memory Bible verse, so I switched the subject. "Did you notice the sideboard? I cleaned it up."

She twisted around in her chair and looked. "Looks good. You didn't throw anything away, did you? I need those papers."

"No, Mom, I didn't throw anything away. Hey, I was looking

at those Town Reports, and you know what? The one from the year I was born, where the babies are all listed, that page is missing. Like, it's torn out."

"Hay is for horses," my mother corrected me. "Don't 'hey' me. And don't say 'like' at the beginning of a sentence."

"Okay, I won't. But Mom, what about the page that's torn out? Do you have it?"

She looked down at her empty plate, then helped herself to another slice of the veggie pizza. "I'm sure it's here somewhere," she said vaguely. "Things get moved around. We should talk about it." Did she mean talk about the missing page, or about things getting moved? She pushed the pizza box toward me. "You can have the rest of this one. I'm going to help Harry finish up in the barn."

At least she didn't want me to come to the barn with her, so I said all right and asked, "Can I call Thea about homework?"

"May I," my mother nudged.

"Yes, may I call Thea now?"

"After seven, so her family can have some peace at suppertime," she replied. "And before you start work, wash out the glasses and put the paper plates in the trash, please."

It took just a moment for her to step into barn boots and pull a barn jacket over her sweatshirt, and she bumped through the porch and out the door. I stood alone in the kitchen again, which was a good thing, because the phone rang right at that moment, and I was the one who answered it.

The crisp clear voice of Mrs. Toussaint came through the phone so loudly that I held it away from my ear. "Good evening. This is Jennie Toussaint. I would like to speak with Shawna Lee, please."

"This is Shawna, Mrs. Toussaint."

"Thank you. Very good. Shawna, when we talked earlier, I told you that the historical society possesses no journals or diaries of doctors from the period before the Civil War. And that is quite true. However—" Mrs. Toussaint paused.

I couldn't bear the suspense. "However?"

She gave a short cough. "However, in surveying the letters in my personal collection, I find several sheets of correspondence to my grandmother, from Mrs. Nancy Woodward. That would be Doctor Woodward's wife. The letters date from 1857 and 1859."

"Can I—I mean, may I see them, Mrs. Toussaint? Please?"

"Yes, of course. I've decided to make a set of photocopies for the historical society, and a second set for you. You may collect them a week from Saturday at the historical society library."

"Thank you!"

Clues! Who knew what could be in those letters? There could be secrets about the Underground Railroad, maybe even mention of Thea's house! It was ten minutes to seven, and I just had to call and tell Thea, even though my mother had said to wait for seven o'clock.

The Warwicks were done with supper anyway. On the phone, Thea and I speculated about the letters and planned out the trip to Barnet, to the Goodwillie House, for this coming Saturday. In the background, I heard her father telling Thea she should get off the phone.

"Let's do the science homework together," Thea proposed. "I bet I could come over for an hour anyway. Can I come over to your house right now?"

"Sure!" Mom and Harry wouldn't mind. And if they came in while Thea and I were working—well, then maybe we could work upstairs in my room, instead of at the kitchen table. That way, whether it was *Jeopardy* or *Entertainment Tonight* that Harry and Mom had on the TV, Thea wouldn't notice. The way her family banned TV during the week made me worried that what Mom and Harry watched might look like a waste of time to Thea, not to mention distracting—although someone with two younger brothers must get distracted a lot, anyway.

I ran upstairs to make my bed and pick up some stuff from the floor, ran back downstairs to grab two TV tables for working, and when Thea came knocking, I already had a plate of gingersnaps ready and two glasses of ice water, since Thea didn't seem to like drinking milk very much. Together we carried the snacks and our bookbags to my room.

But the floor worked better for spreading out the books and papers. Even though it was bumpy from the old boards, the carpet in my room leveled it out enough. At first it was hard to focus on anything except wondering about the letters Mrs. Toussaint had, and the trip to see the fugitive slave hiding place in Barnet. Still, we pulled out our worksheets and began marking the hair colors, eye colors, even skin colors, like the biology assignment wanted.

"You can tell these worksheets came from the Internet," I pointed out. "Skin color! Nobody in this part of Vermont has different skin color. At least, not in North Upton."

"Oh." Thea sighed. "This has to be one of the last places in America that's all the same. Okay."

Thea marked in her mother's hair and eye colors, then the ones for her father. "Perfect," she announced. "Dark hair for both parents, and so is mine. And eye color for my mother, blue, and for my father, green. Green is incomplete dominance between blue and brown," she rattled off. "And I have green eyes, so I got a brown eye gene from my father, for sure."

She looked at my chart. "You have to mark the connections for dominant trait or incomplete dominance," she reminded me. "Your mother has brown eyes, you do too—what about your father?"

I hesitated. "I guess I don't know. I never asked my mother about that. Wait a minute, I'll get his picture from downstairs." I ran down, then back up, taking the stairs two at a time.

"Give it to me," Thea said. "Do you have a magnifying glass?"

We peered at the faded color of the wedding photo from thirty-one years before. My mother had been a lot thinner then; she looked like Alice's photo, more than she looked like herself now. Thea tipped the picture into the light.

"Blue eyes," she announced. "Your father had blue eyes."

I started to mark that onto the chart, then stopped. "Can't be. That wouldn't work for me to have brown eyes. Blue eyes means he'd have two blue genes, and he'd have to give one of them to the embryo. So then I'd have green eyes, but they're totally brown. He must have had green eyes, so he could give me a brown eye gene."

Thea nodded uncertainly. "Your logic is right," she admitted. "Green is what it should be. But they look blue in this picture."

"Maybe the color on the photo faded over the years."

"Maybe."

I penciled "green" into the eye color circle for "Father" on the worksheet. I could double-check with my mother later. Quickly, I finished the chart, and then we did the section on smooth and wrinkled peas, the experiment Mendel did way back in the eighteen hundreds—definitely cool. And when we graphed the third and fourth generations of peas and how the proportions came out in the seeds, I could see a math expression that fit the relationship. Thea saw it too.

"Let's write it down and maybe we'll get extra credit," she proposed.

She checked the bedside clock and packed her papers and books. "Gotta go."

As soon as I opened my bedroom door we could hear the low hum of the television downstairs. I hurried to explain: "My mother and Harry are back in from milking, and they like to unwind for a little, so they watch this show."

"Oh, that's cool," Thea reassured me. "Your parents are normal. Mine are just weird about TV." She flashed me a smile.

Whew. All that worrying I'd done about Thea thinking my parents were strange for watching TV, and she thought they were normal.

When we reached the kitchen, my mother called out, "Shawna? Who's that with you?"

"It's Thea, Mom."

"Hi, Thea!" My mother knew her, of course, from back when she visited the Warwicks when they first moved in across the road. Harry didn't, though, so he stood up and came to the kitchen. He must have changed his sweatshirt when he came in from the barn, because he wore a clean one, and his jeans looked okay, too. When he put his hands on the table to lean on it and say hello, I saw Thea look at his wide farming fingers and stained nails. But she acted normal and just said she was glad to meet him.

"Thea's got to go now," I reminded them, and walked out onto the porch, turning on the outside light. I took a flashlight from the shelf by the door, said I'd be right back, and walked with Thea around the dark end of the barn, to the circle of the safety light by the road. The windows in her house glowed golden. I could see the outline of one of her brothers upstairs.

"See you!" we called to each other, as Thea crossed the road and went up the path to her own kitchen door.

As I walked back around the barn, I flicked the flashlight off and stuffed it into my back pocket. I stopped in the darkest part of the yard to look up at the sky.

You could tell winter was coming soon. Not just from the cold snap of the air, but the way the air vanished from sight, nothing between the ground and the bright stars. I could see so many of them that the sky was almost white in places, especially where the Milky Way hung. A whisker of moon crouched over the hills—appearing or vanishing? I reminded myself: If the curve looked like a lower-case *d*, the moon was DEE-creasing, and if it bulged like a lower-case *b*, it was getting BEE-bigger. Decreasing, then. Tomorrow night there'd be no moon at all.

When I was little, I pretended the stars made a path for God and the angels to walk along. And for thunder, either God was mad at me or the angels were moving furniture around in heaven. Everybody knows that lightning is a sign of God's power. So everything I knew about God back then was either scary or comforting, like Jesus cuddling the lambs and always loving me. "Jesus loves me, this I know, For the Bible tells me so, Little ones to Him belong, They are weak but He is strong."

Under this fierce night sky, with all around me the scent of the nearby barn but also the wet cold smell of leaves on the ground in the darkness underfoot, I looked for God in the sky.

Having a best friend should mean saying thank you to God, a big thank you. I kicked at the leaves, making sure there were no rocks or sticky piles of cow manure, then knelt next to the barn and put one hand against the rough wood so I could tip my head backward and look at the heavens more. God, mighty God.

Cold wetness seeped through the knees of my jeans. I closed my eyes and bent my head, hands folded in my lap. You bow your head to God because God is Lord, but also because God hates stiff-necked people like his earliest ones were. I rolled my head down closer to my chest to be more humble.

"Dear Lord, I just want to say thank you for Thea. Lord, just keep her safe, please. Help me to be good, and to be a good friend back to her." The smallness of being me seemed cold and wet, too. "Help me please to keep having a best friend. And God, please," I switched to automatic, "please just watch over Mom and Harry and Alice and Carl and Emerson and me, and watch over us in the night please, Lord. In Jesus's name and for His sake, Amen."

Folded into a small dark kneeling self against the wet leaves and grass, I stayed small a moment longer. Beyond the farmyard, in the fields, a few crickets made slow chirping sounds, too cold to sing properly. I heard a scuffling from the cow barn, bulky animals changing position. A cat pushed against me, warm and meowing, so I opened my eyes and stroked him. Sammy, patrolling. He rubbed his head on my legs, and I stroked his back, but he didn't want to be picked up, and poured himself away from my arms when I started to lift him. He stalked around the barn, toward the porch.

I stood up. From being closed, now my eyes saw better in the starlight. Up over the edge of the house roof I saw the pattern of the stars that outline Orion, the hunter, with three stars in a row for his sword. I turned to face north and picked out the stars of the Big Dipper, then the Little Dipper and the North Star. "Follow the drinking gourd," the slaves told each other. Follow the constellations that pulled them north.

A hundred and fifty years ago, a black girl could have stood right here, looking for those stars. And then what happened to her? Did she hide in the little room in the cellar of the Warwicks' house? Ride north with someone from North Upton to take care of her?

The code from the secret room: I needed to solve it, to get to the rest of our evidence. I walked to my own kitchen door and back into the warm kitchen. From my bookbag, I pulled out the notes. I lined up the columns of letters and numbers, and also a copy of the list from Henry Dearborn's journal. I let the numbers talk to me, the ones with all those multiples of six and twelve, and a complete certainty came with them. Who counts humans in dozens and half dozens? Nobody does. The numbers in this code definitely weren't about people.

I looked at the clock. No, I wouldn't call Thea now. I'd sleep on the idea. Maybe by morning I could see some other explanation.

ALL DAY THURSDAY I worried about the code and the secret room. The more I thought about the numbers and letters, the more sure I was that something else, something that wasn't escaped slaves at all, hid in the lists. Each time I started to say something to Thea, though, someone interrupted. When could I get some time with just my friend?

After school, everyone from our grade plus the sixth and seventh graders went to the gym to meet in committees for the dance. Thea joined the music committee, and I saw the Willson twins pushing close to her. I couldn't do anything about it, though, because my group was refreshments. Miss Calkins passed around a list for each of us to sign up for something. "Dozens, ladies and gentlemen," she warbled. "You are signing up for how many dozens of something. We need twelve dozen altogether, plus the punch of course. Mrs. Toussaint is donating the punch."

I signed up for three dozen "black as midnight" brownies, easy enough. All the names on the list came in Halloween versions: jack-o-lantern cookies, haunted house doughnuts. Apples were on the list too, for bobbing—Maryellen Bryce signed up for those, which meant she'd bring store-bought apples. Maryellen Bryce was way too snotty to want to have wormy old farm apples in her teeth!

Plus I marked the list of jobs, saying I'd come early and put food onto plates. Probably Thea would come early too, to help set up the music. I looked across the gym at her committee. Who was that, anyway, standing next to her? Miss Calkins told us that we were done, so I went over to the music committee to investigate. Oh—the Willson girls' older cousin, Josh. That meant the high school bus must already have come into the village.

"Yeah, that's okay," Josh was saying to the twins. "Miley Cyrus, she's all right. And I'll bring the Black Eyed Peas, sure. But don't you want to do, like, some seventies music? It's more fun, for a party like this. I could bring, like, some Beatles and The Stones."

"'Satisfaction,' I like that one!" Thea waved her hands enthusiastically. "I've got Led Zeppelin, too, with 'Stairway to Heaven,' and maybe Sly and the Family Stone, 'Dance to the Music,' that would work, wouldn't it?"

Everybody else looked kind of vague, but Josh nodded and kept saying, "Yeah, yeah, that's cool, you really have a lot of this kind of music, don't you?"

"Kind of," Thea answered. "Anyway, I'll bring a couple dozen CDs from that group. But nobody else is going to handle them, right, just you? I don't want scratches, you know?"

"Yeah, no problem," Josh told her. "You can even help if you want."

The Willson twins now stood a bit apart from Thea and Josh with a couple of other girls. Powers of two, I saw mathematically: two to the zero power was one, and that was me; two to the first power was two, and that was Thea and Josh; two to the second power, which is two squared, that's four, which was Merry and Marsha Willson and the two others; two to the power of three would be eight, and the fourth power was sixteen, and I scanned the gym, looking for groups that size. Maybe there were eight in the decoration committee, but it was breaking up from its location under the basketball hoop. I nodded at Adam Langmaid as he came up and, quick as a sheepdog, separated Marsha from the group. Merry seemed okay with it, and I saw a twin-speak glance flash from her to Marsha.

Turning back to Thea, I said, “Hey Thea, are you almost ready?”

She nodded and pulled her bookbag strap over one shoulder, then stuck the other hand out to shake hands with Josh Willson. “Nice to meet you,” she told him. “See you next week at the dance.”

We slipped outside. Thea giggled. “Did you see how surprised he was about shaking hands with me?”

“Yeah! You made him act mature, all right.”

“Mature? Oh. I guess. I just did it so I could find out if he had warm hands or cold ones. And whether he has a good grip.”

“So which does he have, warm or cold?”

“Warm.” Thea spun in a circle, smiling. “Warm strong hands and a good grip, and he held on just long enough. Do you think he’s available?”

I stared. “You mean, to go out with? Maybe. I could ask Merry or Marsha.”

“No, don’t! I’ll find out. Those two are dumb as a box of rocks, and I don’t want them knowing I’m interested in their cousin. You know?”

Wow! I didn’t know what to say, so I just nodded. But inside, I felt as warm as if I were Josh Willson’s hand: Thea didn’t like Marsha and Merry better than me, even though they’d asked her for her music CDs. She thought they were dumb. And that meant she didn’t think that I was dumb. Well, of course, I’m not. But some people could think so. Thea didn’t. Thea really liked me better.

“I’m going to borrow my dad’s digital camera for when we go to Barnet,” Thea was saying. “So we’ll have pictures of everything we see there. You better bring your notebook, you can be the note-taker, right?”

"Right. What time are we leaving on Saturday?"

"Nine-thirty. You better come over to my house at nine, just to be sure."

"Okay. Hey, Thea?"

"What?"

"I think I might have figured out something more about the code. Come on over to my house, and I'll show you. I've got the papers up in my room."

"Cool! I've got to go home first, but I'll come across as soon as I can. What did you figure out? Tell me now!"

"It's the sixes and twelves in the numbers," I began. "But it's better if I show you."

"I'll be right there." She dashed up the path toward her kitchen door, and I trudged around our barn, past the corner where I'd prayed the night before, and up the porch steps. As usual, the kitchen was empty, but an aroma of beef stew hung in the air. I opened the crock-pot to stir it, grabbed two doughnuts from the glass jar by the phone, and hauled my heavy bookbag up the stairs.

Actually, the notes about the code were in the bookbag. Why did I tell Thea they were in my room? Well, anyway, now my bookbag was in my room and so were the notes. I pulled them out and spread them across the bed.

The Dearborn journal notes I divided up to put year by year with the code lists: 1850, then 1851, and so on. Then I pulled the social studies textbook out of my bookbag and found the timeline called "Causes of the Civil War."

Downstairs the door banged and I heard Thea call out, "Shawna?"

"Up here! Come on up."

Together we prowled from dates to lists, and from book to papers and the map. Then we made a graph with different colors for stage arrivals at Henry Dearborn's inn and numbers from the hiding-place list. We looked at each other and shared our assessment: Those numbers and names? They couldn't possibly be fugitive slaves. "There would have had to be hundreds of them," Thea groaned. "No way. Not all the way up here in North Upton. What do you think the numbers really mean?"

"Honestly?" I grimaced. "In the cellar of the inn? I'm thinking beer or something. I mean, wouldn't an innkeeper have beer and stuff in the cellar, keeping it cool? And then the sixes and twelves in the numbers fit really well after all, for, like, cases of beer. I know it's not taking us closer to proving anything about the fugitives, but it's all I can come up with. Beer or eggs," I added reluctantly.

Thea flopped her head down on her arms and mumbled, "I bet you're right." She rolled over and stared at the ceiling, then twisted so she was looking at me upside down. "We have to tell my father. Before those people come to do the video!"

So we piled up the papers, went across the road, and found Mr. Warwick at his computer. His office room didn't look a bit like the rest of the house—the tables were made of glass and metal, and the chairs had leather seats and armrests. He waved at us to sit down and said, "Don't interrupt me yet, wait five minutes. I'm almost through."

Sitting there and being quiet made five minutes seem like fifteen. Actually, it was six minutes and forty-five seconds; there was a big digital clock on the desk and I counted the pulsing light between the hour and minutes in order to know how many seconds. That was four hundred and five seconds all together. I almost said so out loud.

Thea did most of the talking. "Dad, if you look at our numbers and our graph, you can see—the code from our hidden room, it can't be people. The numbers are too big. And see how they match up with when the stage brought people to the inn? We've done three years of the numbers, and a graph, too."

Thea's father frowned and licked a finger to separate the pages. He looked especially at our graph. He used the calculator on his computer to multiply a couple of things. Then he stacked the pages back together.

"I know you girls are trying hard on this, but you're wrong," he announced. "I've been reading more about Vermont during the eighteen-fifties. It was a hotbed of rebellion against federal law." He obviously liked that, because he laughed and slapped a hand on the pages of our work. "A mere four years into the decade, Vermont passed its own law to protect fugitive slaves who came here on the Underground Railroad. And believe it or not, two men from North Upton were in the legislature, making sure that law got written. You two are mistaken. North Upton might have been small, but it mattered."

He pulled out one of our pages again. "Thea, sweetie, just divide all your numbers by six—or multiply them by point one seven, which does the same thing."

He was right about the fraction being point one seven, but it was quicker to just divide by six, and in my head, I saw the divided list settling again into the pattern of ones, twos, threes, and an occasional four, the way I'd worked it out earlier.

Thea gave a hesitant nod. "Those are better numbers, Dad. But why? Why divide them all like that?"

"Because you girls are right, these numbers don't fit with a simple count of people hiding there." He nodded at me and looked back at Thea. "But we can see them as multiples of sixes and twelves. Things were distributed in dozens and half dozens. So the numbers must be a count of what the innkeepers were providing for the fugitives as they arrived. Half a dozen sewing needles. Or a dozen eggs, okay? Even something to drink, you're right, although I don't think this inn served beer. They had ale back then. But honey," he patted Thea's arm reassuringly, "I don't know why you'd want to doubt that this was a hiding place for the runaway slaves. Professor Thomas from the college is already sure of it. He says it's a perfect link to the sites in Barnet and Brownington, the missing location on the map he's been building of the Underground Railroad in Vermont."

Standing up, he waved us back out of his room. "You girls don't need to worry about this. North Upton is a very special village. And finding this hiding place is perfect for the town's future." His hair flopped in his eyes and he tossed it back with an energetic swing of his head, his wide smile and excited eyes making him look a lot like his little boys. "This is what it takes to put North Upton on the map. You tell your parents, too, Shawna—tell them we'll have tourists here by the spring, as well as historians and photographers. See what they think! Good things are coming down the pike!"

And with that, he shut his door behind us and we stood in the hallway, staring at each other in nearly complete confusion.

From the kitchen came sounds of supper cooking, and down the hall the other way, I heard the news from a TV or radio. For a long moment, neither of us spoke.

Finally Thea said, "He could be right."

"I guess," I admitted. But we both knew he'd pushed to a conclusion that went beyond the evidence—just like that picture book had done. There must be some other way to convince Mr. Warwick to back down.

We shrugged, at almost the same moment, and said "Saturday—" We laughed, and Thea added, "Jinx! Pinkie fingers!"

Curling our pinkies together took care of the jinx from saying the same thing at the same time. I let Thea say the whole thing for both of us: "On Saturday we'll go see the hiding place in Barnet. And then we'll know more. And maybe we can prove it to him."

I agreed. "That one's the real thing. So we'll see how much it's like the secret room here."

Down the hall the phone rang, and then Thea's mother called out, "Thea? Someone named Josh wants to talk to you. Five minutes to dinner, so keep it short!"

I made a quick sign of fingers to my ear and lips—call me later!—and Thea grinned and said, "After dinner." She hurried toward the phone, and I slipped through the kitchen behind her, and out the door toward my own home.

WALKING ACROSS THE road alone, in the almost-darkness, the cold surprised me. Underfoot, puddles on the road had shriveled and frozen. My sneakers slipped against the icy surface. The farther I got from Thea's house, the colder things seemed, outside and in. Josh Willson calling Thea: He must have a crush on her. Well, anyone would. Thin, pretty, knows a lot of music, smiles and laughs a lot. Has a secret room in her house, too.

She better not show the secret room to Josh. Just thinking about it made me scared. What if she didn't want to be best friends, if Josh was calling her up? Merry and Marsha didn't like me the way they used to; we were too different, and honestly, neither one of them appealed to me as a friend lately, anyway. Some of the boys at school were okay, but a lot of the girls my age seemed like they were losing their ability to think, and to get excited about new stuff (besides boys). Last year had been lonely. It was still so new, in many ways, having a real friend across the road.

I trudged through the musty-smelling porch, into the kitchen, and flicked on the overhead light. Everybody else's mothers were home after school to take care of them. Where was mine? The barn? Or up at our hunting camp? No note. And no snack left out for me, either. I spotted Sammy, curled up on Harry's armchair in the living room.

No note; that probably meant Mom was in the barn. I went back out to the porch, stepped into my barn boots, and tramped toward the lit doorway at the milkhouse. It felt good to get inside again, into the steamy warmth of the milkroom and then the barn. My mother was spreading sawdust toward the back. Harry stood next to a cow in the first row, injecting medicine into her neck. Must be milk fever. I nodded and said, "Hey."

"Is for horses," Harry tossed back at me, with a short nod. "Hey, yourself. Looking for your mother?"

"I see her."

I detoured over to the grain box and inspected the kittens. Their eyes were open now and their fur, longer and silky, showed different colors. I picked up one that had brown and black and some orange, with a white patch on its face. In my hand, it twisted and curled, seeking its mother's familiar belly. I lifted it close to my face to smell the baby smell of it and nuzzled it with my nose. Then I put it back into the box, right up against one of the mother cat's milky nipples. It grabbed eagerly with its small snout and sucked thirstily, pushing tiny paws rhythmically against the furry belly.

My mother came up behind me with the sawdust cart. "Want to help?"

"Not really," I sighed. "But I will, some. I'll finish the sawdust. Then I've got to go find a snack. I'm starving."

"Have some cheese and crackers," she suggested. "There's beef stew in the crockpot, and I'll make biscuits when I come in. How was school?"

"Okay, I guess. I signed up to bring brownies to the Halloween dance. Three dozen."

She nodded. "You can do those yourself, there are plenty of boxes of brownie mix in the cupboard. By the way, do you think your friend Thea might like to come to church over in St. Johnsbury with us tomorrow night? The missionaries from Africa are showing slides, and there'll be lots of other teenagers, too. I think they're doing a drumming circle after the slide show, the way they taught praise songs over in Ghana or Nigeria or something."

But I was already shaking my head. "Nope. Thea's not into church. I don't think her family ever goes."

"But you could still invite her."

"No way!" In front of me, a cow stamped, then twitched her hind end. Automatically, I moved away from the animal, just in time, before a spray of liquid poop ejected from her. It mostly went down into the gutter. I took the sawdust shovel and heaved a scoopful onto the rest of the mess, scraped it into the gutter, and threw fresh sawdust behind the cow. Harry liked a clean floor to milk from. So did my mother.

She was still standing behind me, probably waiting for me to change my mind about bringing Thea to Friday night praise service. I finally said, "All right, I'll ask her. Okay? Now can I just get this done, so I can go in for my snack?"

"Okay. Thank you, Shawna, for helping out."

I ducked around the next cow and shoveled faster, watching my mother head back toward the milkroom to get the other milking pump.

The clock over the milkroom doorway said four thirty. Maybe two hours until Thea would call me. How much would Josh get in the way of us being best friends?

When the phone finally rang after supper, I grabbed it and pulled against the long cord until I could sit inside the pantry, with the door partly shut. "What did he want?" I asked Thea right away.

"Oh, just to talk about music. He wanted to know which Beatles CDs I've got." Thea laughed. "I have them all. Hey Shawna, he said something about a teen night tomorrow at some extra church you go to, not here in North Upton though. I didn't know he goes to the same church you do!"

"Yeah. Well, my mom wanted me to invite you for tomorrow evening anyway," I admitted. "We go to church here in North Upton for most Sundays, but for teen events, we get together with the bigger church. Do you want to come with us? It's actually supposed to be a history kind of talk, with music, even."

"Awesome! I'm sure I can, just let me check. What time?"

"Six, for the supper, and the program starts at seven. We usually get home about nine."

"Just a minute."

Thea came back and said she could go with us to teen night. I said it would be great, but I didn't say much else because I didn't want to have to talk about Josh anymore. So I was glad when she asked instead, "What did you think about what my dad said? About the college professor and all?"

I admitted the college professor could be right. After all, he knew more than we did. Still, Thea and I agreed the trip to Barnet was even more important now. We needed to see the other hiding place, not just for our project, but because Thea's dad was making such a big deal of all this. After all, he was new in town; maybe he could be a little bit mistaken about some things.

When we finished talking, I stayed in the pantry on the floor a little longer, with the phone next to me. Life seemed very confusing this evening. It was October twenty-third, and I should be thinking about Halloween candy and getting excited about Mom's hunting season coming up. That's how it always was.

Instead, I was worrying about some piece of Vermont history; I was worrying about my new best friend and the way a boy from my own church could mess up our friendship; and my stomach was growling. I took the phone back out into the kitchen and opened the cookie jar. Then the phone rang again.

"Shawna?" Alice's voice came tense and hurried. "Let me speak to Mom, would you? I'm trying to get my tickets for the plane." My mother was already there, reaching for the receiver.

How could I have forgotten? Alice was coming for Thanksgiving. Judging by Carl and Emerson's reactions, that ought to be on my list of big worries, too. What would she think of me, anyway?

Studying in the kitchen seemed a really bad idea, as Mom's voice began to tense up to match Alice's, and Harry turned down the TV to listen in.

Me, I didn't want to hear it.

FRIDAY-EVENING PRAISE service at the big church in town is supposed to be this major teen-friendly thing. The trouble is, our parents keep forgetting we're not really into balloons and coloring anymore. So the table decorations and activities that go with supper are truly juvenile. Still, sitting with Thea made it better, and I could tell she was having fun. Josh didn't try to hog the conversation, either.

It's hard to hear people well in the church hall, because the ceiling is so high that voices echo too much. There's a sound system for whoever is up on the stage, giving a talk or playing some kind of music. Tonight there were drums on the stage: not the pastor's son's drum set, but African drums, about a dozen, decorated in brown and white patterns, and all different heights, from a tiny one the size of a coffee mug, to a huge one more than a foot across and easily three feet tall. A tape played in the background during the supper, and I heard a mix of voices and music in another language. But I could tell some of the songs, like "Our God Is an Awesome God," which I recognized right away. Josh pointed out the familiar tunes to Thea. It turned out she hardly knew any of them.

"We only went to church a couple of times in Connecticut, like for Christmas Eve," Thea explained. "My parents weren't really that into going there, and I guess I never thought that much about the services. Nothing against your church, though," she added quickly.

For a moment, I froze. Even though Mom and I had talked about people who "didn't do church," it hit me that without any church or Bible study, Thea might not "get" a part of me that I thought was really important.

A window opened in my thoughts. My friend was already here with me, right? I could just be myself and watch what God might do in the meantime. "Well, I kind of like this place—it's nice," I admitted carefully. "Plus, I like memorizing for Bible study, because it comes easy for me. And—well, there are a lot of numbers in the Bible. You can find some great patterns in the twelves, and threes, and all. And infinity!"

She nodded. "Yeah, I get it. And absolutely, even Einstein said if you look into the night sky or do a lot of science and math, you've got to admit there's a God out there. I'm just not so sure about the Jesus part. I mean, how can anyone be sure what someone said two thousand years ago anyway? And the part about him dying, well, today people die in worse ways in Iraq or when they're tortured in prisons. That's what I mean about not being so sure."

Holy cow. What should I say? I looked at Josh. But he didn't seem worried. On his plate there were three kinds of lasagna, plus garlic bread and salad, and he mostly was eating. He looked up and said with his mouth full, "Jesus is there for those people too. That's what's cool about it. Hey, do you think we could borrow those drums for the school dance?"

"No way!" I made a face at Josh, and we all laughed. I saw Merry and Marsha noticing, but they were stuck at the front table because they were in the praise group for the evening. Ha! I grabbed a platter of frosted chocolate cupcakes and shared them around our table. The background music suddenly stopped, and everyone looked at the stage. Pastor Wilkins and Pastor Allen stood at the microphone, with a half-circle of five people—three older teens, two adults—forming behind them. Everyone lowered their heads for prayer.

"Heavenly Father, we just want to thank you for bringing us together in such joy and fellowship with friends and family and these amazing missionaries of your Word. Bless our friendships, our love, and our ears tonight, that we might hear your Word for us and commit ourselves to being the Light of the World. In Jesus's name and for his sake, Amen."

"Amen," we all said back, even Thea, and the drums began rippling, five sets of hands pounding on them, soft at first, then louder, then with calls in some foreign language coming up into the air as if birds from Africa had hidden among the drums. It was a whole family that came with the evening speaker, and they were calling out as they beat the rhythms. Josh's hands slapped the edge of the table gently with the sounds. I thought about what Thea had said: warm, strong hands. Hmm.

Up on stage, the drums quieted, and a spotlight focused on a woman with long white hair, standing at the microphone. Everyone else moved to chairs at the back of the stage, and she started talking. It was weird, how it seemed to fit into my life, because she told stories of how a lot of church hymns came from places in Europe, but others grew out of how black people sang them for comfort and strength when they got kidnapped from Africa and enslaved in America. She even talked about songs getting translated into African languages, and then coming back to America in modern days, and she taught us all how to sing "Jesus Loves Me" in Swahili. "Yesu anipenda," we said over and over, and some other lines, too. When everyone seemed to have the sounds, sort of, she called her teenaged kids back to the African drums and they kept us company as we sang it through a couple of times.

Thea sat with her eyes closed, her shoulders moving with the beat. Josh's hands kept going on the table, and the vibrations ran up my arms, making my heart pound hard. Everyone seemed alone inside the music.

Then the drums went softer and all the family up on the stage sang. It started quietly, foreign, blurred in with the drums. It rose in the wide space above us. The words flew and danced, and suddenly I realized I knew what they were: "And He will raise you up on eagle's wings, Bear you on the breath of dawn, Make you to shine like the sun." The whole room was singing now for the last line: "And hold you, hold you in the palm of His hand."

Magically, we were one person, one body, one breath. Thea too? I looked quickly, and saw that her eyes were still shut, but she was smiling and her face was tipped upward. The drums slowed, quieted, and one of the kids on stage started to talk.

I don't remember exactly what those kids said that night, except I know it was about being called to sing, to preach, and to listen. What I do remember though—and will never ever forget, and I don't think Thea will, either—was the ending. That was what all the other drums were for: The missionaries called into the audience, pointed to people, called them up to play with them. The short boy pointed to me, but I shook my head and he smiled at me and pointed to someone else instead. Josh went up; so did Michael Willson, Marsha and Merry's brother. So did a couple of younger kids.

The drums started gently, everyone trying to look at the others to get what was supposed to happen. The woman, the mother of the teens on stage, sang a different song in Swahili, really quietly. Someone turned off the overhead lights, so just the table candles and the stage lights burned. Then we all sang her song together in English instead: "Amazing Grace." People all around were tearing up as they sang. I teared up a little, too.

Thea sang all the words. When it ended, and everyone started to quietly pick up their things to leave, she came over right next to me and whispered.

"You know who wrote the words to 'Amazing Grace,' don't you, Shawna?"

"Who?"

"A slave-ship captain. Get it? Shawna, we have to find out more about the Underground Railroad. It's, like, meant for us to know."

Every hair on my head, my arms, even the skin of my face prickled with the spirit touching us in that moment. And I knew the answer to my wondering from earlier in the evening, too: My new friend wasn't going to be turned off by what I believed, by what I was feeling.

Josh left with his own parents; Thea and I rode home in the backseat of my mother's Subaru. We didn't say anything much until my mother pulled up in front of Thea's house to drop her off.

"Tomorrow," we promised each other, as we said a hushed good-night. "Tomorrow, we'll both figure it out."

MRS. WARWICK'S MINIVAN slowed at the driveway and Thea read the sign out loud. "'The Goodwillie House. 1791.' Mom, this is it."

She bounced on the front seat, one arm out the window, pointing. Right behind her, I leaned forward to see it. Ordinary looking, I thought—just a small, white-painted, wooden house with a circular driveway in the front yard, its flower gardens brown from the frosty nights. A brick chimney stuck up from the center of the roof, and toward one side was a second one, not as big. Neither one had smoke coming out. Flowered curtains hung in the windows, and as we pulled into the driveway, I could see through the glassed front storm door into a dark hallway.

Beside me, Teddy kicked in his car seat. "Out! Out!"

"Just a minute, sweetheart," Mrs. Warwick told him as she unbuckled her own seatbelt. "I'm coming. Girls, you go on ahead, I'll meet you inside."

Thea patted her pocket where the digital camera sat, and I tugged our bag of stuff out of the back of the wagon. The metal case of the tape measure clunked against the big flashlight that

Harry had loaned to me. There were two big pads of graph paper too, and pencils, to chart the hiding place in the Goodwillie House.

On the wet grass, it was easy to see where someone had already gone into the house ahead of us. We followed the shoe marks and our sneakers squeaked, slipping some. Thea knocked at the door, and someone called, "Come on in!"

We pressed past the rattly wooden door with three windows in it, trying to wipe our feet on a mat woven from strips of cloth that sat just inside the door. As my eyes began to adjust, I noticed old photographs in frames on the walls of the hallway, and in front of us, a cross-stitched sampler that showed all the letters of the alphabet.

"Come on into the kitchen," called the woman's voice, thin and old-sounding. Thea followed the voice, and I followed Thea—to a door on the left into a kitchen that looked a lot like the one at home, but smaller. A very thin, white-haired woman stood at the gray Formica-topped kitchen table, folding dish towels. "Just let me get these into the cupboard and I'll give you a tour. Which one of you is Shawna Lee?"

I cleared my throat. "That's me. Are you Mrs. McGuire?"

"Miss," the lady corrected me. "Miss McGuire. So you're Connie Lee's baby, are you? Come on in, I won't bite."

"Yes ma'am. And she's Connie Quinn now," I added.

"Of course she is, married that nice Harry Quinn who helped her keep the farm. Still milking, is he?"

"Yes, and my mother does, too."

"Of course she does." Even without looking down, her thin hands kept folding the towels on the table. "Always a good worker, Connie was. I was her teacher in fourth and fifth grades, you know. No, you didn't know that? I was. You tell your mother to give you more information. Tell her Miss McGuire thinks you're old enough to know a few things." The last towel snapped onto the top of the stack, and the old teacher leaned toward me and patted my arm. "You are old enough, aren't you?"

I was confused, but nodded. "Yes ma'am. I'm almost fourteen."

Sparkling blue eyes surprised me with a sharp glance. "Fourteen. And I'm seventy. Do you know fractions?"

"One fifth," I answered right away.

Moving close beside me, Thea added, "Twenty percent. We're twenty percent as old as you. Ma'am," she hurried to say at the end.

"That's correct. Very good. And you're Thea Warwick, I presume. Yes? Good. Now then, are you ready? Where are your notebooks? You're planning to take notes as I speak with you, isn't that right?"

"Yes ma'am," we said together, and I pulled our notebooks out of the backpack, then slung it over one of my shoulders, feeling the clunk of the flashlight and tape measure against my back.

A squeak and thump of the front storm door told us Thea's mother and Teddy had just come in. It took a few minutes for more introductions, and Mrs. Warwick kept one hand clamped on Teddy, saying to him, "Don't touch anything, sweetheart. Just stay with Mommy now."

"Oh, he can touch the things that are at his level," Miss McGuire offered. "Nothing glass or china, but there are children's toys and such that he's welcome to touch—if he does it gently." She bent over and peered into Teddy's face. "You'll be gentle, won't you, young man? Your mother will help you." Without waiting for an answer, she pulled back up straight, wheeled, and led us into a part of the kitchen that hadn't been visible from the hall doorway. "The brick oven," she announced briskly. "The bricks you see here were made in the brickyard down the hill. Bread and pies, of course, were baked here, and a small fire could keep the oven warm all day."

Hands flying, arms up and down to point in one direction and another, she whirled us past a metal stove—"the first sheet iron stove seen in Barnet, built by the Reverend Goodwillie's brother Joseph, amazing to the women"—and crowded us into a tiny bedroom with a narrow bed with a faded quilt. A brown wooden cradle at Teddy's level caught his attention and he rocked it enthusiastically.

"Are you being gentle?" Miss McGuire asked him, and he pulled back and hid behind Mrs. Warwick's leg until she picked him up and held him on her hip.

"And this was the maid's bedroom?" Mrs. Warwick made a guess. But not a good one.

"Not at all," corrected the teacher. "Although the Goodwillie family prospered here, servants would have been too costly in this rough Scottish settlement. No, my dear, this was the borning room—now then, you explain to the girls what that means."

We didn't need an explanation, but we listened politely as Mrs. Warwick spoke up, for all the world like a senior student reciting for the teacher. "The babies for the Goodwillie family would be born here, in this warm snug room behind the oven, and"—she glanced at Miss McGuire for confirmation—"I presume a midwife would attend the births?"

"That's correct. The room could also be used for an invalid—say, if someone contracted a heavy cold that led into pneumonia." She whirled through the next doorway. "And here, the parlor."

We followed into the next room, a mostly boring one with pictures and stiff chairs and an old organ. Two ordinary bedrooms, separated by a more or less up-to-date bathroom, and then another stiffly formal room, with a dining table and matching chairs, made up the rest of the main floor.

"We'll go up to the attic," Miss McGuire announced, "where the toy collection is. Your young man will enjoy that, with his mother's help, while you young ladies see the dress closets and the old silk gowns and of course the corsets and other undergarments." Her voice floated up the stairs ahead of her and we scrambled to keep up.

At the top of the stairs everyone stopped and stared: In front of us and around us was an amazing amount of things, from stamp collections to army uniforms to women's clothes and even a big table full of old toys.

"Some crop storage would have taken place here, of course,"

the teacher continued. "Make sure you write in your notes, girls, that anything needing drying would be hung up here, two hundred years ago and even one hundred. Straight through the Second World War, as a matter of fact. Herbs. Flowers. Medicinal remedies grown in the garden." She waved up at fasteners along the inside of the roof, some of them nails, some hooks, even a long iron rod fastened in place. Then she led us through the clothes collections in two little attic rooms, and opened two big scrapbooks in front of us, where letters rested under plastic, among newspaper articles mostly yellow and brown with age.

I watched Thea. She seemed especially excited that we could touch the things around us. Her hands, delicate and slender, cupped each stiff scrapbook page both front and back as she turned them, supporting the pasted in letters and greeting cards, dried flowers, and yellowed news clippings. "Eighteen twenty-nine," she read aloud, "dedication of the brick church." She looked at Miss McGuire: "It's a wooden church, though, isn't it?"

The neat white-haired head bobbed. "It is. The one you have on the page there burned and was replaced. Mrs. Thomas Goodwillie painted a picture of the brick church, though. When we go back downstairs, you can look at her painting."

I tapped Thea's shoulder. "Go later," I suggested. "Go to the eighteen fifties. To the Underground Railroad times."

Behind us the voices of Mrs. Warwick and Teddy continued to talk about the toys in the other rooms. The sounds faded into background as I focused entirely on the pages in the scrapbook. Thea said, "Here, a letter from eighteen fifty-three. With, let's see, a sermon I guess, by the minister." She flashed me an excited look. "It's about the right of all men to be free. It's about the slaves!"

Miss McGuire slipped a thin white hand, ridged with blue veins, under the page and turned it carefully. "The Reverend Goodwillie spoke for the Union, you know. Like all the Scots here, he believed nothing should break apart the joining of the states, the Union that God had made." She bent closer to the page, pointed to a paragraph, then moved her hand to the next page. "And with the minister from Peacham, he preached very movingly about Daniel Webster, and how Webster placed the Union before all else."

I wanted to hear more. I asked, "And didn't he tell people that they had a duty to help the slaves who escaped, the ones who were headed for Canada?"

"Well, we don't know that he did," Miss McGuire back-pedaled. "Natural rights, God-given freedoms, yes, and we know that he preached the end of slavery from this pulpit here. But he didn't tell people to break the law outright."

Thea was still turning the scrapbook pages. "There should be some letters here about the Underground Railroad, and the fugitive slaves that he hid in his house," she said. "But I can't find them. And I'm all the way to eighteen sixty-one, with letters about the battles and the soldiers. Look at this one, 'David Somers has enlisted as a private in Third Regiment, Company A,'" she said, quickly translating from the abbreviations like Pvt. and Rgt. on the page.

"Oh my, no," the elderly teacher responded. "No, I'm quite sure there are no mentions in the letters about the people being hidden here. It was all kept quite secret, you know." Her voice dipped low as if someone could hear the secret and get in trouble even now. "People whispered to each other about it, but I'm sure nobody would be so rash as to write anything down."

"Then, can we see where they hid the fugitives?" I was tired of the letters. I wanted to see the hiding place, and measure it and draw it, and see how much like the one in Thea's cellar it would be. "I mean, may we? Please?"

"That would be in the cellar, of course. We'll need to turn out all the lights up here first." Miss McGuire turned around, and led the way back to the staircase. Now Teddy's voice was below us. A door thumped and I couldn't hear him anymore. Mrs. Warwick must be with him someplace downstairs. "This way, girls."

Thea first, me following, bag in my arms so it wouldn't swing into any of the pictures on the walls, we went down the narrow stairway with its small steps. People were smaller in the old days, I reminded myself. Smaller people, smaller stairs, smaller beds, smaller hiding places.

I expected to go down a set of stairs from the kitchen or something, but Miss McGuire led us out the front door and all the way around to the other side of the house, where the ground sloped downward, so there was a regular-size door in the cellar wall. Undoing a padlock with a large key from a cluster she held, Miss McGuire stepped into the darkness and fumbled for a light switch. I held my breath for a moment, staring ahead, looking for signs and for the next door, the one that would lead to a secret room like the one at the Warwicks' house. Thea stood by the doorway, waiting for the teacher to say we could come in.

"Over there, girls." She pointed toward the left, into a dark corner. "Go right through the opening into the root cellar. The hiding place is just beyond it, between the two walls of the cellar, one true, one false. You'll see for yourselves, it was specially built, and nobody would have seen it was there if they didn't already know."

Thea said, "Thank you very much. It will take us a little while, because we need to measure everything, for our school project. Is that all right?"

"Of course. I can make some tea for your mother while we wait for you. Take all the time you need."

She watched as we stepped carefully into the underground part of the Goodwillie House, staring into the shadows toward what we both wanted to know about.

Underfoot, the cellar floor felt greasy with a damp sweat on the packed dirt. I fumbled in the backpack and pulled out the big flashlight. Up above us, a thump was followed by a wail and Mrs. Warwick's sharp voice.

Miss McGuire jumped and turned, calling over her shoulder, "When you girls have explored, come back to the kitchen. Don't try to lock the outer door, I'll do that myself." She vanished, leaving the door hanging open, a large square of daylight coming partway into the cellar, and the one bulb of the overhead light barely taking the darkness out of the rest of the space.

Shovels, rakes, and other tools hung neatly against the walls. Empty wooden boxes, the kind for apples, sat in short stacks, and a wheelbarrow piled with garden hoses stood in our way. I flicked the switch on the flashlight, and Thea eased around the wheelbarrow handles, moving toward the lower corner of the cellar. I held the light so she could see where she was going, which meant it wasn't lit up much near the wheelbarrow as I squeezed past it myself, and the backpack, back over my shoulder again, caught on the coil of garden hoses so I had to stop and fix them. I lifted the light again toward the corner and saw Thea already disappearing through an opening like a doorway ahead of me. "Wait up!"

It was really a doorway, framed with wood, and an old hinge showed there had been a door across it in the past, but it wasn't there now. When I stepped into the root cellar, the dampness got twice as damp and cold around me. "Wow! I hope they had lots of blankets for the people hiding here."

"Yeah, really."

In the corner of this smaller but empty, rock-walled space, a cement wall leaned slightly into the room. The flashlight revealed an opening beyond it. Together, we leaned through the opening, expecting to see shelves for beds, and maybe writing on the wall, like at Thea's house. This was the real thing, for sure—the place where people desperate to escape the cruel Southern masters and the money-hungry slave hunters would shiver and be safe for a night or two, until they could rush to the safety of Canada, a mere sixty miles to the north.

At first, though, all we could see was, well, nothing. Just a stone wall beyond the cement one. It tilted a little away from us, just as the cement inside wall had tilted toward us. Between the two, a space about two feet across at floor level, and maybe three feet across at shoulder height, stretched out of sight.

"Give me the flashlight," Thea said, and she stepped inside the space, shining the light up, down, and along the walls. I crowded in, too, staring.

There were no shelves. No places where shelves could have fastened. No hooks or nails. No writing. Just an old wooden handle from a shovel or rake, lying on the damp dirt under our feet. It was the biggest disappointment I could have ever dreamed of.

Thea hissed softly, considering the space. Carefully, she crouched down, spreading her arms from one wall to the other, hands pressed flat against the rough sides. The flashlight wobbled and dipped. "I'll hold it now," I offered.

"No, just come down here, like me," Thea insisted. "As if we were hiding here."

I didn't want to, but I did what she said. One knee at a time, I moved down to sit against the inner wall, back propped, knees bent.

Thea turned off the flashlight.

Into the cramped dark space, there came a tiny breath of air from the open cellar doorway. But no light. From the little square of daylight in the larger cellar room, the walls and doorway into the root cellar blocked almost everything, and the twist into the space between the cellar walls took care of the rest. I couldn't even see Thea's eyes, or my own self.

"This is what it was like," Thea whispered. "Hiding here, without making a sound. No light, no moving. Even the slightest sound could give them away. The vicious slave hunters with their guns and shackles paced nearby, unable to discover the trembling victims of the South's cruel plantation owners."

I understood she was writing a page out loud. So I added to it: "In the northern cold, their black bodies shivered, accustomed to hot sun. But the solid stone walls on which they leaned their whip-scarred backs comforted them somehow, and they whispered together the Lord's Prayer."

"They said it under their breath," Thea corrected me. "Afraid even to whisper, they huddled against each other. The scent of fear rose sharp and acrid in the confined space. A baby clutched too tightly gave a whimper, and its mother clamped a hand over the tiny face."

"No, pressed it to her breast to suckle," I suggested. "With the rough wool blanket pulled close around them, to muffle even that soft sound."

"Good!" Thea clicked the switch, and suddenly we were back in our own place, our own time, our own selves. But shivering. My knees felt locked into place. I stared at Thea, knowing for sure that nobody else, not my mother or my brothers, or anyone else at school, could ever know what this was like. Just Thea and me.

"This was the real thing," Thea confirmed, still whispering.

Suddenly she stood up. "Come on. We have to measure it. I'll hold the light, you get the tape measure out. Where's my notebook?"

It took almost twenty minutes to make sure we had all the measurements—the four feet ten inches length of the space, the height of five feet more or less, the width across the floor of twenty-two inches and at the ceiling of forty-one. We went back into the root cellar and drew the proportions of that space, too, so we could do a better diagram of how it all fit into the underneath of the house, and we measured that largest rectangle carefully, making sure there was no space not accounted for. Some dirt smudged the notebook pages, but Thea said that was okay; we'd make a better drawing when we got home.

Outside at last in the bright sunlight, I blinked and brushed dirt off my flannel shirt. Thea told me to turn around, and she brushed the back of it for me, where I'd scraped against the root cellar walls, squeezing around the wheelbarrow. I checked her sweater too, but it was pretty clean.

We both dusted off our knees as best we could, packed everything back into the bookbag, and went back around the house and into the chilly little kitchen.

I looked at the ordinary table and chairs, the electric burners and little refrigerator wedged into a cubby beyond the old iron stove, and Miss McGuire and Mrs. Warwick washing teacups and drying them and putting them away, while Teddy pushed a wooden truck around the floor. Did the Goodwillie family do this, to cover up for their black runaways hiding in the cellar, when the bounty hunters came riding through the neighborhood, trying to capture the escaped slaves? The family would use old-fashioned kitchen things, of course. I imagined bread baking in the brick oven, and someone churning butter or something.

"Are you all done?" Thea's mother asked us. We both nodded, saying thanks again to Miss McGuire.

"I'll go lock the door, then," said Miss McGuire. Whisking off her red-checked apron, she slipped past us, keys in hand.

"Tell me all about it," said Mrs. Warwick over her shoulder as she scooped up Teddy and put the toy truck away in the hallway. "Is it just like ours?"

"No, Mom, it's completely different," Thea began. "It's way more hidden, and it's pretty damp and uncomfortable. I don't think there were beds or anything, either. There isn't even room."

"Oh, then your father should see it, I think, with the people from the college. I expect they're coming here anyway when they film all the Underground Railroad places." She led Teddy out the front door and turned him loose to run in the yard. "Turn off the kitchen lights, girls. Miss McGuire is here to lock up."

The retired teacher was back already, and she asked to see our drawings of the cellar. I tugged Thea's notebook out of my backpack and showed her the sketches, with the measurements all penciled in.

"Well done," she approved. "Our historical society would like a copy, of course, and a copy of your school paper when you finish it. Could your mother send that to us?"

"I guess," I said, and Thea agreed.

"Miss McGuire, could we ask you something?" Thea handed me back the notebook and went on. "The hiding place at my house has more room in it, and places for shelves that people could sleep on. But the one here doesn't look like people could stretch out at night, if there was more than one person. How did they manage?"

"Oh my dear, of course they weren't there at night. It's not like it was in Boston, with Southern ships in the harbor and kidnappers snatching fugitives to take them back in chains, you know. I doubt if even one slave chaser per year came to this part of Vermont. Clearly, if one did, whoever was here at the Goodwillie home only stood in the darkness for an hour or so until the stranger was headed down the road again."

She clucked at the surprise in our faces. "Read your history, girls. Study. Of course the people in Barnet were proud of standing up for justice, being part of the Underground Railroad. But think about it, this far north—why, some of the black people simply became laborers for the farmers, sometimes even staying for years before going on across the border into Canada. There was no hurry when they'd come this far already."

With a wave of her arms, she had us out the door, and carrying her own canvas bag of books, she stepped out into the sunshine. "Ah, that feels better. Who is teaching history in North Upton this year?"

"Mr. Harris," Thea replied.

"Jerry Harris? You tell him, please, that Miss McGuire sends her regards. He was always a hard worker. Go sit down with him and tell him your ideas before you start to write your report, girls. He'll make sure you're seeing things in terms of what actually happened. Kindly ask Mrs. Toussaint at the library to give me a call when she has a chance, too."

Mrs. Warwick had Teddy strapped into his car seat, and she came back over to thank Miss McGuire again for opening the house to us.

"No trouble at all. I wish all the students came here more often. And these girls have done a fine job getting the details onto paper. You'll send me a copy of the girls' final report, won't you, dear?"

A round of shoulder pats and more thanks, and we were in the car, headed into town for Mrs. Warwick to shop for groceries before going back to North Upton. In the front seat, Thea lowered the sun visor and adjusted it so that the mirror on it reflected her face to me, my face to hers. We stared at each other, knowing we were sharing the same thought:

If fugitive slaves didn't need to be hidden for more than an hour or so at a time up here, what was the explanation for the very different hiding place at the Warwicks' house? Our research told a different story from what Mr. Warwick believed. Could we get him to listen to us before tomorrow's camera crew from the college arrived?

I HAD NO CHANCE to help Thea talk with her father that afternoon, and my mother wouldn't promise anything about the evening, either. As soon as we'd unloaded Mrs. Warwick's groceries for her, I crossed the road to check in, and my mother insisted that I vacuum the first floor, then help her take a wagon-load of stuff—canned food, soda, clean blankets—up to the hunting cabin on the ridge. I called Thea to tell her I couldn't come over until later. She said not to worry about it. If she could get her dad to sit down and listen in the meantime, she'd start filling him in.

When I got off the phone, Harry stood in the kitchen, giving me a funny look. "I could come up to camp with the two of you," he said suddenly. "I'd be glad to."

"No," my mother said loudly, almost angry. "No, Harry, I said I'd do it. Just let me do it. We'll be back later."

What was the big deal about taking the stuff to camp? I wouldn't have minded Harry coming to help carry things. But obviously, my mom had other plans.

She drove the mud-spattered four-wheeler, and I sat on top

of her pile of blankets in the hooked-on wagon, trying to keep everything from bouncing around too much while holding onto the railing as we bumped up the trail.

"Who's milking?" I called over the growl of the smoky little engine.

"Carl and Harry. Watch your head, the branches here are low!"

I ducked.

People from away have this idea that Vermont trees will be all decorated with red and gold leaves through October, maybe even November, because that's when autumn comes to, say, New York or southern Connecticut. But usually the peak of "the colors" here is the last week of September and the first week of October, and from then on, the leaves are on the ground—yellow for a while, but soon just brown. Especially if there's a lot of rain, they fall off early. And that's what it was like in the woods now: slippery brown leaves all over the ground, and the trees pretty much naked. "Stick season," my mother calls it. I gave up trying to talk to her over the noise of the four-wheeler and concentrated on keeping my head down so the dangling branches wouldn't scratch my face and eyes.

The four-wheeler slowed and dipped downward, angling the wagon up, then thumping it back down with a splash as we went through the stream that pretty much divided our farm from the rest of the mountain. On the other side, the trail angled up again, with more rocks and a pair of deep wheel ruts, with the center ridge sticking up between them. The wagon scraped its bottom some on the ridge. I held on tighter.

Brown leaf smells and a faint undertone of something spoiled, maybe last year's leaves turning into moldy soil, or something dead under the bushes—I wrinkled my nose and tried to breathe only through my mouth. Then the trail got even steeper, and we were in the spruce forest, where thick dark evergreens blocked the sun from the ground, and only spare, spindly stems of the summer's weeds stuck up from the soil. The air changed: cooler, and scented with balsam every now and then. Balsam is the most

Christmassy of all the evergreen smells; they put balsam needles inside the little souvenir pillows that you can buy at the tourist shops to take Vermont home with you.

We bounced through another stream bed, this one smaller, and the clearing for our cabin opened in front of us. Now I smelled apples, the half-crushed dropped apples rotting under the two big trees in the front yard of the cabin. On the porch, a red squirrel dashed along the railing, complaining, and vanished up onto the roof.

Grinning at me, Mom climbed off the padded seat and reached a hand up. "Enjoy the ride, Shawna?"

"Mom, you drive like you're crazy!"

She laughed and hugged me across the shoulders. "I figure as long as we're scaring the deer by driving up here, we might as well have some fun on the way!"

Together we unloaded the wagon onto the porch first, the part of the porch that wasn't covered with neatly stacked split maple and birch logs for the fire, and then we moved everything inside. It wasn't locked; my mother always said that a real thief would bust a lock anyway, so it was better to trust God and the neighbors, and if someone really needed something that bad, we should let them have it.

I pulled the long white string dangling near the door, and one of the overhead lights went on. There was a good pile of kindling wood in a neat short row by the woodstove.

"You've been doing a lot up here," I commented.

"Can't split wood during hunting season, can I? Here, pass me the soda, I'll put it under the sink."

This was the best part of coming up to hunting camp: doing things together, knowing how it was all going to go. You didn't know whether anyone would actually get a deer, of course, but you knew there would be long evenings by the stove, eating stew and biscuits and pie, and playing cards, and there'd be early mornings, in the dark of four a.m., hiking out to the deer stand to climb up onto the old gray boards and be above the game trail before the animals started moving. Once I'd turned six and started school, I could only come to camp on weekends, and now I remembered what it was like to be a little kid, staying a week at a time in the bunks, learning to carve with a jackknife, and making the fire turn colors with pinecones dipped in salt. And s'mores every night, crushing half-scorched marshmallows between slabs of chocolate and graham crackers.

Impulsively I asked, "Could we stay here tonight?"

"You know we can't," my mother replied, but her wide smile showed she knew why I'd asked. "Men to feed tonight, church tomorrow. Tell you what, though, I brought a box of Ring Dings and a thermos of coffee, just in case we wanted to sit on the porch for a bit. Let's grab a couple of blankets and head for the rocking chairs."

"Yeah!"

Usually there were enough people at camp that we had to take turns for the three rocking chairs on the porch. Being just the two of us made it perfect. My mother listened while I told about the hiding place at the Goodwillie House, and she asked how things were going with Thea. She said how glad she was that Thea had come to teen night at church. "She seems like a nice girl. Maybe she'll bring her parents to church sometime."

"Maybe." I didn't think it seemed too likely, but I was too comfortable to disagree. Between us, we finished the six Ring Dings, which the hot sweet coffee made taste even better.

"Shawna, there's something else I want to talk with you about," my mother said slowly, stopping the rocking of her chair. "As long as it's just you and me here. And now that you're almost fourteeen."

I groaned. "Not the birds and the bees, Mom. I remember enough from before. And I'm not interested in boys anyway, and if I was, I'd still be a virgin until I was married. You don't have to tell me again."

She smiled faintly, then fell to a serious face again. "It's not that. It's—well, it's partly about Alice. You know she's coming to visit at Thanksgiving."

"Yeah. Carl and Emerson sort of hinted that might be hard.

Are you worried about her coming, Mom?"

She shook her head. "Not really. No. It's just that, well, a long time ago Alice made a mistake, and I did the best I could to help her with it. And now that you're a teenager yourself, Alice wants you to know about what she did."

"Like what? What did she do?" I stopped rocking, too, and stared at my mother.

"She's a good person," Mom said quietly. "She's always been a kind person, too. When Alice was fifteen, she was, well, she was just too kind." She stared at the ground for a long moment, then looked up at me. "She was too kind to a young man, Shawna. Alice got pregnant."

I was stunned. My sister got pregnant when she was a teenager? Nobody ever told me that before. "Did she get married, too?"

"No," said my mother slowly. "The young man was somebody's summer visitor, from away. He went back to New Jersey somewhere, and Alice didn't know she was expecting until almost Christmas. No, we didn't try to find him. We just helped her go away that winter, and then in the spring, to have the baby. And then, you see, it was hard for her, and she didn't want to be a mother when she was only a teenager herself. So we helped her to go to Aunt Janet's in California, and that's where she finished high school, before going to college there."

"Wow," I mused. "I guess I never thought much about why she went there in the first place. No wonder she doesn't like to come back here very much. Did it, like, ruin her life? Will she ever get married to somebody who loves her?"

"I think she'll find the right person some day," my mother said. "She's strong and she's honest and she cares a lot. Aunt Janet says she just started seeing someone, someone from church out there. Maybe when she's here at Thanksgiving she'll tell us about him."

"Good! Maybe she'll bring us a photo. Mom, if Alice gets married in California, we'd go to her wedding, wouldn't we?"

"I'm sure we would."

"Cool." I started rocking again, happy. "Hardly anyone in my class has been to California. And I've never been in a wedding yet. I'd be a bridesmaid, right?"

My mother wasn't rocking, though. She sat very still, watching me. Waiting. Suddenly, I realized what she was expecting. I saw the empty space hanging there in the air, the part she hadn't explained. I asked the question. "So if Alice had a baby and she wasn't married, somebody must have adopted it, right? A good home, right? Was it someone in Vermont?"

"It was," my mother said quietly. "Shawna, honey: It was me."

For a moment, I didn't get it. I stammered, "You adopted a baby? What happened to it? I never knew..."

And then it hit me. "Me? You mean it was me?" My mother was nodding, but also trying to interrupt. I ignored what she was saying. I couldn't hear her, anyway. Just my own voice: "And you lied to me for all these years? You lied to me! You're not even my mother. And you lied, you lied! Oh God, you're my grandmother?"

With that horrible thought yelled into the air, I leaped out of the rocking chair and shouted, "No! You lied to me! I hate you!"

And ran down the trail away from the cabin, as fast and as hard as ever I could.

WHEN I REACHED the first stream that cut across the trail, I realized I couldn't just keep running toward home. Home! What did that mean now? I didn't even belong at home. I had a mother who'd been an unwed teenage slut. That's what Alice was. I had a mother—no, a grandmother—who'd lied to me for my whole life. I had nothing real anymore.

I leaned against the trunk of a poplar tree and threw up. A brown mess of half-dissolved Ring Dings and coffee scattered and slid over the dead leaves at my feet. I choked, and my stomach heaved again. My nose was running. I grappled in my pocket and found a napkin, and blew my nose, and some throw-up came out too, burning. I couldn't stop crying.

But I didn't want to throw up again. So I leaned against the cool smooth trunk of the tree for a moment. I took a long ragged breath and held it. The woods around me held its breath, as if the trees and birds were horrified too. Dear Lord and Jesus, what was I going to do?

Thinking it that way made me realize I'd been swearing at—at whoever she was, my mom, my grandmother, the only person

I'd thought was a hundred percent good and trustable in the world. I'd taken the Lord's name in vain. Even God would hate me now.

Why should I go down the trail toward the farm? I didn't belong there. I was some stupid unwanted baby of a slutty teenager that I always thought was my beautiful older sister. My life didn't even exist.

I left the trail and walked along the edge of the stream, kicking rocks and sticks and leaves into the water. I walked until I couldn't see the trail anymore. And then I kept on walking, downhill, along the stream. I wanted to be lost.

Though my feet kept moving, my mind and my heart began to freeze. Ruined, ruined, was the only word for my life. Every step of my sneakers on a stick or a clump of moss or a rock slapped the word back up at me. Ruined.

The silence in the woods grew bigger, pressing on my ears, my face. Why didn't the birds call?

Oh. I stopped and looked around me. It was almost dark. No wonder nothing was calling. Everything was home for the night. Except me. Home? I started to cry again, this time out loud with a mixed up sigh and wail, tears running down my cheeks. Snot dripped from my nose again. I tried to find the napkin, but I'd lost it. I snuffled against the sleeve of my flannel shirt.

Alice was coming for Thanksgiving. Alice wasn't my sister. Alice wanted me to know. Alice could take over my life—take me out of North Upton school, take me away from my friends, take me away from everything. California? Who cared about California? I wanted my life. I wanted my heart, my self.

I sat down and leaned sideways on a big boulder. It was cold—the cold night air of almost winter settled around me. A flannel shirt wasn't enough for a late October evening in Vermont. What should I do? Make a fire? Ha. I didn't have matches. And even if I knew how to make an Indian fire drill to light some leaves, the leaves around me and the sticks too were too darned wet and cold.

Oh God.

I looked up, even though everyone knows that Heaven isn't really in the sky. I talked out loud.

"Heavenly Father, why did you do this to me? Why did you put me into this family? My mother lied to me. My mother isn't my mother. My sister is my mother, and she probably hates me. Do you hate me? In Jesus's name, amen," I finished automatically.

Breath by breath, I slowed down. With my face still tilted toward the dark sky, I let my eyes close. My whole life was a lie. Ruined.

Little tiny drops of cold moisture settled on my hot cheeks. The dew was falling; maybe it was even frost. My legs and backside, damp and cold against the rock, took over, and with my eyes still shut, I slowly stood up. And opened my eyes.

Across the ragged patch of sky outlined by the bare tree limbs above me, a falling star shot like a green flare, and vanished, more or less in the direction of the farm. As I stared up, trying to decide whether a shooting star meant anything at all, something large gave a snort like a sneeze. It scuffed and rustled, whatever it was, in the very dark bulk of trees and brush just up the hill, where I'd stumbled along the bank of the tumbling, trickling stream.

Live all your life with a mother who hunts, and you know what to do: I yelled as loud as I could, "Go away!" And I bent over and picked up a stone, and threw it into the woods, not where the animal was, but over to the side, like there might be another person over there, starting to move. I heard the animal jump and skitter uphill. I grabbed another rock to hold, just in case, and started downhill again, following the sound of the stream, feeling with my feet sliding just along the ground and trying not to slip or stumble.

I waved one arm and hand back and forth in front of me as I walked. Sometimes I felt a branch that way and ducked under it. With my other hand, I buttoned the top button on my shirt, to close the collar around my neck. It made me a little warmer. "Keep moving," I told myself, "and you won't freeze. All streams go downhill. All hills go down to roads, sooner or later."

Actually, I realized, I knew when this stream would reach the road: about a half mile north of the village, in a stretch of woods I sometimes walked beside on the way to the blueberry field. I didn't really know who the field belonged to, but Carl and Emerson took me with them when I was little, in late summer, to pick berries to bring home. My mother would bake us a blueberry pie then, but only if we did the berry picking.

My mother. My heart ached. I already missed her. She wasn't my real mother after all. She was Carl's and Emerson's and Alice's, but not mine. I started crying again. But I needed both hands to feel my way, so I couldn't keep blowing my nose. I made the tears stop. That made room for being angry instead.

It was the Ninth Commandment: Thou shalt not lie. When I was five years old, I already could say all Ten Commandments, from "Thou shalt have no other Gods before me," to "Thou shalt not covet"—which really went on to say, "Thou shalt not covet thy neighbor's wife or ass." Meaning donkey, of course.

My own mother, my whole family, had broken the Ninth Commandment. They'd lied to me. All my life, they'd told me a lie.

I tripped at a dip in the ground, and banged my shoulder, grabbing a tree so I wouldn't fall down. "Slow and steady," I told myself. Slow down.

I could feel an emptiness in my stomach. Probably it was making me weak. The thought frightened me and made it harder to slow down.

"God takes care of the weak." The thought came automatically. I heard a Bible song in my head, and I thought I might be safer to sing it out loud, so the night animals would back off. Some of them might be along the stream, too.

"Jesus loves, me this I know," I croaked out. "For the Bible tells me so." My throat hurt from crying hard and from throwing up. My voice sounded weird. I pushed to make it a little louder anyway. I didn't want to meet a skunk or a porcupine. Bears were shy and didn't worry me all that much, but it would be awful to get sprayed by a startled skunk. Louder. "Little ones to Him belong. They are weak but He is strong. Yes, Jesus loves me; yes, Jesus loves me; yes, Jesus loves me; The Bible tells me so."

Okay, Jesus loves me even if I'm weak. That's good. Keep walking. But Jesus says, God says, don't lie. Don't lie to me.

Don't think about that part. Keep walking. Slow and steady. Sing. Or talk out loud.

I started saying the Ten Commandments. One God. No idols. Don't swear. Keep the Sabbath. Those were short versions, and I knew them easily. Soon I'd finished them. Okay, I need a challenge: Focus. Say the long versions, all of them, from Exodus. Out loud, I called them into the dark trees, refusing to think about the rest of my life.

"I am the Lord your God, who brought you out of Egypt, out of the land of slavery. You shall have no other gods before me. You shall not make for yourself an idol in the form of anything in heaven above or in the waters below. You shall not bow down to them or worship them."

I moved away from the stream bank to circle a thick clump of cedar, its fragrance rising in my face as my arm kept brushing against the flat cold fronds that were its needles. "You shall not misuse the name of the Lord your God, for the Lord will not hold anyone guiltless who misuses His name." I had misused His holy name, when I yelled at my mother on the cabin porch. I stopped for a moment and prayed an apology with my eyes shut. Maybe I was being brought out of Egypt, out of the land of slavery.

Slavery.

With the word, my life fell back into my chest and I choked for a moment, then took a huge breath. Slavery. Thea and me and our project about the hiding places. Tonight was the night we needed to convince her father, to tell him the hiding place at Thea's house might not be a hiding place from the Underground Railroad. Thea needed me to help.

So I couldn't keep going slow and steady now. Eyes open, arms spread, feet scuffing, I moved as quickly downhill as I dared. And now the stars were out, and a little light reached toward me— not enough to see the ground well, but enough to outline the tree branches and clumps of weeds and bushes around me. In the stream, to the left of me, star reflections sparkled on the flat parts and flickered among the quicker bits.

The sound of the stream changed. Ahead of me I could see more stars, and all at once I heard a truck's deep unmuffled engine. I was coming to the road.

By the time I reached the roadway, the truck was already gone. My legs ached, my nose wouldn't work from being so stuffed up from crying, and my head ached too.

From behind me, from away from the village, lights and the rumble of a car came. I turned around. The car pulled up beside me, braking with a squeal and a jerk, and Emerson, tall strong Emerson, Emerson with his arms open to grab me and hold me and want me, took me into an enormous hug that lasted forever.

Once again, I burst into tears, and wailed into the rough denim chest of Emerson's jacket: "She lied to me. Mom lied to me. She's not really my mother. She doesn't love me. Oh Emerson, you're not really my brother and nobody wants me and what am I going to do?"

Emerson's arms squeezed tighter, even though I was dripping tears and more on his jacket, and his head came down against mine, and his hands rubbed my back.

"Mom's always loved you for your whole life, Shawna-Fawna," he growled, using the old name he used to say to tease me when I was little. "We've all loved you. We always have, and we always will. Even Alice. And you can't say Mom's not your real mother and mean it, Shawna. She's done everything a real mother does, and then some. And right now—" he tipped my head back so I looked into his face. "Right now, Shawna, Mom's out there on the mountain, trying to find you. So is everybody else. So let's go home and ring the big old bell out front, and call them all back from the dark. Okay?"

I snuffled, and Emerson handed me his own handkerchief.

"Okay?" he repeated. "Come on, Shawna-Fawna, tell me

you heard what I said."

I wiped my face and blew my nose. "Okay for now," I answered grudgingly. "I heard you. But I'm not going to pretend I don't know the truth."

"Good girl," Emerson answered. "The truth will set you free. Remember? Let's go home."

HOME.

I wasn't sure what it meant, or who my family was, or who I was. But after Emerson rang the big old dinner bell at the corner of the barn really loud and long, we went inside, into the warm kitchen, and Midnight wound around my legs. I reached down to pick up the cat, and he purred, rubbing his head under my chin.

"Emerson? I don't feel so great," I told my big brother.

He snorted. "You missed supper. So did the rest of us. Get some chili out of the crock-pot while I start the coffee."

I pushed Midnight away and sat down to eat. Emerson was right, I was starving. I could have starved to death on the mountain. I shivered.

"Where's M—" I hesitated.

"Don't be dumb, Shawna, she's still Mom, even if you're confused. We'll sort it all out. Mom came roaring down here on the four-wheeler to get us all looking for you. Then she headed back up to camp, to walk down along the stream. She said you'd gone that way."

"But I didn't see her."

"Nope, she's probably half an hour behind you, even with a flashlight. Give her a chance. She sent me to drive back and forth along the road, and Carl and your friend Theresa went to wait at the camp. They've got the four-wheeler. Harry took over the milking so we could all be out there."

"Not Theresa, her name's Thea," I corrected him. "What's Thea doing with Carl?"

"I guess she came looking for you. She was here when Mom came racing into the kitchen and said you were hiking down the mountain in the dark. She wanted to help."

How embarrassing. I put my head down on my arm and hid my eyes. My very first best friend, right in the middle of the biggest family catastrophe of my life.

I remembered Thea talking in the kitchen before, looking at my brothers' photos on the fridge. "She said Carl was cute," I said out loud.

"What? Take your face out of your sweatshirt if you want to tell me something. What did you say, Shawna?"

"I said, she said Carl was cute. She saw his picture and she said he was cute!"

Emerson grinned. "Then she better like the smell of cow poop as well as his cute face. Carl was in the middle of milking, you know. Speaking of faces, why don't you go wash yours, before the others come in. Your hands could use some cleaning up, too."

I grinned back at him, weakly, then mopped chili off my face and went upstairs to the use the bathroom. And when I saw my reflection, I realized I'd better change my clothes, too. What a mess.

Back in the kitchen, that's what I said to Emerson: "What a mess. Emerson, why didn't anybody tell me? Why did you all lie to me? Why didn't you tell me the truth?"

He sighed, and sat down opposite me at the kitchen table. "When?" he asked, very seriously. "When do you think we should have told you? When you were two? Or three?" His lips worked for a moment, as if he didn't like the taste of what he'd said. "And besides, after Alice left, it's almost like we forgot. I mean, Mom did the adoption papers way back, and you've just always been my kid sister."

"What about Alice? What about when she called here? Did she want to know about me?"

"Always!" Emerson thumped the table in emphasis. "Always, she always wanted to know about you, and get pictures, and your report cards and everything. She's proud of you. So are all of us. You're a good kid, Shawna. And a lot better than Alice was when she was your age."

"Did Alice get in a lot of trouble?"

I didn't get an answer from Emerson for that, because the door banged open. It was Carl. He was already talking to Emerson. "Where'd you find her? Is she okay?"

"She's fine! See?"

Carl burst across the room and grabbed me up out of my chair. "And we always said you were so smart. What kind of dumb little sister are you, running into the woods at night without a flashlight or a friend? Hey, your friend's here, she was worried about you, too!"

Thea stood just inside the kitchen door, unsure of herself. "Shawna, are you okay? Really?"

"Really," I assured her. Of course, I knew my nose and eyes were still red from crying half the way down the mountain, but I didn't want Thea to think I'd been scared in the woods. "I sang out loud and talked and the bears and wolves and stuff all ran away from me."

"Wolves?" She stared, and clutched her sweater around her.

Emerson cut in. "She's kidding you, Thea. No wolves in North Upton. They've been gone for a hundred years. Come on in and have some chili. Shawna, get your friend a bowl and a spoon. Where are your manners?" He reached across and knocked a fist lightly against my arm. "Up and at 'em, kiddo."

Carl looked at the clock, then at Emerson. "Harry's got to be about done milking, or close to it. Don't you think so?"

"Probably," Emerson agreed. "Shawna, get a bowl for Carl, too. Coffee's almost ready. Here, Thea, you can sit over on this side. I'll slice some bread. Carl, grab the butter off the sideboard, would you?"

"Uh, no chili for me, thanks," Thea said quickly, and I was about to be confused but then remembered and blushed as I realized there was meat in it.

"I can warm up some vegetable soup in the microwave," I offered. "It goes well with Mom's bread."

"Okay—thanks!"

So when my mother—no, Emerson and Carl and Alice's mother—or is your grandmother also your mother if she properly adopts you?—anyway, when she walked in fifteen minutes later, kicking off her boots on the porch and dumping a flashlight and backpack on the sideboard, half of the chili was eaten, and almost all of a loaf of bread, and Harry was at the kitchen sink washing his hands, standing there in his socks and telling me over his shoulder to put the new milk into the fridge and get out another bottle of orange soda.

I stood up to face my mother as she walked toward me. "I found my own way down," I told her.

"I see that. Looks like the Lord took pretty good care of you on the way. Talk about Daniel and the lions, or Shawna and the bears." She hesitated, arms halfway out to me.

For a long moment, I didn't reach out at all, but I saw the pain in her eyes. In fact, it looked like she'd been crying, too.

So I stepped forward into the same old hug I'd always had from my mother. And into her chest I said again, "You lied to me. You all did."

"I guess you're right," she finally admitted. She rubbed the top of my head. "I'm sorry, Shawna. Let's get the truth on the table, clean and clear, now."

Harry came over and put his arms around both of us. "I like that idea," he rumbled. "But a man's gotta eat, and the same with a mountain rescue team. Sit down, Connie. Emerson's getting you a bowl of chili. Then we'll talk until it's all talked out."

The only person who didn't know what was really going on was Thea. This was definitely embarrassing. I said, "Um, Thea, maybe you want to go home?" Then I remembered. "Oh gosh, did you talk with your father? Do you need me to go with you?"

She shook her head. "He's gone to town now. He took my brothers to a movie. I came to see if you wanted to do homework." She swallowed hard. "I guess I should go home."

"No way," Carl intervened. "No way, Thea. No way, Shawna. Let's get this all cleared up. Thea's in on it tonight. She's your best friend, and she went right up the mountain with me, because she wanted you to be safe. No more secrets here, anyway. Let's do it."

Everyone else nodded, and I finally agreed. "But she gets to sit by me, not by you, Carl!"

They all laughed, especially Emerson, and Thea got a little red in the face, and the rest of the evening—really, the rest of my life—started over.

While Mom dug into her bowl of chili and Emerson passed around mugs of coffee, Thea called her house and said she'd be home in another hour. Then I couldn't wait any longer, and I started to explain to Thea.

"So I didn't know about this until today, up at our hunting camp, when my m—when my m—when my mother"—oh, it was hard to say it—"when she told me that my sister Alice got, um, got pregnant, when she was, like, fifteen."

Thea nodded, very serious.

Even though there was a lot I wanted to say about that, wanted to scream really, I was screamed out for the night. So I just told it the way my mother had told me: "And Alice had the baby, and my mother adopted the baby, because Alice wasn't ready to be a mother yet. And Alice went to California to finish high school. And the baby was me."

Such a short story that way. I couldn't believe I'd said it in such a little bit of words. Almost fourteen years of my life and now everything needed a new frame, a new set of explanations and, well, stories. Thea was still nodding.

"Yeah," said Thea, and I could tell she was trying to make it okay for me, "in Connecticut I knew someone where that happened. I mean, I knew this girl who got pregnant. It was weird because she wasn't really, like, a slutty person. Nobody could believe it. She stayed in school, and she had the baby over Christmas break. I don't think the baby got adopted by her mother, though. I think she had to give it away at one of those homes or something." My friend's face twisted in apology. "She wasn't really a friend of mine, just somebody in the class ahead of me. So I didn't know all that much. You know?"

Emerson cut in. "That's a lot like what happened with Alice. Alice wasn't fast or anything. But, well, this flatlander kid was here and she met him at a picnic, and Alice always tried to make people feel good, feel part of things. Carl and me, we figured that's kind of what happened but it got carried away." He looked at Carl. "We should have checked up on her more."

Carl agreed. "I never did like that guy all that much. I should have listened to my gut, told him to get lost, and Alice would have been okay."

Now my mother put a hand on Carl's arm. "You don't know that for sure, Carl. And in a lot of ways, Alice is very much okay right now. The Lord's just got a different path for her. And she's coming home for Thanksgiving."

"Praise the Lord," Harry said quietly.

"That's what I don't understand, though," I choked as I started crying again. "Is Alice going to take me to California? Do I have to call Alice 'Mom' or something? I don't want to go to California," I wailed.

"No way," Emerson declared as he threw an arm over my shoulders. "No way you're going to California. Is she, Mom?"

"That's not why Alice is coming," my mother agreed. "She's not coming to take you away from home, Shawna. She's coming to say she's sorry, though, and to talk with all of us. She's trying to be family again, in a new way. And Shawna," she pushed a handful of Kleenex into my hand, "honey, you don't have to call Alice anything except Alice, unless you want to."

Everyone went quiet for a moment, looking at me. Thea didn't say anything. I looked at Mom, looked at Harry, looked at how sad they both seemed to be. Finally I spoke. "I guess I'll stick with the names I've already got for everyone," I said slowly. My mother still looked strained. So I went on. "I guess it was a pretty big deal that I didn't have to get sent away to someplace else. It was a good thing to be adopted, even if I didn't know about it. And you're my Mom, even if you're not exactly my mother," I admitted, watching Mom's face and the tiny nod that she gave. Thea nodded too, which gave me more courage. "Thanks. Thanks, all of you, for being my family." I gulped. "But don't you ever, ever lie to me again! I'm still mad at you all."

Carl snorted. "Come on, Shawna, let us off the hook a little bit more. Nobody lied, exactly. You just don't tell a little kid some things. Admit it! Give Mom a break."

Everyone waited for me to say something. Finally I got up from my seat and went around the table to where my mother was. I felt awkward, but I hugged her across her shoulders, and she rubbed my back. "Thanks, Shawna," she said quietly.

"I love you," I whispered.

"Me too, you," she said against the top of my head.

I let go of my mother and looked up. Thea was smiling at me, her eyes shining. So I guess something was right, after all. Heat crept up my neck and into my face. I had to say something to get everyone to stop looking so sappy. I fumbled: "So hey, is there any dessert?"

And there was, and it was chocolate ice cream, and Harry scooped good big bowls full for everyone.

Meanwhile, I managed to get back to my chair, next to Thea, and asked her, "What about your father?"

She wrinkled her face and shrugged. "So far, he thinks we should let the college people come do the filming tomorrow, and see what they say afterward. He says you and I aren't experts and the professor is, and we should wait and tell them tomorrow what we're thinking."

Together we sighed. We both had serious doubts now about

the hiding place at Thea's house, but nobody important wanted to hear them.

"I guess we'll have to wait, then," I agreed. "I'll make better drawings of the place at the Goodwillie House, after church tomorrow. What time is the video crew coming?"

"Three o'clock. I'll write down what Miss McGuire told us, too."

Bowls of chocolate ice cream reached our side of the table, and I said, "Okay, I'll come at two-thirty, then."

It was good to have a plan for tomorrow. Still, I peeked up on the wall at Alice's framed picture there, and realized I had absolutely positively no plan at all for when she'd arrive at Thanksgiving, or even for the next time my big sister, who was also my birth mother, would call on the phone.

Lucky for me, the phone didn't ring at all that evening, and I slept like a log until the alarm got me up to help in the barn before Sunday morning service.

SITTING IN CHURCH on Sunday, I felt as though my head would burst from trying to hold too many ideas all at once. Alice, my sister Alice, got pregnant when she was a teenager and I didn't know about it. Well, of course I didn't know about it when it happened because I wasn't born yet. In church we learn about not getting into trouble, about saving yourself for when you get married, when it's God's will to make love and have babies. And if you mess around before you're at least engaged, people call you a slut. And in order to get pregnant, Alice must have messed around.

But my mother and my brothers said that Alice wasn't a slut. And they helped her have her baby. And the baby was me. And they adopted me. So did that make Alice into a good person again? It couldn't make her a virgin again. Somehow it didn't really make her my mother, either, and I tried to figure out why.

I missed most of the sermon, although I know it was from John 14, where Jesus says, "Do not let your hearts be troubled. Trust in God; trust also in me. In my Father's house are many rooms." In my mind, Alice's life became a room, and my life was a room, too. And Thea's, even though she didn't go to church.

Finally I decided it probably had something to do with love. Not the kind that's just saying the words, but the kind that you give to a baby when you change its diapers without throwing up from the smell. And the kind when you make supper for someone every single night, like Mom and Harry did for me and whichever of Emerson or Carl or both happened to be there. I guess love and family were kind of stuck together like that. But that didn't mean I was ready to say it was right for everyone to lie to me. No way.

On the way home from church, we passed Mrs. Toussaint's house, where two dead deer hung upside down from a tree in the front yard. One had a big rack of antlers; the other just had little spike horns, but still, it seemed pretty big, hanging there like that to drain. When she saw the two bucks, Mom gave a soft whistle.

"Two of them, and it's only bow and arrow season," she marveled. "I guess Jennie Toussaint's nephews really got lucky this year."

I leaned over into the front seat, between Mom and Harry. "Mom, is that big one the buck you've been tracking up on the ridge? Did they get your deer?"

Harry took one hand off the steering wheel and patted her leg in sympathy. But she shook her head. "No, I doubt it. Mine's a good size, but not as big as that one. Besides, Toussaints hunt up in Wheelock mostly. They just hang their deer down at her place to show off to the village. No, Shawna, I imagine my deer's still up there." She looked worried anyway. "I better not take the four-wheeler up there again until rifle season opens. No sense spooking them with the smell or the noise of it."

I counted out loud. "Two weeks and six days: that's twenty days until the season opens. They'll forget that we were there yesterday, won't they? Up at the cabin?"

"Sure they will. Sure." Mom caught my eye in the mirror. "Don't worry, Shawna. I always take things up to camp at the end of October with the four-wheeler, and it's never stopped me from finding my own deer if I worked hard for it."

At home, I checked the time: I should be over at Thea's by two-thirty, maybe earlier. Lunch, dishes to wash from breakfast and lunch both, and change into jeans—and I'd need an hour to make the drawings of the hiding place from the Goodwillie House, I figured. I'd have to hurry.

Thea met me at the door of her house before I even had a chance to knock. "I was watching from upstairs. Come on!"

At the far end of the hallway, Thea's younger brothers came out from the TV room and Thaddeus, his hair sticking up and shirt untucked, grinned and said, "Hey." Little Teddy had his thumb in his mouth and was pulling on his brother's leg. Thaddeus bent down and lifted the toddler in a football hoist, running back into the other room. They were allowed to do that on Sunday? I ducked up the stairs behind Thea, expecting to hear a grownup yelling, but nothing happened.

"Is your mother home?" I asked as Thea closed her bedroom door behind us.

"Yes, she's in the kitchen, I think. It's okay, she knows we're doing stuff for the college professor to see. Look what I've got!" She waved toward the pages lined up across the rug, pages with charts of the visitors to the inn that she'd done from my scribbled Dearborn journal notes, and a list of the lines of code from the basement room, and a few more with typing on them—details from her notes on what Mrs. Toussaint, Mr. Harris, and Miss McGuire had told us.

"Awesome!" I pulled out my drawings of the hiding place and cellar from the Goodwillie House, and of the hidden room in Thea's basement, with all the dimensions inked onto them in neat block numbers and letters. We added those to the line-up.

"Know what? This looks like we've got most of our history project display pulled together," Thea said. She was right. It looked so good already.

"And we've got until December. We should have pictures, though. And maybe a model of how the dimensions in your cellar hide the room."

"Can you do that? Make a model?"

"Sure. All we need is some of those foam-core boards that everyone uses to put displays on, and I could cut them up into walls and fit them together."

Anybody could see, looking at the numbers and floor plans, that the two hidden places were entirely different. Especially a college professor. At least, that's what we thought.

But we were wrong.

The video crew arrived at almost quarter after three. Thea and her dad had already answered the door for three other people before that, though.

The first was Mrs. Toussaint. In spite of her white hair and creased skin, she looked as eager as a kid. "Thank you so much for inviting me," she said to Thea's father. "May I see the hidden room?"

"Let's all wait and go downstairs together," Mr. Warwick suggested. "Here's my wife, Barb. Come on into the dining room—we'll all gather there before going down."

All gather? What was going on? Standing on the stairs, I looked up at Thea, still in the upstairs hall. She shrugged. I went back up and whispered to her, "Do you know?"

"Not really. I've been up here working."

Who else had her father invited? We gathered all our pages in a careful stack and went down to the dining room.

"And here's my daughter now," Mr. Warwick said.

"Oh, I already know your daughter, of course." The librarian smiled at Thea and me. "And Shawna Lee. Girls, what's that you've got?"

"Our information," I answered while Thea began to spread out the pages along the center of the table. "We've got notes from the journal you showed us, and information from Mr. Harris, and from Miss McGuire at the Goodwillie House, too. And here are the drawings of the two places."

Mrs. Toussaint beamed. "Research! Both library research and in-person investigation. Excellent." She leaned over the table to read from the pages. "Millicent McGuire of course is a wonderful resource herself."

"And she said to ask you to give her a call, please," Thea added quickly.

Someone knocked at the kitchen door. Mr. Warwick went to answer the door, while Mrs. Warwick poured apple cider into small glasses. Good—anyone serving cider must be planning to bring out donuts sooner or later, I figured.

I recognized a voice in the hall: Pastor Wilkins. What on earth? And another voice that I didn't know. A moment later, three people came in: Pastor Wilkins, Mr. Warwick, and someone I knew I should know, but I couldn't think of his name. Mr. Warwick made introductions to his wife: "Barb, you know Pastor Wilkins already, and this is Steve Cobleigh, the selectman."

Oh. Mr. Cobleigh. Of course I'd seen him before. He smiled at me across the dining table, his face a little crooked and his blue eyes scrunching smaller from the big grin. I liked the way he paid attention to us girls right away. "Remind me who these young ladies are, Bill. One must be yours, and isn't this Connie Quinn's girl?"

"My daughter Thea, and her classmate Shawna," Mr. Warwick replied. "And those are my sons, Thaddeus and Ted," he added as the boys peeked around the doorway. "Boys, you can come in and get some cider, but then I want you to stay in the other room, the way we agreed."

People glanced at our papers on the table, but mostly they looked at the drawings of the two hiding places: the one from the Goodwillie House, and the one downstairs, underneath us. Mrs. Warwick went to answer the door again, and I moved so I could see down the hall. This time it was the film crew from the college, all right. Two college students, one a boy and one a girl, came in carrying big black duffel bags of equipment that looked really heavy. Behind them, already talking to Mrs. Warwick, was the professor—Dr. Thomas. "Yes, thanks, it's been a great day," he said as he came toward the dining room, dodging around the students. "Leave the bags by the door a minute," he told them, beckoning them into the dining room with everyone else. He continued, "We've been to Peacham, at the Johnson house, where

William Lloyd Garrison used to visit, you know. And before that, the Goodwillie House, of course. Yours is our last stop today."

With the professor and the students crowded into the dining room too, nobody paid attention to our papers any more. Introductions criss-crossed the room like a web. Then, finally, we were all headed down the cellar stairs, except for Thea's mom, who said she'd let her husband "do the honors."

Thea and I hung back while the newest visitors crowded into the small space of the hidden room. The two college students knelt on the cellar floor just outside the room, snapping together black metal stands and unwrapping a big video camera. I heard Mrs. Toussaint's voice rise the clearest above all the men: "Oh, my. Gracious! Just look at that. Aim that lamp of yours on the walls here, would you, young man? Now, I suppose you're all working on whose handwriting that would be. Not Henry Dearborn's, certainly; I'm very familiar with his, from his journals. No, I would say this is a much less educated script, don't you think?" I couldn't see her expression from where I stood. What did she mean by that?

Dr. Thomas replied, "Quite right, Mrs. Toussaint. James and Karyn, we'll need some close shots of the handwriting. This could be the first real evidence left behind of some of the fugitive slaves themselves."

"Oh, I doubt that, Dr. Thomas," the librarian cut in. "I think this is all one hand or at most two people's writing on the wall. That would indicated the tally was being kept for some time by someone who belonged here in the house, keeping track of who passed through." She paused, then added more quietly, "Who, or what."

Pastor Wilkins sounded excited as he took his turn explaining. "It could even have been the minister here in the village," he guessed. "The Reverend John Stanton preached several times at North Church against slavery, even before the Civil War, and of course all the way through it. He could have been central in the Underground Railroad station here."

"We need a list of all the pastors in all the local churches at that time," the professor called out. "Karyn, make a note of that. There should be portraits of the ministers available, to feed into the video. Are the lights ready?"

"Just about ready," the girl said, standing up awkwardly and switching on a very bright white light that turned the cellar walls silvery gray. The boy lifted onto his shoulder the camera, about two feet long with a lens that reached another six inches forward. I could tell it was heavy by the way he tipped to balance it.

Mr. Cobleigh came out of the little room, with Mrs. Toussaint and the others following, just leaving the professor inside as the students pushed in with the light stand and the camera that had the thick black stem of a microphone sticking up near the front of it.

"Five, four, three," the boy said, giving a nod to the professor, who began a smooth speech just at the point in my mind's ear when I could hear the unspoken "zero" from the count.

"We're in a hiding place for fugitive slaves in the cellar of a former inn, in the village of North Upton, Vermont. Note the faint lines along the walls where shelf-like sleeping platforms must have been fastened, to fit the maximum number of black persons into this small space as they hid from the notorious slave hunts that terrorized northern New England under the Fugitive Slave Law. Here at my left, markings on the wall suggest someone kept a tally of the individuals who passed through this small but significant place, a safety and a haven for the lives being saved." He beckoned to Mr. Warwick, who took Thea's hand and pulled her along, inside the little room.

"This is William Warwick, whose family lives in the former stagecoach inn today. Mr. Warwick, tell us how this discovery was made. You just realized this week that your home included a possible Underground Railroad site, is that right?"

"That's right, Dr. Thomas," Mr. Warwick said, nodding at the camera that was now focused on him. "And actually, the discovery of the room was made by my daughter Thea, here."

Thea spoke right up. "By two of us," she corrected her father. "My friend Shawna Lee and I were measuring the house dimensions for a math project for school." She made a "come here" motion with one hand, but I shook my head—no way I was going in front of any video camera—and I pointed back at her. So she kept going. "We found the room because the dimensions outside and inside showed something must be here. But we're still doing historical research to figure out what the room was for."

"Of course, of course," said the professor. The camera swung back to his face. "A great deal of research will be needed to ensure that this is indeed an Underground Railroad hiding place. Of course, with a verified site in nearby Barnet, and active conductors for the route north in such local towns as Peacham and Hardwick, it seems very likely that further research will verify this site as well. Note the convenience of the location: Escaping slaves costumed to look like ordinary farm workers or rural guests could be brought on the stagecoach among the regular passengers. In their support for liberty and the Union, Vermonters would do all in their power to see justice served and escort the runaways to freedom in Canada, just another sixty miles to the north."

Then there were video sweeps of the entire cellar, and of the stairs down, and then the students went outside to "capture images" of the outside of Thea's house. Meanwhile, the rest of us went back to the dining room, where Mrs. Warwick had fresh cups of cider waiting, and a bowl of pretzel sticks. It wasn't a very big bowl. I took some and tried to eat them slowly while I listened to the others.

Mr. Cobleigh had his pocket calendar out and was checking with Thea's dad. "The selectmen could all visit before our next meeting," he explained. "And the town clerk. She needs to be up on this, for the phone calls that will probably come after the news program. When did you say this will air?"

The professor had his calendar out, too. "Sunday, November thirteenth. That will give the class some time to work on laying in still photos and interviewing some other local experts. I've contacted the news station in Burlington, and they've agreed to show it, too. James and Karyn, make sure background music is on your list for tomorrow." He made some notes.

I asked, "Don't you want to wait for more research first?"

"No, no, that's not necessary. We can always do a second program." He looked at me for a moment and said, "You're not the Warwick daughter, are you? I thought she was—oh, there she is. So you're the other young lady who helped with the discovery, are you? Good for the two of you." But that was enough for him, it seemed, because he turned back to Mr. Warwick right away and said, "You mentioned a web site for this, didn't you? We'll need that, to put it on the screen at the end of the program."

"Sure, just a minute, I'll give you a card."

Web site? Thea shot a look at me, and I followed her out into the hall.

"My dad spent this entire morning designing a new web site for the town," she explained. "With pictures. He said we can use it as part of our project if we want to."

"But why? I mean, why is he doing all this so fast?"

Mrs. Toussaint spoke from behind me, making me jump. "It's good for the town," she said. "People are excited, and everyone wants to get in on this. With a web site, you can put the photos there, even a film, I believe. So people can look and see, and feel part of this. It's a big thing for North Upton to have a discovery like you girls have made."

I backed away against the wall and asked, "But what if it's not really an Underground Railroad hiding place? What if the research says it was something else?" The children's book about the messages hidden in patches and quilts, the one that made Mr. Harris so mad, was on my mind. "Won't people get angry?"

The librarian smiled and patted my shoulder. "Then that will be news, too," she reassured me. "There's a saying in the newspaper business, 'All publicity is good publicity.' Don't worry. You girls go ahead with your project, and let Mr. Cobleigh and the selectmen go ahead with theirs. It will be fine."

I wasn't so sure. Thea must have felt the same, because she started to say, "But Mrs. Toussaint," when the college students came back in from outside, and the hallway became too full of people and voices.

Mrs. Toussaint bent close to me and whispered, "Tell your friend we'll talk about it next Saturday, when you two come back to the library." Standing straight again, she called back into the dining room, "Thank you so much, William and Barbara, and Dr. Thomas, I'll be expecting your call for use of the photographs at our historical society. I'm afraid I need to get going now." And with a whirl of her long dark skirt and a nod at the two of us, the librarian whisked down the hall and out of the house.

Thea asked me what the whisper had been, and I told her.

"At least *somebody* is listening to us," she said. "I just wish my dad would, too." She pursed her mouth and twisted it to one side. "I guess nobody's parents are perfect, you know what I mean?"

"Yeah," I agreed. "I know." We twisted our pinkies together for a moment, partners against the rest of the world.

We looked inside the dining room and listened for a moment to the chaos of conversations going on, then slipped upstairs to Thea's room and closed the door for some peace and quiet.

"Okay, we can't do much about this until next weekend, when we go see Mrs. Toussaint again," Thea decided. "So tell me what the dance is going to be like on Friday, okay? Don't forget, I'm the new girl here. You've got to tell me what to expect, and then we can make a plan."

THERE WERE FIVE days until Friday, the day of the Halloween dance at school—and the strangest thing was that nothing strange happened in them. Alice didn't call, at least as far as I knew. And I definitely didn't want to talk with her anyway. I felt weird at home, uneasy, as if the floors and walls had moved around in the night. What I used to know about myself and my family was—well, it wasn't completely wrong, but it was missing such a big part. I blamed my mother and Harry for not trusting me with the truth. But what I felt about Alice was even more awful. Each time I thought about her being pregnant—about me being born from her—it gave me the creeps. New evidence about Alice, as far as I was concerned, had turned her into somebody I really didn't want to see.

Thea and I couldn't work on our history project until Saturday, when we'd visit Mrs. Toussaint again. I didn't try to talk about it at school, either. I wanted some ordinary time without so much stress.

On Thursday after supper, I needed to bake the three dozen brownies I'd promised to bring, and Thea promised she'd come across the road to help. We could do our math homework while the brownies were in the oven.

When Thea knocked at the kitchen door and I called to her to come in, she called back to me, "No, you come out first—it's snowing!"

Sure enough. You couldn't see any snow on the ground, because it melted as soon as it got there. But on the dark blue of Thea's sweater sleeve, little chunks of white kept landing, then vanishing. They didn't look like the single snowflakes like in books and photos, but more like grains of sand—lumpy little bits. Thea looked at me in the porch light and asked, "Will there be a whole foot of it in the morning?"

"No, not yet. It'll melt tonight. But it's the beginning of winter, for sure."

Inside, Thea set down her bookbag, and I called out to Mom and Harry, "It's snowing!" I explained to Thea: "A little snow is great for hunting season. You can see the tracks better."

With three boxes of brownie mix out on the table, I was ready to start baking. Thea emptied the mixes into my mother's biggest mixing bowl, and I added eggs, oil, and water.

"Why so much?" she asked me.

"Each box is supposed to make three dozen, but that's only if you cut them really small. Nobody wants brownies that small, not really. So you need two boxes. But we need some for here too, so Mom and Harry can have a couple, plus you and me. So ... three boxes."

"Got it."

Math homework was easy, of course, just graphs of parabolic curves and writing some equations. Thea and I finished at almost the same moment. The timer still showed ten minutes more for the brownies in the oven.

"So did you decide what you're wearing for the dance?"

I shook my head. "Maybe my newest sweater, I guess. And corduroys."

"You're kidding! Shawna, don't people dress up for school dances here?"

"Well, yeah, some people do. But I don't really care what I wear, you know?"

Thea rolled her eyes at me. So when we took the brownies out of the oven and set them to cool, she insisted on exploring my clothes upstairs.

"Where are your skirts?"

I showed her, in the closet. "I just have them for church. I don't really like them much."

"Yeah, I can see why." She held up a plaid wool skirt that made me look like a Scottish sheepdog or something. "These just aren't you, anyway." She pulled out two T-shirts, one green, one blue, and a pair of black pants I'd mostly forgotten about, with the tags still on them. "This would work better for you, and you should wear the blue shirt over the green, like this, see? Plus maybe a belt or a sash or something, to make it pop. And you'll want something sparkly, maybe around your neck. Where's your jewelry?"

I dug out the shoebox where I kept necklaces and earrings. I didn't have much, though, and I was a little embarrassed to show it to Thea, who probably had ten times as much of this stuff as I did. "Okay, this chain with the rhinestones will work. And you can borrow some dangly earrings from me—good thing your ears are pierced! And—your mother won't get mad if you wear a little bit of eye makeup, will she?"

"I don't think so." Actually, I knew my mother wouldn't mind. She'd given me some makeup for my thirteenth birthday. I just felt stupid about it. I pulled out the eyeliner and eye shadow and mascara. Thea nodded her approval.

"And lip gloss. It's much more real than those old lipsticks. I've got extra—you can use some. So tomorrow after school, after we all decorate the gym, you can put on these clothes and come over to my house, and we'll do our makeup together." She pawed through the shoes on the floor of the closet, grunting. "You know what? Wear some fuzzy socks. I bet we'll all dance in socks anyway, so shoes won't matter."

That was a relief. I asked, "What about you?"

Thea grinned. "I've got a gypsy skirt and blouse and I'm wearing big hoop earnings. It won't go with the music really, but I'm planning to have fun!"

She leaned close to speak really quietly, although nobody else would have heard her, anyway: "I bet I can get Josh to kiss me by the end of the dance."

I didn't know what to say.

My friend bounced on my bed in a huge belly flop, and laughed. "Anyway, it's going to be fun. Are you sure we won't get a foot of snow tonight?"

My turn to laugh. A foot of snow, on October 30? No way.

In the morning, there was a half-inch of snow on the ground. The green prickles of grass stems poked through. It wasn't cold enough to bother wearing mittens, but I tugged the hood of my sweatshirt up over my head, and I threw on a down vest for the walk to school.

On the way, I noticed carved pumpkins at a couple of houses, and I told Thea they'd probably all have candles in them later, for the little kids going from house to house for trick-or-treat. "What will your little brothers be tonight?"

"Oh, Thaddeus is going to be a wizard, with a magic wand, and my mother's gluing stars and glitter onto a hat for him. I think Teddy will do the cowboy thing again, it's about the only kind of dress-up he likes to do." We laughed together.

The Willson twins came around the side of the school, from the parking lot, and rushed toward Thea. "Somebody just asked us for the movie music from 'Moulin Rouge,'" Merry Willson said breathlessly. Marsha finished, "So do you have that on a CD, Thea?"

"Probably." Thea shrugged, pulling off her bookbag to go inside the building. "Listen, I'll check when I get home, and if I have it, I'll bring it tonight. Your cousin's still going to do the DJ thing, right?"

She was so calm and casual! The Willson girls obviously never guessed that Thea had plans for their cousin Josh. I held back a smile, but something must have showed a little, because

Thea suddenly turned around so the others didn't see her face, winked at me, and punched my shoulder lightly.

In homeroom, I scribbled a one-paragraph summary of *Uncle Tom's Cabin,* and then the bell rang and the push of classes and clock took over. At two in the afternoon, all the sixth, seventh, and eighth graders reported to the gym to decorate: orange and black crepe paper to drape on things, plus cutouts of bats and black cats for the walls, and miniature yellow pumpkins to stack on the tables where the refreshments would go. I noticed there weren't any cutouts of witches this year. The year before, my mother and a couple of other moms had talked with the principal about steering Halloween away from any kind of devil worship, including witches and warlocks and things like that. Maybe Mom wouldn't find out that Thea's brother was going trick-or-treating as a wizard. But unless Harry was the one answering the door in the evening—which wasn't too likely, because he'd be in the barn—probably Thaddeus Wizard Warwick would be right at our kitchen door, getting a Hershey bar from my mother. Oh well. I just hoped Mrs. Warwick wasn't making his costume too weird.

Miss Calkins called out for all of us to pay attention, and slowly the gym quieted. "It's quarter to three now, and anyone riding the bus home or getting a ride with their parents should go back to their classrooms now. Those of you who live in the village can stay until three-thirty, and then I expect you all to go home and get changed for the dance." A ripple of concern spread among the boys, who were looking at each other to find out what "get changed for the dance" meant. Miss Calkins continued, "No, you don't have to wear school clothes tonight, but I expect everyone to dress for the weather, please, and just a reminder, there will be no false teeth or fangs allowed on school property. And no objects inside noses or ears, either."

"What?" Thea stared at me. I laughed—lots of other people were laughing, too.

"Last year, one of the kids choked on his plastic teeth," I explained. "The ambulance had to come and everything. And the year before, Maryellen Bryce brought a bag of glow-in-the-dark earrings, and Michael Willson stuffed one up his nose and had to go to the hospital to get it taken out!"

"Jeez!"

"Let me guess, that never happened in Connecticut," I teased.

"No way! But there was this one time," my friend leaned toward me, "these two boys, I didn't really see this but I heard about it, these two boys were doing magic tricks and one of the teachers said they made his watch disappear. Everybody had to empty their pockets and everything, but it never turned up. Their class had detention for, like, a month, and still nobody found it."

"Why did the teacher let them do magic with his watch, anyway?"

Thea shrugged, and passed me one end of a roll of crepe paper to hold while she unrolled the rest, twisting as she went. "Who knows? Can you hold that up over your head, so I can see how it will reach across the doorway?"

At three-thirty, we went home, and I promised to be at Thea's at five with my T-shirts, black pants, and eye makeup. The snow had melted during the day, but it was cold anyway, and I was glad to get inside our house. A note on the kitchen table said, "SHAWNA come help in barn? Harry."

Just what I didn't need. I poured a tall glass of milk. In the fridge a leftover serving of apple crisp in a bowl looked like it was getting dried out; I ate it so it wouldn't spoil. Besides, it's good to have fruit for a snack. I drained my milk, changed into old jeans and a ratty old sweatshirt and barn boots, and went back outside. It was snowing again, just a little bit, and almost dark already.

In the milkroom, Harry stood up from the water controls under the bulk tank and said "Thank goodness you're here! Your mother's still up on the hill and I had a broken water line, so I'm late starting. I know you've got Halloween to do, but can you bed the cows for me?"

He meant, would I scrape the manure into the gutters and

shovel clean sawdust behind all the cows and heifers—like on Sunday mornings.

"Yeah, I guess. But I'll have to go at four-thirty, to take a shower and get over to Thea's for the dance, okay?"

Harry glanced up at the clock. That would be just forty-five minutes. "I'll take any time you can give," he said. "Thanks, kiddo. And maybe your mother will be back by then."

So I loaded a cart with fragrant cedar sawdust and started scraping and shoveling, with just a quick peek at the kittens in the grain box first. They'd opened their eyes, and they were so cute. Thea could help name them, I decided.

I left the barn at exactly four-thirty, and there was no sign yet of my mother. Harry waved and called out, "Thanks," as I shoved the sawdust cart back into the corner. All the stalls were done, and Harry had the grain shoveled out and was partway down the first row of cows with the milking machine. Not bad.

Inside the house, I made sure the porch light wasn't on; same with the kitchen. I didn't want trick-or-treaters coming while I was in the shower! I popped two slices of frozen pizza into the microwave. Washing my hair from the barn smell took a little longer than I wanted it to, but even so, at just five after five, I had on the T-shirts and black slacks, my winter jacket over them, the eye makeup and jewelry in a plastic bag, and at the last minute I remembered to bring the brownies, too. Leaning over a paper plate, I hurried to eat the pizza, holding the two slices together like a sandwich so I wouldn't get tomato sauce on me. Then I put the basket of Halloween candy out in the porch and turned the outside light back on, so kids would know there was candy for them and so Mom could see when she came down from the hill. As I slipped out the door, I heard the phone ringing behind me, but whoever it was could leave a message.

Picking my way carefully across the yard in the light snow, careful not to slip on the wet grass, I watched the ground in front of me—and realized there were tracks from two deer going right along the driveway. Somehow they'd walked through while I was inside, either in the barn or in the house. I smiled: Mom was up on the hill, and the deer were at our house. Funny.

At Thea's house, my hands were too full to open the door, so I pushed the doorbell. Kids' feet ran toward it, Thaddeus and Teddy both yelling, "I'll get it, it's my turn." Wow, they were cute in their costumes! Each carried a hat—Thaddeus a silver-blue wizard's hat with silver stars sparkling, and Teddy a little straw cowboy hat. He wore cowboy boots, too, and a red neckerchief, plus a miniature decorated vest. Next to the door stood a plate of individually wrapped granola bars decorated with black and orange ribbons, and he tried to give me one. I said no, thanks anyway.

"Hey Thea, Shawna's here," Thaddeus called up the stairs.

Mrs. Warwick leaned out of the kitchen into the hall and waved, one hand holding the telephone. As I crossed the hall to go up, I heard her say goodbye to someone and start moving Thea's little brothers into coats to go trick-or-treating. Mr. Warwick came into the hall too, saying, "Go ahead, I'll take care of the door."

Thea wore the gypsy skirt and blouse she'd described, with a long red sash at the waist. Her hoop earrings looked terrific. I closed the bedroom door behind me and watched her in front of her mirror, spreading blue eye shadow on her lids. Her closet stood open, and inside it, neatly hung clothes in matching colors lined up across the space. I looked to see if she'd mind my touching them, and she said right away, "Go ahead. My mom just made me clean it. By tomorrow it'll be a mess again. The ones on the left are my yoga pants and tops. I used to do that a lot in Connecticut. You know, yoga exercises?" I lifted a color-matched set and saw the impossibly slim legs of the pants and some Asian design on the top. "You'd like yoga," she added. "Maybe we can start a group at school." My stomach twisted into a knot at the thought of wearing stretchy things like that in front of Merry and Marsha and Maryellen. Yikes. I quickly shut the closet door.

Finished with her eyes, Thea switched to a tube of lip gloss and at the same time waved me toward the bed, where a tangle of sashes and belts waited. "Here, pick one of these. I'll get out the necklaces too—just a minute while I do this."

In a clear space on the rug, I set down my jacket and the brownies, then sorted through the chaos on the bed. Why did she have so many? I didn't like most of the thin sashes, but I found a heavy belt with bright squares and triangles on it.

Thea leaned across the bed and laughed. "You found a math belt—all geometry. Let's see how it looks." She held it up against my shirt, then handed it back to me. I wrapped it around my waist.

She shook her head. "You've got to keep it looser, so it rides down on your hips some. Can I fix it for you?"

She made the belt really loose and tugged it into an angle over the second layer of T-shirt. Not bad. I pulled out my eyeliner and mascara. "I'll go to the bathroom and do these."

"No, do them right here, it's fine." Thea swept a clear place on top of her dresser, and I looked at myself in the mirror. I'd only tried the eye stuff once, when my mother first gave it to me. I fumbled with the tubes, embarrassed. The first line of eyeliner looked crooked and amateur.

"Do it again," Thea ordered. "Right on top of the first line. Let it be wide, that's fine, the shadow will blur the edge of it."

I got the eyeliner and mascara on finally, and stood with my eyes closed while Thea added eye shadow from a compact full of colors. Her fingers were warm and small and felt strange on my eyelids. She smoothed color onto each lid twice.

"Okay, you can open your eyes. But don't go away. I'm putting on some blusher for you."

She dabbed some of the powder on my cheeks, and handed me a little tub of lip gloss. The face looking back at me, with rose cheeks, green eye shadow, and a finger slick of shiny lip gloss, was a stranger. I moved my lips carefully, and I could see the reflected lips move too. Thea peeked over my shoulder. "Ooh, Shawna, you look great! What about me, do I look okay?"

"You look amazing!" I assured her. "And those earrings make you look, well, really like a gypsy dancer. But better!"

We laughed together. I stared into the mirror again. Mom might not like this this, I thought. She'd hate how different I looked. Would Alice approve, though? And would that be good, or awful?

"Let's go," Thea urged. "Come on!"

Outside, it was dark and cold, except where the barn safety light lit the roadway. Only one set of car tracks was there, but as we got closer to the school, there were lots of footprints. In front of the McGill house I saw a cluster of kids, maybe second grade age. Mrs. McGill was putting candy into their treat bags. I didn't see Mrs. Warwick and Thaddeus and Teddy, though. They must have gone around a corner or inside one of the houses. Jack-o'-lanterns glowed all over the village. The school lights lit the far end of town, and two cars came from behind us, pulling in to drop off some kids.

We left our coats and our snow-wet shoes in the hall, padding into the gym in our socks. I was glad Thea had suggested fuzzy socks—other girls had brightly colored socks on, too. For once, I fit in. A cluster of people at the refreshments table caught my gaze.

"I'd better go put my brownies there," I told Thea. She nodded and headed toward a big decorated booth where lights flashed on the sound equipment and two tall boys, one of them probably Josh, were sorting a stack of CDs.

The refreshments table looked pathetic. Somebody's paper plate of tiny sugar cookies with orange gumdrops on top sat alone at one end, and a block of cheese and box of crackers perched next to a cutting board. The empty punchbowl waited for ingredients. Paper plates and cups in wrappers sat in the middle of it all.

I set the brownies down and opened the paper plates, to divide up the brownies into two arrangements. I tucked the lame little sugar cookies among them, making the table look like more like party food. Miss Calkins arrived and unloaded three half-gallon bottles of orange soda, a bag of ice, and a plastic container of lemon sherbet. Well, so it wasn't going to be a very fancy punch after all—at least I knew how to put all this together. Armed with an ice cream scoop, I got to work: ice into the bowl, then the soda, and scoops of sherbet floating on top. The teacher passed me a punch ladle, and said, "Looks great, Shawna. Now could you do something with the rest of it?"

While I'd been scooping sherbet, more food had arrived, mostly in plastic bags, damp with melted snowflakes from being carried from cars and houses. I found graham cracker teddy bears, Oreos, apple-raisin bars, even a bag of miniature chocolate bars. Arranging everything on serving plates looked a lot better than leaving them in the packages. I stuck the wrappers into one of the bigger bags, shoved it under the table, brushed off some crumbs, and looked around.

The gym had filled right up. Some kids did have costumes on, even though it was a dance. There must have been at least seven ghosts and a couple of witches. I spotted Maryellen Bryce, in a princess tiara and pink dress. Lame! Thea's outfit was a hundred times better. Where was Thea, anyway?

I walked over to the "sound booth" and pushed through a ring of eighth graders. There she was: standing behind Josh Willson, leaning over his shoulder to pick out CDs for the stack he'd be playing. Thea leaned further, so the neckline of her blouse dipped some, and I swear I could see the red flush moving up Josh's neck to his face.

The last thing I wanted to think about was Alice, but how could I help it? Seeing Thea tease Josh, I knew I could be seeing a replay of Alice when she was fifteen. I wanted to do something about it, so I said, "Hey! Hey Josh, can you make announcements on that thing? Can you announce that the refreshments are ready?"

He fumbled and found a microphone, and Thea leaned back and winked at me. She came out of the sound booth and said in a low voice, "Do you know if he can dance?"

"No idea!" I leaned closer and whispered, "Slow it down some, he won't be able to play the music right if you get him all worked up like that!" I was worried, too: "You only want him to kiss you at the end, right? He's going to think something else if you keep leaning over him that way!"

Thea shrugged. "Yeah, I guess you're right. Anyway, I made an impression. Hey, that's a David Archuleta song, isn't it? That's not one of mine. Maybe Josh brought it himself. Come one, let's dance!"

There were only girls dancing anyway, kind of just moving around and a couple of them pretending to sing. So we stood with a group of them under the basketball hoop, and I could see right away that Thea knew some real dance moves. It got everyone trying to do more of them. After a couple of minutes, I backed away and stood against the cool painted concrete wall to watch.

Alan Everts's younger brother came to stand against the same wall. I couldn't think of his name for a minute. He was tall, much taller than the other seventh graders. "Hey," I said.

"Hey. You're Shawna, right? Shawna Lee?"

"Yeah."

"I thought so. But you look different, dressed up. Hey, I'm Kyle. My brother is Alan, you know?"

"I guess."

Even though I wasn't saying much, he kept talking. "Your brother Carl was the best basketball player. I saw him at Upton High, back when I was a little kid. Didn't he play for the University of Vermont, too?"

"Some." I looked at Kyle Everts sideways. He had brown hair that was almost red, and it stuck up at the front. Looking upward and from the side, I noticed how his cheeks, with tiny dark pinpoints, showed he'd started to shave. It made me feel funny about talking with him. He wasn't just a kid anymore. "Carl was a forward, actually, on the Catamounts. But he broke his ankle senior year."

"Oh wow, I didn't know. Sorry to hear it. So, does he still play at all? Do you think he'd maybe come coach a little, if we asked him?"

"Maybe." I nodded. "He might, I guess. You could ask."

"Cool!" He lingered a moment longer, then said really quickly, "Anyway, I like your costume." And he turned and headed for the refreshments table, without looking back at me. I stared after him, amazed.

Thea suddenly grabbed my arm. "Come on, I've been looking all over for you. Let's get some punch, I'm dying from the heat in here."

Mr. Harris and his wife stood next to the punchbowl, and Mrs. Harris handed us half cups of soda with sherbet. "Here, girls! You look like you could use a cool drink." She called over her shoulder, "Michael, bring those other bottles of orange soda over here, would you please?"

My brownies were almost gone, I saw. I took two Oreos; they tasted all right with the orange soda, but milk would have been better with them. Thea didn't eat anything.

She tugged at my sleeve and nodded toward Mr. Harris at the other side of the table. "Come on." I followed her around. Mr. Harris was talking with Michael Willson. Thea waited for a break and said, "Excuse me. Mr. Harris?"

Michael Willson drifted off. Mr. Harris smiled and asked, "Are you having a good time? You young ladies look terrific tonight." He mostly looked at Thea when he said that. Not surprising, considering she was the thin one in the gypsy skirt. He added, "I see the two of you are putting North Upton on the map. Did you see the paper this evening?"

Thea said, "No, sir. What do you mean?"

I muttered "Uh-oh" under my breath.

"The hiding place, of course! There's a front-page article about how the college is featuring it for the November television special on the Underground Railroad. I have to say, I'd really like to see it myself." He pulled a notebook out of his jacket pocket. "Maybe tomorrow afternoon? There's nothing like actually seeing one of these places, is there?"

I closed my eyes for a moment. Thea hesitated, then said, "I'm not sure what my parents are doing this weekend. Could you call the house in the morning? I'll tell my dad you'll be calling."

"Of course, of course. Your phone number's in the book, isn't it? I'll call your father tomorrow. Don't let me keep you—I see they want you out in the dance."

A circle of kids had formed on the gym floor and people were calling for Thea and me to come be part of it. "Cha-cha slide!" called out a couple of voices. "Come on!"

"Macarena!" said someone else, but the group pushed for the cha-cha slide instead.

"Go ahead," I told Thea. "I've got to get another drink, maybe I'll do it later."

Actually, I slipped out of the gym to the girls' room, which was cool and quiet and empty, and I splashed my face with cold water and patted my cheeks dry, trying not to get the mascara wet. No way was I going to slide around on the gym floor and look stupid in front of everyone. Whew! Who knew Halloween could be so stressful?

I stood in the hallway for a bit, listening to the music and the voices, trying not to think too much. The hiding place at Thea's. Alice. The history project. The video crew, the TV show, the newspaper. Life kept getting more complicated.

By eight o'clock, I was wishing it was over, and I kept looking for ways to slip away from the noise and confusion. The food was gone. I needed to get home. I used a spoon to scoop out the last of the melted lemon sherbet at the bottom of the punchbowl.

Finally it was almost nine, and a lot of people helped clean up, pulling down the crepe paper streamers and packing up the sound booth and all. I saw Thea helping Josh sort out whose music was whose, and figured I'd stay a little back from them, so Thea could try out her plan. Kyle Everts came up and said good night to me and asked if he could call our house to talk with Carl about basketball, and I said sure. But mostly I felt like I was watching Thea, trying to tell when she was going to do it.

When only a few people were still in the gym, and Mr. and Mrs. Harris headed out, with just Miss Calkins left to shut off the lights as we finished, I helped Thea and Josh carry boxes out to Josh's mother's car. I suddenly realized he must have a junior driver's license, the kind where you can't carry passengers under age twenty-one, and you're not supposed to drive after dark, either. Well, his house was just at the other end of the village—nobody would really care if he drove that far.

Miss Calkins came out behind us, locking the door. "Do you girls need a ride?" she asked.

"No thanks," I told her. "We're just down the road."

"All right." She looked at the three of us—Josh, Thea, me. "Joshua, you're taking that car straight home, aren't you?"

"Yes, ma'am." He brushed some snow off the windshield, got into the car, and started it, with the window open on the driver side. "See you."

"See you," Thea and I both said. We stepped out of the schoolyard and began the walk toward our houses. I couldn't see Thea's face—the schoolyard lamp was behind her—but I thought she must really be disappointed. Or maybe she'd changed her mind. She hunched down into her jacket collar.

"Good night," Miss Calkins called, as she pulled out of the parking lot, and her car headed through the lightly swirling snow toward the road to Upton Corners.

From behind us came car headlights. Josh pulled up next to us. A quick look at Thea convinced me she'd expected this, and I said, "I'll meet you down the road. OK?"

"Good," she said in a low breathless voice. I hurried to put some space between us. But I could hear their voices behind me.

Josh called out his window. "I think I've got one of your CDs here by mistake, Thea."

And she said, "Oh, thanks."

Then there was silence, except for the rumble of the car engine. It took all my self-discipline not to turn around and peek. I walked ahead steadily, slowly, and very quietly, so I could keep listening.

Slipping, scuffling steps behind me and the backing up of the car sounds and lights convinced me that whatever had happened was over. I finally peeked: Thea caught up with me, spun me around in place, then skipped on ahead.

"Yes!" she called out to me. "This is so much better than Connecticut! It's actually snowing already!" She whirled around and ducked back toward me, suddenly serious. "You're not mad at me, right? Please, Shawna, say you're not mad."

"Of course I'm not mad! Why would I be mad at you?"

The melting snow made Thea look like she had tears on her face. She stood close to me and said intensely, "My best friend in Connecticut hated me, really hated me, for talking to this boy she liked. She told everybody I was a slut. And everybody believed her. I didn't even have one friend after that, and all the boys kept staring at me. I couldn't stand it." A real tear trickled into the snow droplets.

I punched Thea's shoulder gently. "Anybody can see you're not a slut. You're just pretty, and probably she was jealous. And stupid. I bet she couldn't even solve basic algebra. Am I right? Am I?"

"Yeah, you are." She swept a hand across her face and sniffed hard, "Shawna, you're the best part about living here. Don't ever change, okay? You're as special as a prime number!"

A prime number? I giggled, and to my relief, so did Thea. She twirled in a circle again, and then said, "Snow! First snow!" She took off, running, her open jacket swinging wide around her. I followed. Laughing, we raced each other, and slipped and slid in the fresh white snow, and I bent to scoop up a handful for a loose snowball.

I threw it as high as I could in the air, and it fell apart, pieces tumbling down in the light of the streetlamp by our barn. Thea tagged my shoulder. All the jack-o'-lanterns were dark or taken inside, and only a couple of houses had inside lights glowing—no outside lights on at all.

Thea tagged me again. "I saw Kyle Everts come talk to you twice!" she whooped. "What a night!"

"What a night!" I echoed. Guiltily, I realized it must be really late for the village to be so dark. I hushed my voice down and said, "Gotta run. See you in the morning!"

"See you!"

I ran and slid across the lawn and up the porch steps, then pulled up and tiptoed in through the porch and the kitchen door. On the kitchen table stood a bowl of Halloween candy corn and a note folded like a tent to stand up: "Sleep tight, and set your alarm for seven. Mrs. Toussaint wants you at ten-thirty. Alice called to say hi. Love you. Mom."

THE MOUNTAIN IN my dream grew steeper and icier as I climbed: Rocks rose from the path, cased with ice, and my boots kept slipping. Someplace lower on the mountain, something powerful and dark growled, a winter bear awake when it shouldn't be, climbing behind me. I scrambled harder against the rock in front of me. My heart pounded and my arms trembled from pulling upward. The wind tore at the slope, and ice from the rocks above tore loose and began to fall on me. Each icicle pattering down the rock face rang with danger.

When I forced open my eyes to escape the dream, I found my alarm clock ringing. I slapped the ringer button to the off position, and closed my eyes again, trying to remember what day it was and why I was supposed to get up. My legs ached—oh yeah, the dance at school, and sliding home afterward through the snowy night. I rolled over and squinted at the window, which was open a few inches. I was freezing.

A hot shower, that's what I needed. I sat up and looked around, still groggy. My black pants and the T-shirts lay on the floor. Thea's geometric belt hung over my chair.

When I stood up, I noticed my pillowcase had black smudges on it. Uh-oh. I should have washed off the mascara before I'd gone to bed. I tugged the pillowcase free, balled it up small, and pushed it into the bottom of the basket of dirty laundry in the hall. Carrying my bathrobe, I thumped down the stairs toward the shower.

I could smell coffee. I peered into the kitchen, but Harry and Mom weren't there. Maybe Mom had plugged in the pot before she went to the barn. A package of toaster waffles sat at the table next to my plate.

By the time I'd showered and dressed, it was almost eight o'clock, and I could hear voices downstairs. It turned out to be Mom and Emerson and Carl, talking about who was going to do which days in the barn during hunting season.

"I've got to be at the store on Fridays and Saturdays," Emerson insisted, "and Tuesdays are delivery days. So I can't do those. Give me the Monday mornings and the Wednesday and Thursday evenings." Carl marked the calendar. My mother stirred sugar into a big mug of coffee and nodded.

"Morning, Shawna-Fawna, how was the Halloween dance? Did any of the boys dance at all?" Carl grinned at me.

"Okay, I guess. Yeah, some of the boys danced. It was all right. Hey Carl, one of the kids is going to call you. His name is Kyle Everts. He wants to know if you can coach basketball or something." I yawned and accepted a mug from my mother. Coffee for me, too. Maybe it would help me wake up.

Carl patted the calendar page. "No time for anything until Mom gets her deer," he teased. "She'll probably hold off on shooting, just to keep us all working in the barn. You'll help Harry on Sunday mornings, right? And how about Friday evenings? Then you can sleep in on Saturday mornings, I'll take those."

"How come I couldn't sleep in today?" I complained. "It's Saturday now."

My mother looked up from the calendar. "Yes, it is. And you haven't done any chores at home all week, plus I'm thinking you have something to get ready for church, don't you?"

Ugh. Laundry. Dishes. Bible study. I groaned out loud, and everybody laughed at me.

The phone rang, and I turned toward it, then realized it might be Alice. Everything normal felt suddenly strange, as I wondered what I would say to her. Mom stood up to answer it instead. "Sure, Thea, she's right here, just a moment."

What a relief. With everyone listening, though, I kept it short. We'd meet at the library at ten-thirty. My mother buttered me a pair of freshly cooked waffles, and I poured maple syrup over them and tried to wake up the rest of the way.

At twenty after ten, I escaped from house chores and burst out the door into the crisp fresh day. A sharp November wind blew, but the sky was bright blue with just a few clouds scudding past, and about half the snow from the night had vanished. The grass still was green, even though the trees were bare. Overhead a vee of a dozen geese honked. They seemed to be headed north instead of south, but maybe they needed a food break in some field first. I zipped my sweatshirt the rest of the way up, stuffed my hands in its warm pockets, and drew in the cool air, fresh and brook-sweet. The aroma of the barn in the air didn't spoil it; barns were natural, just part of the world of animals and, well, life. Underneath all this was a rich delicious scent that said change was coming. I suppose it was the dead leaves breathing upward from the ground, mixed with a hint of snow in the wind.

A flash of white hat up ahead woke me up even more: Thea was already at the schoolyard, sitting on the railing, waiting for me to go into the library with her. I hurried.

"He's already called me twice," Thea announced, continuing from the night before. She laughed. "I only talked with him once. I told my brother to say I'd call him back, the other time."

"Why?"

"To make sure he doesn't think I'm easy!" She laughed again, her cheeks bright red with November and with delight. "You can't just pay all your attention to a boy, not ever. You have to be centered in yourself, and just kind of swing out from there toward someone else, but always make sure you swing back to center, you know."

I didn't know, and I was fascinated. "You mean, you let Josh kiss you, but you're not going to go out with him? Won't that hurt his feelings?"

"That's not the point. I might go out with him, sure. But not yet! And besides, he didn't kiss me." My friend shook her head so that her hair bounced. "I kissed him instead. And, of course," she added nonchalantly, "he kissed me back."

She swung down from the railing. "Come on, let's go see what Mrs. Toussaint has for us. Aren't you curious?"

Of course I was! But even more curious about Thea and how she could say such strange things. I wondered whether Alice knew what Thea knew. Maybe she didn't. Maybe that's why she got pregnant.

Ick. I didn't want to think about it, but it kept coming back. Absolutely the last thing I wanted to imagine was my older sister making out with some boy from out of town. I shook my head to get rid of the picture and followed Thea inside into the dim hallway. Lights in the library glowed ahead of us, and we slid along the waxed floor and spun into the room full of books.

Mrs. Toussaint wasn't at the desk. We hesitated there, not sure what to do, but then she came in a moment later and apologized for keeping us waiting. "Why don't you both sit down, and we'll look at these letters together?"

First she showed us the actual letters, the originals, with their thick paper and brown, old-fashioned handwriting with lots of flourishes. Then she placed a photocopy in front of us, six sheets thick, and while she held the originals, Thea and I struggled to read the letters out loud.

"Read the dates aloud, too," Mrs. Toussaint instructed. "That way you pay attention to them. What season is the doctor's wife writing in?"

"Spring," I replied. "The fifth of April, eighteen fifty-seven."

"Good," the librarian nodded. "So think about spring blizzards, and the ice letting go on the lakes, and birds returning.

Think about mud season. Think about no fresh fruits or vegetables for months. And wood heat. And no baths all winter."

Thea added, "President Lincoln? And the Civil War about to start?"

"Not yet. President James Buchanan, who would be remembered for utterly failing to hold the nation back from war. President Lincoln doesn't get elected until eighteen-sixty and takes office in March of that year. The war begins in eighteen sixty-one, so we're not there yet."

The numbers made a map in my mind. I noticed and said out loud, "And the earliest settlers in North Upton must have been dying off. The new generation would be in charge."

"That's correct. You may read aloud from the first paragraph." The way she talked to us in her teacher voice felt like school, but I reminded myself that Mrs. Toussaint was once a reporter. Maybe they acted that way, too, when they were digging for facts.

I read out loud:

> *"Dear Charlotte. I fear it has been many weeks since your letter arrived here, and I beg your forgiveness for this long wait. One might think winter to be a good season for correspondence, but scarlet fever struck so many in the village this winter that John has hardly been the father and husband to us all, and I have spent many an hour carrying firewood from the shed myself. John C., who should have spent some of the winter months at the village school, suffered a chest inflammation since the New Year and is only now returning to health, so I have been also a nurse. And when the minister is away to Upton Center, I have been called to read the Lord's Prayer at many a North Upton bedside. So you see that your little sister has fulfilled all the roles of woman, and some of man, in this long season. Hence forgive me, my dear one, for this long silence.*
>
> *"Nor have we been immune here from the events of the nation. Young men of three families here in the village departed last summer for Kansas, one to print a newspaper there, and two others for the sake of land but also to stake a claim to the state's*

entry into the Union as free states. As much as scarlet fever, this passion to advance an end to slave holding decreases our farms and families. I need hardly say to what end John himself has labored many a night, as the stage arrives at Henry Dearborn's inn with its manifold woes and troubles."

Mrs. Toussaint's lifted hand stopped me. "John C. was the son of Dr. and Mrs. Woodward," she filled in. "He was born in eighteen forty-eight."

I scribbled the information in my notebook. "And Charlotte was Mrs. Woodward's sister, obviously living outside the village."

"Charlotte Adams Russell," said the librarian. "Living in Boston." She gave more instructions: "Look up the Kansas-Nebraska debates, and the Fugitive Slave Act. Look up Vermont's personal liberty law, the one enacted in eighteen fifty-eight, before you read the second letter. And here," she handed another page to Thea, "here is a partial family tree of Doctor Woodward and one also of the Dearborn family. And you'll want this photocopy of the births and deaths and marriages for those years, from the town records. You may work at the large table, ladies. Let me know if you have questions."

Questions? Of course I had questions! Still, Thea and I could do a lot of this on our own. I saw the pattern Mrs. Toussaint was putting in front of us: picking out details in each part of the letter, leading us to more information, painting the scenes. Right away, when I saw on the family tree that Charlotte Adams Russell was fifteen years older than her sister Nancy, who was married to the doctor, I could picture how it was for them: how Nancy Woodward might want to tell her older sister some of the problems of village life, but wouldn't want to seem "little" or like a "country mouse." And how she'd want letters but at the same time not want them.

Like me and Alice.

We finished reading the first letter together, then did the second. It seemed cryptic in places. Part of it talked about a lending library at the doctor's house of books and tracts and things that outlined the case against slavery, and how the minister kept borrowing them and then sharing them so it was hard to get them gathered back. Part of it, like the first letter, was about people who were sick, and one that died.

The last paragraph sent shivers down my back:

"Dearest sister, I know you will want to hear about your parcel so kindly sent on the stage from Boston. Let me assure you it was made most welcome. John tells me that the parcel has been forwarded safely toward Coventry and then Canada. God bless the kind hearts around us."

I tugged at Thea's sleeve. "Maybe this is one of those coded messages. Let's see what we can find about the stage line to Canada. It could go from North Upton through Coventry to Canada, and wouldn't that be the way to send people north if there was danger?" I added, because she might not know about it, "Coventry's a little town up by the Canada border." We looked at each other, wild with speculation.

Thea headed back to the librarian's desk. "Are there any books here that show the stagecoach routes, Mrs. Toussaint?"

"No, I'm afraid not. But"—a pause, and then the librarian finished, "why don't you use the state archive web site? I know the school computers won't let you access that, but I can from here. They may have some maps of what you need."

Pecking at the computer keys, we explored the Vermont state web site and found the state historical society. We typed "North Upton" into the search box but found no matches. Discouraging. Mrs. Toussaint said, "Of course, one always does better with the actual materials. A class trip to Barre, perhaps, to visit the archives in person?"

I didn't think that was too likely, at least, not before our project was due. Thea scrolled the cursor down along the side of the page, looking at other links. "Wait!"

We saw it at the same time: Vermont in the Civil War. Thea clicked the mouse and the computer jumped us to a different history site, one without the dark green borders of the state site.

Again we used the search box—and this time, bingo! There was a map!

We read it silently, then stared at each other: Somebody in the state government, worried about which tourist locations were really part of the Underground Railroad in the 1800s, had mapped them all.

And North Upton was completely surrounded by them.

We printed out the information from the computer, two copies. Then, back at the big library table, we sat in silence for a long moment. If only we had our own computers, and a way to get onto the Internet without having to go into Mr. Warwick's office, we could have known about this sooner. It mattered.

Thea pushed the letters written by Mrs. Woodward toward me. As she touched the first one, she said, "Evidence of connection between the doctor and the stage arrivals at the inn." I agreed. "And this," she said carefully, not wanting to conclude more than the second letter really said, "this is evidence of connection through the North Upton doctor's wife, to something that traveled north from Boston to the Canadian border."

I added to the stack a copy of the map from the "Friends of Freedom" survey that tested the evidence for the towns in Vermont. I pointed to each dot all around our village: in Barnet, Peacham, St. Johnsbury, and Hardwick. "The stage line links them through North Upton," I added. "So it's geometry after all: You can't cross between these places without including your family's inn, Thea. Whether or not people hid in the secret room, people in this town must have been helping."

Now everything had turned inside out. We didn't have to link the "code" to fugitive slaves. The letters and numbers we'd found could mean something else completely, something that had to do with lots of packages or containers or food and drink for the stagecoach arrivals.

But the little room in the cellar of Thea's house might still be a hiding place for something important after all. At the very least, I thought, the people who owned and visited the inn must have been involved somehow in the Underground Railroad.

And the doctor and his wife. And Nancy Woodward's sister in Boston, sending someone or something secretly north, so close to the border with Canada.

That moment, I knew, would be frozen in my mind forever. We had only part of the story, part of the evidence, but Thea and I were sure: The Underground Railroad had moved something or someone right past where we were sitting, right down the road, in the Warwicks' house in North Upton, Vermont.

WHEN WE LEFT the library, we strategized about the project for the history fair. How could we convince Mr. Harris that we were being careful with the truth? And what should we show to Thea's father, and when?

Thea invited me into her house, but it was almost one o'clock. I wanted to check in at home, and she suggested coming over to my house around three so we could show each other our book report drafts for English. She added, "And that will give me time to think about whether to call Josh back today!"

We laughed, and I headed up my own driveway. My sweatshirt hung open in the warmer afternoon. The rumble and smelly smoke of a diesel engine told me Harry was doing something mechanical at the barn. I dodged into the house, hoping I could reach my room without being spotted and maybe tagged to help.

Thank goodness, there was nobody in the kitchen. I leaned into the refrigerator and pulled out a container of meatballs on noodles, and started it heating up in the microwave. The phone beside the fridge rang and without thinking, I picked it up. "Yeah? Hello?"

"Shawna? It's me. Alice." I could hear her start one of those deep breaths again.

I said the first thing that came to me: "You're not my mother. And you're a liar."

"You know what, Shawna? You're right. And I forgive you for saying that. So I'm calling to ask you to forgive me, too. I didn't mean to do this to you. God has a better plan for you and me now."

I couldn't help it. I screamed into the phone: "Just because you're into church doesn't mean you get to tell me what to do. I hate you! Don't ever call me again!"

And I hung up. I cried then, cried like on the trail down the mountain in the dark, cried until my nose ran and my throat swelled and choked and the ding of the microwave getting done almost vanished in how hard I was crying.

My whole world was upside down and inside out. I thought I'd liked Alice before, but why should I like her now? Alice gave me away, I told myself. She didn't want me. What does she expect, thanks for dumping me? I cried longer and harder.

Then I blew my nose, and splashed my face with cold water, and lay on the living room couch until my stomach growled so hard that I couldn't ignore it any longer, and I ate half a bowl of noodles with meatballs, but I couldn't eat anything else. No matter how much I ate, it wasn't going to help. I felt totally lost, and horrible. What kind of person was Alice, to do this to me? And what kind of person was I, to scream at her that way? I shivered.

At two-thirty, I pulled out a page of notebook paper and my copy of *Uncle Tom's Cabin* and made myself start to write. It was bad enough that Thea knew about Alice and last weekend—I wasn't going to say how upset I felt. No way. Who would want me for a best friend if I all I could talk about was the most awful part of my life?

I wiped my nose on the back of my hand and, looking at the pages I'd already bookmarked, as well as the stuff on the back of the book, I drafted the first two paragraphs quickly:

In her 1852 best-selling novel of slavery and the American South, Uncle Tom's Cabin, *New England writer Harriet Beecher Stowe tells the story of a group of slaves all related or connected to a God-fearing man named Tom, the slave that the book is named for. There are three important parts of the story. The first is the escape of an enslaved mother, named Dinah, who is chased by slave-catchers and dogs but who carries her young son with her across the melting ice of the Ohio River, to freedom. Second is the story of Tom himself, sold from the hands of a kind but dead master into the brutal hands of Simon Legree. This evil and godless owner or master illustrates how cruel and violent a man can become. The third important story is of the escape of two light-skinned women slaves named Emmeline and Cassy, who eventually join their family members in a new liberated life in Africa.*

People say that this novel moved people into being willing to go to war to liberate the slaves. Supposedly, when President Abraham Lincoln met the author, he said to her, "So this is the little lady who made this big war." Obviously the book did not create the war. Slavery and the conflict over what states can choose to do when they are part of one country, the United States of America, created the war. But I also see what President Lincoln meant, because emotions are a big part of historical decisions. This book could have changed enough emotions so that people were willing to go to war.

I hesitated before tackling the third paragraph, which was supposed to compare or contrast the story with our own lives. Well, it was only a draft, wasn't it?

I see a pattern in Uncle Tom's Cabin *where the author talks about being Christian as the key to appreciating people as human beings. Slavery and the selling and owning of human beings were cruel and vicious and not morally right. Harriet Beecher Stowe made her story show that people who prayed with all their heart would make the right choices and would help free the slaves. I think this is only partly true, because many people who pray and believe in Christ and go to church are still making very bad choices. In my opinion, if somebody has power or control over somebody else, they will probably not make the best choices for the other person.*

Now I was really stuck. What I meant was, I had personal evidence that Alice and my mother—my grandmother—my adopted mother, that was what Mom was—anyway, I had evidence that praying and being Christian didn't make their decisions perfect.

In fact, I saw that for Alice to give me away was a lot like people thinking they could sell other people.

Just as I started to get really angry again about the whole thing with my family, I heard Thea knock at the porch door. "Come on in!" I put a cookie into my mouth to help swallow how mad I felt, and turned to clear a place at the table for Thea. No way was I going to let all this out in front of her again, if I could possibly help it.

As Thea came in, the phone started to ring. I stared at the black receiver. It kept on ringing as Thea dropped her bag on the floor and took off her jacket.

"Aren't you going to answer it? It can't be Josh," she joked. "He doesn't know I'm here."

"No," I said slowly. I was caught. It could be Alice. But how could I say that without opening up what I didn't want to talk about with Thea? So on the fourth ring, I picked up the phone, cleared my throat, and in a low and half-strangled voice, I forced out, "Hello?"

"Um, hello," came the uncertain voice on the other end. It wasn't Alice. "Um, this is Kyle Everts. Is this Shawna?"

Thea could hear him—the phone was clear and loud. She grinned and waved both hands in the air. "Yes-s-s!" she whispered. "You go, girl!"

I said quickly, "Hey, Kyle. Yeah, this is Shawna. Listen, Carl's not here right now, and he's got a separate phone number anyway." I rattled it off. "Got it?"

"Sure. I guess so." Kyle continued, "But you know, since he's not there, do you have a couple minutes to talk anyway?"

"Not now. No, sorry. Maybe later. After supper, maybe." I wasn't even going to say that much, but with Thea watching and bouncing up and down, what else could I say? "Try after seven, okay? I gotta go now. Bye!"

I hung up the phone and my friend whooped, jumping out of her chair. "See what some sparkles and makeup will do? Shawna, you rock!"

"I don't think that's it. He just wants to talk to Carl, that's all."

"Yeah, sure. And if that's all, why does he want to call you later? I'm telling you, this is the best weekend we've had in just about forever. This is awesome!"

I didn't think it was awesome. I also didn't think Kyle Everts wanted to talk to some overweight girl with math aptitude. But I cracked a smile for Thea's sake, and said, "I guess! So what's going on at your house, anyway?" I reached for another cookie.

"You won't believe this," Thea bubbled. "My dad's built the new web site for Upton already, with a big part for North Upton, and you and I are on it!"

"No way!"

"Way. Hey, don't eat another cookie." She reached over and slapped my hand, startling me. "Two is enough."

I blinked, confused. "What?"

"Shawna, listen—we're best friends, right? So just like you telling me about North Upton school dances and stuff, I'm going to tell you how to look cool. And the first rule is, you have to think before you eat more junk food." She leaned over and grabbed my arm. "Second rule is, you have to keep liking me, even if you don't like what I tell you. Deal?"

I scowled and pulled back from her hand. "It's not your business," I protested. "I need that cookie."

"Nope. Wrong. It is my business, and you *don't* need it, you just want it. Trust me, I know. I know it like I know the square root of sixty-four."

"Eight," I said automatically.

Thea pushed the cookies to the other side of the table. "Yeah.

And the square root of two hundred and twenty-five?"

"Fifteen."

"Right. So each time you start to eat junk food, do a harder square root and think about me instead." She changed the subject, just in time before I had to decide whether to get mad or more embarrassed or burst into tears. "Hey, come on, let's get these book reports done, and then you've got to come over to my house and look at the web site. People are already e-mailing from other places. This whole town is going to be famous, and it's all because of you and me."

Famous. That was the last thing I needed right now: more people who knew everything about my life.

AT FIVE-THIRTY, just when Thea and I were packing up all our papers—including the math graphing assignment, which was so easy that it barely took ten minutes—my mother pulled into the driveway and beeped the horn. When I stuck my head out the porch door, she said, "Come on, I need some help here!" She put a huge box of Chinese take-out containers, smelling wonderful, into my arms, while she went back to the truck to get the groceries.

In the kitchen, she asked Thea, "Would you like to stay for supper? I brought plenty." Who could resist fried rice and hot-and-sour soup, that's what I figured—and I guess Thea felt the same. It wasn't junk food, either. My hand was fine but Thea's slap still smarted. Was she watching everything I ate? That seemed unfair.

Still, she said yes to supper at our house. Her parents said she could stay, and then invited me and Mom to come across the road for dessert at seven. I wondered why they wanted my mother, and I figured she'd say no because of having to do farm stuff, but Carl and Harry had the barn covered, so Mom could come.

When we got across to the big house, the reason for the invitation turned out to be partly just "being neighbors"—I could tell from the questions that the Warwicks asked, they wanted to know more about the family of the girl who kept doing things with their daughter. Had Thea told them about Alice and the terrible discovery? I didn't think so. Mr. Warwick just seemed happy that we were a team for all the history research, and Mrs. Warwick said things like, "Who else in your family is good with numbers like Shawna is?" Tiny bowls of fresh berries with some kind of lemony cream on top and cinnamon-spiced hot cider kept people passing things for a few minutes. I was still hungry after my bowl, but, glancing over at Thea, I tried filling myself up with squares and square roots instead. I counted up to twenty-five squared (six hundred and twenty-five) and back down again. It didn't really work, but at least it kept me distracted from my rumbling stomach for a while.

The grownups got to talking about the Warwicks' house, and my mother began telling stories of people who had lived there and the changes they made, like adding electricity and turning the front yard into flower gardens instead of where horses used to wait. I didn't realize it was all so new. My mother pointed out that in the 1930s, during the Great Depression, people in the village mostly couldn't drive their cars because they couldn't afford gasoline, but they could go to town with a horse and wagon.

"Why didn't the Dearborn family drive, though?" Mr. Warwick asked. "With so many rooms to rent, they must still have done all right."

My mother shook her head. "No, there was no tourism here during the thirties," she explained. "In fact, here in the country, people were better off than in the cities, because everyone could grow vegetables, raise chickens, cut wood. Big city people were hit hard, and people just didn't take vacations at all for a while. And then the war came, so things stayed very tight until the end of the Second World War in nineteen forty-five."

Mrs. Warwick said, "That's so sad. So all these rooms just sat empty for fifteen years or so?"

"No, they weren't empty at all." Mom shifted in her chair, adjusting her blue denim skirt. "From what my folks said, there were as many as thirty people living here in the Dearborn house during the worst of the Depression. Anyone related to Charles and Mary Dearborn tended to come this way, at least for a few years."

"Thirty people here, and only one and a half bathrooms?" A squeal of dismay came from Mrs. Warwick.

My mother grinned. "Those bathrooms were added in the sixties. In the Depression, people used outhouses, and took their weekly bath in the kitchen." Ee-ew.

Thea pulled out the family tree of the Dearborns that Mrs. Toussaint had given us, and we located Charles Dearborn and filled in his wife and children, as my mother gave us more details. With Thea's parents nodding so eagerly, my normally quiet mother kept talking. "It wasn't as bad as you might think," she explained. "Actually, people around here lived pretty much as usual during the Depression. All the women in the village kept their cellars full of canned goods, while the men made sure there was plenty of meat. My parents used to say that Charlie Dearborn was always a good manager of whatever came his way, and he was able to set aside enough during the war to start a grain business in St. Johnsbury afterward." She paused, reflecting. "People move up here now, like you folks have, but after the war, a lot of families drifted away. Once they connected with the outside world, the way the Dearborns did, it seemed like all the grown children wanted the better life down in Connecticut. After Charlie's death, Mary moved down there too, and the house sat empty for a while."

Mrs. Warwick said it must have been sad to see the house empty. My mother agreed.

"Of course, I didn't live across the road here until I married my husband Franklin. He passed away, you know." Everyone made the usual sympathetic comments.

My mother continued, "But then I remarried, so I've been

here all along since nineteen seventy. There was a meditation center in your house for a while in the seventies, and it became an artists' cooperative in the eighties. But nobody kept it up very well, so it was quite a relief when the Morrison brothers bought the place as an investment and began bringing it back into good condition. And now we have good neighbors!" Everyone smiled, back into cheerfulness. "Now I wonder, could I have a little tour and see what you all have done here? And of course, I'd love to see the hiding place that the girls discovered."

While her parents showed the main floor and then the upstairs, Thea started a movie on TV for her brothers and then we went down to the cellar. You could see that her parents had cleaned and rearranged things, to make it easier for people to get to the hidden room. There was a new light, too, a kind of spotlight to shine into the corner. Definitely not our secret any more.

"It's okay," Thea decided. "I mean, it's not as interesting when it's not our own place, but I can hardly wait for the television program about it, you know? We'll have the best project for the history fair, anyway. And," she lowered her voice, "that stupid Maryellen Bryce is never ever getting into my house to see this. Not ever!"

"What did she do? What happened?" There must be something Thea hadn't told me.

"In the girls' room at the dance. I didn't see her. I was in one of the stalls, the one at the end. And she was talking on a cell phone, telling someone that the 'flatlander girl' was crawling all over Josh Willson." Thea balled up her fists. Her voice sounded like she was going to cry. "I didn't crawl all over him! I didn't! I hate her, you know? She is such a snotty, arrogant"—she lowered her voice to a hiss—"bitchy pain."

I nodded, a few times too many. "And you shouldn't ever listen to a word she says. She's just mean." I gave Thea a sideways hug. "You should have told me sooner. She's never been nice. And probably she's jealous, too. Josh really likes you, I can tell."

"Anyway," Thea said, "I'm not a flatlander anymore. I've

been in Vermont for four months already. I'm a Vermonter now, too."

Oops. Umm. I couldn't exactly tell Thea that nobody was going to call her or her family Vermonters for a long, long time. People from away were still people from away. But she looked so hurt. It must have been awful to be hiding in the girls' room, trapped by Maryellen Bryce and her meanness. I changed the subject for her: "Anyway, Josh was totally into having you help with the music. Nobody else around here knows music like you do. And look at the CD collection you've got already."

Thea told me, "Josh called again after lunch. We talked for a while about the band he's started. He's all right, you know?"

"He's not just all right. He's hot!"

So we were laughing when the others came down the stairs, and my mother looked happy, starting to laugh with us. "You girls are quite a pair. Oh my, look at this little room. How on earth did you notice it?"

By the time the story was told again, Mr. Warwick looked like he was bursting to say something. He waited until everyone got back to the dining room, though, to bring it up.

"So ladies, I have an idea and I wonder whether you might help me put it into action. I'd like to hear more stories about this house and about the old days in North Upton village. Do you think we could get people to come to a meeting later this year to share stories? It would be a good way to start collecting them, don't you think?"

Personally, I thought it would also be a good way to get stuck in a room with a lot of older people who couldn't hear each other properly.

But my mother was agreeing, and she started suggesting different people who'd want to come. "Mrs. Toussaint, of course, and the historical society. In fact, those ladies might want to be a sponsor of the meeting, and some of them are very good cooks. You'll want refreshments, of course."

Obviously that hadn't occurred to Mr. Warwick, but he started writing down suggestions and phone numbers, and then he said, "Wait, wait! You haven't seen the web site yet!" And we all crowded into his office to look at his computer, where Upton and North Upton photos led to pictures of the hidden room and a little written part about how Vermonters all wanted to help runaway slaves escape to freedom on the Underground Railroad.

"When you girls have your school report done, I'll put that onto the web site too," Thea's father offered. He pointed out the photo of the two of us, taken just before Thea had gone in front of the video camera. Thank goodness, you couldn't see much of me because I was behind Thea.

My mother looked at me, and maybe she noticed the dark thought flicker past. At any rate, she said we needed to get home and get ready for church the next day, and a few minutes later, we were out in the cold night air together, crossing the frozen roadway and circling the dark little machinery barn, toward our own house.

It was peaceful to be just the two of us, after all the talk and noise of the visit. Neither one of us said anything, but half of a yellow November moon hung over the hillside, ringed with thin clouds, and we slowed down, taking our time to reach our own waiting doorway.

At least when kids at school said I was fat, I could think about someday being thin or rich or whatever. But Thea—coming from Connecticut, she was always and forever going to be a flatlander. Well, we'd have the best history project in the whole town, and that would show a few people.

DOING BARN CHORES before church meant that every Sunday started with too much work. This time, it also started with too much weather: a drenching icy rain that thawed the top of the ground and turned it into a muddy, manure-slipping mess. The wind whipped through the barn and my sweatshirt wasn't warm enough, but I refused to go back to the house to dig out a barn jacket. I just wanted to get chores over with.

Harry and Mom didn't make it any easier, either. Everyone was in a bad mood. The gutter cleaner broke down so the manure couldn't get moved out of the barn, and I had to shovel it into a wheelbarrow before spreading sawdust.

After two hours of both sweating and shivering, I stacked my rakes and shovel in the corner and headed for the shower. Mom was late coming in, and Harry stayed in the barn, skipping church completely. And as if that wasn't enough, when we came out of church, we had a flat tire and had to stand in the rain while some of the men from church changed it. I thought we could have at least gone back inside, but my mother insisted that we stay out there and "appreciate" what Mr. Somers and Mr. Gray were doing for us.

In the car on the way home, we fought. Alice was arriving in three weeks. I said I didn't want to see her or speak to her. I said she was a liar and a slut and I hated her. I said I'd rather leave home completely than have to share the house with her for Thanksgiving. And I said the only reason my mother had adopted me was to get someone else to work in the cow barn for free, and I wasn't going to do it anymore.

My mother didn't say a whole lot back to me. But just as we reached the village, I started in on Harry. I couldn't stop. I said he probably just felt sorry for my mother and all of us and that that was the only reason he married her. I said he didn't love me and nobody did, and nobody ever would. And then I said he was dumb.

That was the straw that broke the camel's back, I guess. My mother pulled the station wagon to the side of the road. "Out!" she snapped. "Get out of the car! You can walk from here to home. Maybe by then you'll remember who your family is. And if you haven't straightened yourself out by the time you get home, I'll do something else to make sure."

I slammed the car door behind me, and my mother gunned the engine and took off.

No way that I was going to walk through the whole village like this. No way at all. I kicked at the road, then left it, cutting across into the woods that ran along the river. The rain dripped down my collar, and soaked into my sneakers. Life was a rainstorm, a permanent November of misery. I doubted if even God cared.

Tramping through bare trees during a November rainstorm didn't cure my anger. It only gave me a headache. No animals, no tracks—I watched the ground, knowing it was already bow and arrow season, knowing the deer would be way up the mountain, not down by the river. But I didn't even see any signs of raccoons or coyotes or foxes. And every bare set of branches that I brushed past sent extra water down my neck. The river tumbled next to me, thick and muddy and loud.

I cut out of the trees and across the last field and stomped into the house, kicking off my boots in the porch and throwing my soaking wet coat onto a chair. "See what you did to me," I yelled at my mother, who wasn't my mother.

Too late, I realized she was on the phone. "We'll be right over," she was saying. "Give us five minutes to change."

She hung up. "Shawna, go towel off, use the hair dryer on your hair, and put on some warm clothes for outside. Hurry up, honey. Your friend's little brother is missing. They think he's in the woods or along the river. We've got to go help."

In a whirl, I stripped off my soggy clothes and the soaked socks that bunched up and resisted, and pulled on sweatpants and a sweatshirt. My mother checked the sweats: "Go out to the porch and pull on your old snowsuit over those, so at least it will be a little bit waterproof. And I told you, use the hair dryer, you're not going back out with wet hair."

I blew hot air with the hair dryer for a moment, then tugged my sweatshirt hood up over my hair and zipped my old blue snowsuit on over everything. From the porch I could hear trucks arriving across the road, other searchers coming. "Come on, Mom!"

Out of the kitchen she came, also rigged out in a snowsuit, her feet jammed into her waterproof hunting boots. I pushed my feet into a pair of barn boots. My mother pressed a flashlight into my hand and carried one herself.

Between our house and Thea's were half a dozen trucks and the fire truck as well, plus a bunch of people, mostly grownups, but a few teenagers, too. We packed into the Warwicks' mudroom. A whistle blew and the head of the rescue squad, Mr. Perkins, got everyone's attention and silence. I stared at his round bald head and bulky shoulders. I'd never paid much attention to him before. He had a thin reedy voice, out of proportion to the rest of his body.

"First rule, nobody searches alone. We'll have five groups, and each one needs to take a radio unit along. Cell phones aren't reliable enough. Raise your hand if you already know Teddy

Warwick pretty well."

Thea and her mother, strained and pale, raised their hands, and so did her father, whose hair and face were already very wet with the rain. After a moment, I raised mine, and so did my mother.

"Good, that's five of you—count off now, one through five."

My mother figured out what Mr. Perkins wanted and called out, "One!"

I yelled "Two" and Thea and her parents followed with three, four, and five. Her brother Thaddeus tried to get into the count but Mr. Perkins told him he had to be base crew at the phone, with Mrs. Toussaint.

Then everyone else counted off, and we gathered by number. My group of "two's" had Jeff Perkins, a grown son of Mr. Perkins, for radio and leader. There were two other people, parents that I didn't know well—Mr. Johnson and Mrs. Lafontaine. I spotted Mr. Cobleigh in the group with my mother. I wanted to be with Thea, who was a "three," but I could only wave across to her. "We'll find him," I called out.

"Quiet again, please, for a moment," hollered Mr. Perkins. "Listen up, and the sooner you do, the sooner we can start searching." He read from a clipboard. "Group one, you'll go up the trail toward the ridge. Go as far as the first brook and then if you haven't seen any sign of the boy, start downhill along the brook.

"Group two, take the road over to the school, then walk along this side of the river all the way back to here. Group three, also take the road to the school, then walk the far side of the river. Group four, you're behind the house, going into the woods there. After forty-five minutes, no matter what distance you've gone, you turn around and come back to here. And group five, you've got the road toward St. Johnsbury; walk to the four corners, then go down to the river and walk along it back to here. This is a little boy, three years old, so look down and under things. That's where he'll be. Keep calling his name, and stay within sight of the others in your group.

"All groups meet back here in an hour and a half—that will be three-thirty. And we'll map where you've been and get ready for a second loop if we need it. Let's hope we find him in the first loop. Don't lose your group members.

"Last but not least, first priority when you find this little boy is going to be to get him warm. One person from each group grabs a wool blanket on the way out the door. Go!"

Thea's group and mine, the two's and three's, clumped together outside and got sorted out for a moment by the group leaders. Then we were on our way down the road to the school, two's on the left side of the road looking into the high grass along the way, three's on the right side looking up the front yards and porches of the four houses between the Warwicks' house and the school. My side was looking for any knocked down part in the grass that might be where little Teddy had left the road. Jeff Perkins in his yellow rain gear was just ahead of me, so I asked him, "How did Teddy get outside? Who called the rescue squad?"

"Don't know how he got outside, but his folks searched the whole house and he's not in there. They found the porch door open," Jeff said, swishing his long flashlight against the grass and small bare bushes. "I guess his dad already was out for a while looking, and my father was coming down from camp and stopped him. Better to have an organized group, we'll find him faster."

"Oh." It still didn't make sense to me. "Why would he go outside? He's just a little kid and it's cold and raining."

Jeff grunted in agreement. "You wouldn't think he'd be out in this. So the state police are stopping cars out on Route 2, in case somebody picked him up."

"You mean kidnapped him?"

"Yeah. I mean, that's not real likely. But they're checking up at the highway, and we do the local search. Best way to divide it up."

I said a quick prayer inside myself: "Dear God, please help us find Teddy. Don't let him be kidnapped, please, God. In Jesus's name. Amen."

Thea's group, without the high grass to look through, had already reached the school and was on the bridge to the far side of the river. I waved at Thea. She gave me a half wave back, then moved faster as her group leader called something to her.

Jeff Perkins stopped our group, waited for Mrs. Lafontaine to catch up, and led us down to the stony, slippery bank of the river on our side. "Look two ways," he instructed. "Look into the water for clothes, and look along the bank for slip marks. Don't hurry. Worst thing would be to go too fast and miss him. And keep calling his name. Come on, now."

As the river wound away from the road, the trees I'd walked through before separated us from the houses of the village. The rain turned the air gray and dim. It wasn't dusk yet, but I turned on my flashlight and aimed the beam into the jumbled rocks along the water's edge. Mr. Johnson moved ahead of me, but Mrs. Lafontaine was behind me. Suddenly she said, "I think I found a slip mark!"

I called out to Jeff Perkins, and the two men rushed back to us, spreading out a bit so as not to trample what Mrs. Lafontaine had found. Mr. Johnson pointed. "Good eye, Betty, nice catch, but see the prints over here—looks like a couple of deer. Let's spread out again and keep going."

Mr. Johnson stopped us a little further, because he found a hat, but it wasn't a child's hat. We started again. Inside the snowsuit, I was sweating, in spite of my face and hands getting pelted with icy rain. I stuck my hands into my pockets, but then I couldn't balance well, so I pulled them out again and let them be cold.

Jeff Perkins stopped us for the third time and suggested that Mrs. Lafontaine and me be the ones to walk the edge of the river, while he and Mr. Johnson spread a little ways into the trees. Then we went more slowly, everyone swishing the brush around them with their arms. "Teddy!" we called. "Teddy, where are you?"

My group and Thea's connected again as the river reached our farm. Her team came across the wooden bridge that Harry used for haying the upper fields. Everyone who had one checked a watch and agreed we were way too early. "Let's do the farm buildings," Jeff Perkins proposed.

Harry and Carl arrived from town in the truck just then and joined us. Carl brought the twos into the main barn, while Harry opened the tractor shed and machine barn for the three's. I didn't think a three-year-old would go near the big cows with their loud noises and heavy stamping feet, but I checked by the kittens and Mrs. Lafontaine looked inside each calf box just in case. Mr. Johnson climbed the ladder to the hayloft, which I thought was foolish, but I guess he wanted to know we'd looked in the whole barn. Everybody pushed things around, looking behind and under them. It made me realize how much junk there was in the machine barn. Nobody saw anything that looked recently disturbed, although I heard Mr. Johnson say a cuss word when he accidentally stepped on a broken spot on the floor.

Then we circled around the yard. "Look inside and under each vehicle," Mr. Perkins called out.

Nothing and nobody. One of our cats ran out from under Harry's truck, but otherwise, the yard was cold, wet, and empty except for the searchers.

"All right, let's do the Warwick garage and yard while we're at it." We followed the leader of the threes, a man I recognized from the car repair garage in Upton Center, and spread out in a wide circle to walk through every bit of the Warwicks' yard, including the soggy brown flower gardens and around the back where the other gardens were just mud and stems. I saw our old treehouse, but the first step to it was almost out of my own reach; Teddy could never have climbed there.

We gathered by the front porch and went inside. Mrs. Toussaint was on the phone, talking with someone at the state police in town.

Thaddeus pressed up against her, half crying. "When will they find him?"

Mrs. Toussaint hung up the phone and rubbed his shoulders. "He can't be far away. Just wait a bit. They're going to find him soon."

Jeff Perkins spoke into his radio. A crackly reply from the group up on the ridge said they'd just reached the stream and would start down.

Mr. Perkins stomped in, shaking his wet hat in one hand. "I've got group five, from the four corners and the river," he said. "No sign. You?"

"Nothing," agreed Jeff and the other leader.

Harry said, "There's a roadblock out at Upton Center. I came through it on my way home."

"Yeah." Mr. Perkins and Jeff checked the clipboard. "Well," said Mr. Perkins, "I think we need to go door to door through the village next. Check each front porch, talk to each person we can find, get more eyes looking." He turned and looked at me and Thea, where we stood dripping by the doorway.

"You two girls, I don't want you out again, because it's getting dark. How about you do another search of the house? Closets, beds, under and behind things, shake out every blanket, all that. Toy boxes. Anything he could have climbed into or under."

Thea shook her head. "We already looked everywhere, even inside the kitchen cabinets," she protested. "My family already did all that."

"Well, better do it again, girls," Mr. Perkins said. "Or you can help Mrs. Toussaint keep the coffee going in the kitchen if you want. And it would be good if you both ate something, something sweet, with a hot cup of cocoa." He raised his voice. "Anyone else need a hot drink before we head out? Use the bathroom?"

A moment later, the groups pressed back out. One bunch of people headed to the schoolyard and another to the church and cemetery. Two of the other men plus Carl headed over to the farm to find lights that could get set up out by the road. I watched for a moment; it really was dark out. I found the switch for the Warwicks' porch light and turned it on.

I looked at Thea. Her eyes were big and hollow. "If there's nothing else to do, let's try searching the house again together."

We tugged off our boots and dropped our wet hats and outdoor stuff on a chair by the door. Mrs. Toussaint asked Thaddeus if he wanted to look with us, but he refused to leave the phone in case somebody called with news. So we headed upstairs, turning on every light as we went.

I could tell people had looked for Teddy up there already—the tidiness and neatness had vanished. Beds had humps of blankets on them, along with pillows. The bathroom towels hung crooked. Closet doors were open.

I said to Thea, "Let's be systematic. We'll work from one end to the other, together, so we don't miss anything. First of all, do you have an attic?"

Yes, there was an attic, but you had to pull down a set of folding stairs to get there. The string for the stairs barely reached down low enough for parents to pull on it. For Thea to pull it open, she had to stand on a chair. Still, we looked, so we could say we'd covered that part of the graph of the house.

Then we went to the far end of the hallway. A door opened into a second hallway. At the end of the second hall, there was a narrow room that stretched from the front of the house to the back, brightly painted with geometric shapes on the floor and yellow and blue walls. I stared. "What is this?"

"It was the teaching room, I think, when the Zen school was here. Like for yoga, you know? Or something like that. There's another room past here, too." Thea wrestled with two separate latches on the last door, and showed me a storage space where boxes and baskets of clothes stood in rows. "Do you think we have to open them all?"

"Depends. Do you think Teddy could have opened the door into here?"

"No way."

"Yeah. So let's just walk down one row and up the other, so if anything's been moved, we'd see it." We did, but there was nothing, so we backed up into the wildly painted room and double-latched the flat door behind us. The long weird room was empty, so that was done, too. That left us four guest bedrooms to search before reaching the first hallway, the one with the bedrooms that the Warwicks actually used. I'd really only seen Thea's room before, and her parents' room, with its matching furniture and also a small sofa and armchair, surprised me. It was like having a living room upstairs, a living room that included your bed.

"No TV?"

I said it lightly, but Thea tapped on a ceiling-height dresser and explained, "It's in there, but they don't really watch it. We've got to open the doors to it, if this cupboard's big enough for Teddy to crawl into." We did open the doors, and then the two closets, and looked all the way under the bed, and lifted the pile of bedspread and thick down comforter. Everything felt soft, lightweight, warm, and just about new; barely any dust bunnies, let alone a little boy.

In the boys' room, we opened up everything, even the two big wooden toy boxes, and then did the same routine under and on the bed. Thea's room came next, followed by the bathroom, including pulling the shower curtain out of the tub and checking inside the towels closet. Thea took a deep breath, and I could see her shoulders starting to shake.

"Okay," I said to Thea, trying to keep my voice steady. "Let's go downstairs, down to the cellar. I bet nobody's done the cellar as well as we can."

Thea nodded, a little too panicky-looking, and clattering down the steep stairs, she slipped. She grabbed the stair railing and kept herself from falling all the way, but she cried out in pain and, as soon as she got her balance again, cradled her right wrist in her left hand. "Oh God—I think I broke something."

Mrs. Toussaint heard us and came out of the kitchen. "Let me see," she urged. After a moment, she said she thought it was probably just a sprain, and she put together a bag of ice for Thea to hold against it to stop the swelling.

"I can do the cellar," I told Thea.

Her eyes swam with tears, but she said she'd come down with me. "If you'll open boxes and things, I can still help look. We'll do it better if there's both of us."

We told Mrs. Toussaint and Thaddeus that we'd go down. Mrs. Toussaint nodded and went back to making sandwiches to feed the rescue crew. Thaddeus wouldn't move away from the phone.

Thea held open the cellar door while I propped it in place with a chair. Someone had left the cellar light switch on. "We should take flashlights, too," I suggested, but it turned out they were all gone with the search teams.

Down in the damp cellar, where we'd spent so much time measuring and drawing, we began our search pattern in the room at the foot of the stairs. The water tank and furnace stood against one wall, and there was nothing at all around them, just clear, clean floor. Some buckets and brooms stood beyond the stairs. On our cellar map, that was room one.

Room two contained a couple dozen cardboard packing boxes, some of them large enough for a small boy, so I stuck a hand into each one as Thea watched. But they turned out to hold exactly what their labels said: magazines, some books, small children's clothes. A tool bench stood opposite the boxes. Its legs were linked with simple shelves—no place to hide.

In room three, the stacks of split firewood made dark shadows in the corners that the bare overhead bulb couldn't get rid of. I shuffled my feet as I walked into each corner and down the spaces between the stacks, to make sure I wouldn't trip on anything. I heard Thea sniff hard.

"We'll find him," I told her again. "Maybe they've already found him outside. He could be in someone's car being brought home already. Let's just finish the search, though."

She wiped her nose against her left wrist and said in a stuffed-up, quiet voice, "Okay. Let's do the next room."

Room four had no light of its own, and it was pretty big. Some glow from the overhead bulbs of rooms three and five, though, gave enough to see by. A lot of old splintery wood, smelling of dampness, cluttered up the room, along with some pipes. No little kid would try to hide here. Still, just in case, we felt our way through.

And then we entered the room at the north end of the house, where we'd found the hiding place, the secret room at the far end. Thea grabbed my arm, then winced and clutched at her wrist. She croaked: "The door's open!"

We switched on the extra spotlight that Mr. Warwick had rigged up, hurried across to the short doorway, and peered inside. Nothing. I bent down to check under the last low shelf, and gasped: a small red sneaker. I pulled it out and handed it to Thea. "Is it his?"

"Yes!"

We both lay down on the floor to look underneath, and in the change of the way the air smelled, we knew at the same moment: An opening in the wall, barely big enough to wriggle into, led into a dark tunnel. How could we have missed this before?

"Teddy?" Thea called out. "Teddy, are you in there?"

A loud wail startled us both into banging our heads. "Momm-yy! I want Momm-yy!"

"Come on out, Teddy," Thea said, half crying, half laughing. "Mommy wants you too. Come on out of there!"

More wails followed, and scrabbling sounds came at us from the darkness. Thea hushed me and we finally figured out what Teddy was saying as he sobbed: He was stuck.

I looked at Thea. Clearly, she was the thin one, the best person to do it—but with her sprained wrist, could she climb in and get her little brother from the tunnel? I slid backward so she'd have plenty of room to try.

But she was backing out, too. She sat up, biting her lip and looking at me desperately. "I won't be able to crawl," she told me, rocking back and forth, clutching at the arm above her right wrist. "Shawna, can you? Please?"

Teddy's crying grew louder and more frightened and I felt awful for him. What was he doing in there, anyway? I didn't know if I could even fit into the tunnel. I stared at Thea and then said, “I guess. Maybe. It would be better if we had a flashlight, though.”

“I’ll go find one. There’s got to be one somewhere. And I’ll get Mrs. Toussaint. Wait here.” She called into the dark space, “Hang on, Teddy, Shawna’s going to come get you! Don’t cry!” She pulled back and stood up quickly. “Talk to him while I go upstairs, okay? So he won’t be so scared.”

She flew out of the room, and I could hear her racing through the rest of the cellar toward the stairs.

I leaned down again and put my face near the hole. Although it was small, I realized I could widen the opening by pulling back another board. While I tugged at it, I started talking to Teddy. “It’s all right, Teddy, don’t cry. It’s me, Shawna. Can you come here a little ways, Teddy? Come on,” I coaxed him.

He just kept saying in a mournful little cry, “’Tuck! Me ’tuck!”

Suddenly there was another scrabbling sound, and the unmistakable meow of a cat coming from the tunnel. As if in response to my “Come on,” the creature’s cry joined Teddy’s. What on earth?

In a burst of dust and grit, something jumped out of the tunnel onto my arm and pushed up against my face, fur rough with sand, but purr entirely familiar: Midnight, our bigger black cat. What was he doing here? Automatically, I stroked him and rubbed behind his ears. I pulled again on the board, and it finally came loose with a squeal and a shower of dust.

Behind me came a clatter of feet, more than just Thea’s, and several voices: Mrs. Toussaint, and Thaddeus, and Thea, all in a group. Thaddeus was calling out, “Teddy! Teddy!”

Thea gave a short scream. “Omigosh, a cat! A cat just ran up the stairs!”

“It’s my cat, Midnight,” I called out. “Don’t worry about him. Come on!” I heard the group rushing through the other rooms.

“Here,” Thea said breathlessly, pushing a little pocket flashlight into my hand. “Thaddeus had this in his bedroom. It’s all we could find."

Mrs. Toussaint held a pair of candles in her hand, but clearly I couldn't carry them in the small hiding-place room, let alone in the tunnel.

I looked at Thaddeus—maybe he should go in and get Teddy, since he was definitely small enough to fit into the tunnel, no problem. But his face was already screwed-up and puffy from being hysterical. The last thing we needed was another little kid getting stuck in the cellar. Thaddeus called out "Teddy!" again and then he started to cry, too. Mrs. Toussaint folded him in her arms.

In the dim cellar room, lit only from behind, Mrs. Toussaint's face was hard for me to see. But her eyes shone behind her glasses and she squinted a bit, concentrating her gaze at me. She said, "Shawna, the men will come back soon, and so will Mrs. Warwick. But it would be very kind to Teddy if you would go help him now, so he doesn't have to stay in the darkness. Remember, he has probably been down here for three or four hours, and he is cold and only three years old. Will you help him, please, Shawna?"

"Please?" echoed Thea, cradling her wrist like a damaged wing. "Please could you help him?"

Teddy's crying was awful, with his voice little and hoarse. I imagined for a moment what it must feel like, and right away I pictured Emerson and Carl. They would never leave me even five minutes extra in something that scared me. If Thea couldn't go in, and Thaddeus was too scared, then it was up to me, wasn't it?

I pushed the button on the little flashlight. It gave a small circle of yellow light. I sighed heavily, and pulled the hood of my sweatshirt up over my hair, to keep out spiders and dirt. "Yeah, okay. I'm going in."

I knelt on the floor. Thea came in next to me, and crouched next to my leg. "I'll hold your foot, to keep you company," she offered.

"Yeah. Thanks."

I flattened myself against the cold hard dirt floor, and reached into the hole with the hand holding the flashlight. I couldn't see Teddy—he must be further along. But I could see that the tunnel seemed to open up after the first tight part. I pulled my arm back and put the flashlight between my teeth, so it sort of pointed down and forward, and using both hands and my feet, I pushed into the tight and uneven space. Oh God, don't let me get stuck, I prayed. I would be so incredibly embarrassed. I was more afraid of that than of any spiders.

As soon as there was room, I got my hand up next to my face to hold the flashlight again, so I could talk into the dark tunnel ahead of me. "It's all right, Teddy. It's Shawna. I'm coming to get you."

He wailed in a mucousy, bubbly, choking way, "Momm-mee." In the tight space around me, it hurt my ears, even through my hood.

"Ssh-h," I said quietly, trying to sound soothing. "Ssh-h, I'm coming, Teddy, we'll get you out of here and back to your mommy. Ssh-h." The waistband of my corduroys dragged and caught against each snag on the floor, and I had to keep hunching and bunching myself like a caterpillar to get unsnagged and move another few inches forward. I could feel Thea's hand on my ankle for the first bit, and then she let go as I moved deeper into the darkness.

The pressure above my head stopped being there. I twisted sideways and aimed the little flashlight. Hunh. I scrabbled forward a bit more, and I was in something more like a room than a tunnel—low ceiling and a lot of spiderwebs, but there were boards over my head and to both sides of me. I halfway stood up and flashed the light forward. Up ahead was another part that was more tunnel than room, and in the bit of light, I could just see a bit of Teddy's wet, dirty face. I hurried forward and saw more: He was pulling at his foot, the one that still had a shoe on. It was caught in a bundle of wire or fence or something. I smelled a diaper smell, and realized he'd probably wet his pants. Ick.

Just as I got right up to him, saying over and over, "It's all right now, Teddy, it's all right," the flashlight went out. I shook it and pushed the button again, but it wouldn't come back on. Drat. Teddy cried out. I called back behind me, "Flashlight's out. But I've found him. Talk to me, so I can tell which way to go." Thea must have heard me, because she said something muffled, and then I heard Mrs. Toussaint start to talk, too. I couldn't make out the words, though.

Carefully, I squatted in the darkness, reaching for the little boy. His face was all slimy with tears and snot against my hand. Ick again. Well, it couldn't be worse than the barn, could it? I could wash my hands later, I told myself. I patted Teddy's shoulders and pulled him against me, snot and all. "Don't cry now, I'll get you out of here."

But when I tried to pull his foot free, he cried louder. So I sat right against him and followed his legs in the darkness with my hands. Ah! It felt like chicken wire, the little frames of wire all netted together. His foot was caught in it, with some prickly end of wire snagging the shoe. I'd have to bend each one back, in order to get his foot loose.

I closed my eyes to concentrate, and it worked. Less than a minute later, I had him free from the wire. I pulled him onto my lap and rocked him for a moment. "It's all right," I repeated. The wet little hands gripped my shoulder and pulled at some of my hair where it stuck out of the hood, and I had to reach up and undo his grip—which he fastened onto me again, but this time without my hair, thank goodness.

"Okay, Teddy, we're going back out, now. It's all right, it's all right now."

But it wasn't easy. Following the sound of the voices, I inched forward in the underground room. In front of me, any minute, would be the change of height, down to tunnel size again, and I didn't want to bump into that. Holding Teddy with one hand and arm, I felt ahead of me with the other.

There it was. And ahead the tunnel had a bit of light, too, from the cellar. I called forward, "Move away from the opening, so I can see." Thea understood; I heard her explain to Mrs. Toussaint and more light came into the passageway.

But I couldn't squeeze into the tunnel with Teddy clutched to my shoulder. There wasn't room. What should I do? If I had a blanket, I could use it as a sled for him over the floor. I started to ask Thea for one, then realized she wouldn't be able to get it in there. Well, there was only one choice: I pulled off my sweatshirt, wrapping it around the toddler as it came loose.

"Okay, Teddy, I'm going to give you a ride. Thea, call out to Teddy. And watch for his feet!"

He kept grabbing at my hair, and I undid his hands again and again, awkwardly feeding his sweatshirt-wrapped legs into the tunnel and coaxing the rest of him more or less into a lying down position, so I could move him ahead of me, one of my hands under his head, the other pushing ahead to slide his bottom forward.

With nothing to protect my hair or head anymore, I scraped against the tunnel ceiling, feeling spiderwebs and dirt landing on me and on my face. I blew out to get some of them off my lips. The smell of dampness, dirt, and Teddy's soiled pants filled my nostrils. I tried not to breathe, but I had to.

A long moment later, the light at the tunnel mouth vanished as someone's arm, shoulders, and head blocked the way. Someone was reaching in to take hold of Teddy's foot. And then it was done: He was out of the tunnel, and I was out myself a moment later, rolling against the cold floor and grabbing the sleeping shelf to pull myself up to stand, so very glad to be out of the hole.

Thea hugged Teddy hard in spite of her wrist, and Thaddeus pushed up against the two of them. Mrs. Toussaint patted them all and wrapped a blanket around Teddy. She began to shoo us all out into the larger room, and when we all stood in the light, she looked at me and gasped, immediately taking off her own sweater.

I looked down. My shirt was coated with dirt, spiderwebs hung from it in sticky bunches, and I'd torn a shirt button. Also somehow there was a red smear on one sleeve, where I realized I'd scraped an elbow. Mrs. Toussaint insisted on buttoning her warm, snug sweater over me, and I was glad for the warmth, even though I hadn't realized I was cold. With a deft twist, she rolled one sleeve up so the scraped elbow wouldn't bleed more into the fabric.

"Let's get Teddy upstairs and into a warm bath if we can," she suggested to Thaddeus and Thea. "He's probably cold, and we'll wash some of the dirt off him before your mother gets home. And Thaddeus, suppose you call the state police number and tell them we've got your brother, so that they can call all the searchers back. Hmm?"

She motioned us all toward the stairs, like a chicken with a batch of dazed chicks. As Thea started up, balancing Teddy against one shoulder, I noticed Mrs. Toussaint looking back through the cellar toward the hiding place. She turned and caught my eye.

"I thought that tunnel was long gone," she told me.

My mind began to function as I rubbed dirt from my face and stared at her. "Was it an Underground Railroad tunnel?" I asked.

"Not when my mother used it," she answered, and whisked me speechless ahead of her, up the stairs toward the warm, well-lit kitchen and the aromas of cocoa and coffee.

THEA TOOK TEDDY into the bathroom, and Thaddeus ran to get snuggly pajamas for his brother. The two of them coaxed their brother into a warm bath, and the sounds of family teasing and snuggling rolled over me, only a bit blurred, as I sat in the kitchen and let Mrs. Toussaint wash my cuts. She also wiped my face. I tried to take the wet cloth away from her and do it myself, but she told me to drink my hot chocolate and let her work. Then gently, she drew her own comb through my hair, wiping spiderwebs off the comb onto a paper towel. I could smell lavender in her clothes as she leaned close.

"You did a good job, Shawna Lee," the librarian told me. "Hear that little boy splashing in there? You brought him back into his family quickly, and that will make a big difference to him in how he recovers from being alone in the dark. Your mother is going to be very proud of you."

"But she's not really my—" I cut off the words as I realized what I was saying, not knowing how they had started to spill out.

"Not really your mother?" Mrs. Toussaint finished the

sentence without surprise. "No, I suppose she didn't give birth to you. Poor Alice did that. What a sweet girl she was. She just needed a man's attention and affection a little too much, perhaps."

I was stunned. "You know about Alice? You know about my family?"

"Of course I know!" Reading the surge of shame and worry on my face, she went on. "Old women like me sometimes remember that kind of thing, you know, because we care enough to look and notice. But nobody's talked about it in years and years. I doubt that it even comes up when your sister visits home." Her eyes crinkled as she smiled at me. "I've always liked your mother—Connie, I mean—for the way she didn't shame Alice. She just took you right into her heart and life went on again."

"But why didn't anyone tell me?" I burst out. "I had a right to know. People lied to me. My mother lied to me."

"Nonsense! Nobody lied to you. You just know more about it now than you did a month ago—just the way you also know more about this village and the Dearborns now, too. It's good to grow in knowledge. My own grandmother taught me that." She dabbed at my elbow with alcohol, which made my eyes sting, and began to unwrap a Band-Aid.

"I was happier before I knew." Even as I said it, I knew it was a mean, childish thing to say.

"Happier how? Happier because you didn't know that Alice could make mistakes?"

"Not exactly. I guess I knew Alice could make mistakes. But this, this is just so—! If you knew about it all, then, oh, Mrs. Toussaint, was Alice a—a slut?" My heart cramped in pain.

The older woman's voice deepened, slow and serious. "Shawna Lee, who on earth have you been listening to? Don't you know that people are made to love and be loved? You are. Your mother, and I do mean Connie now, is good at loving. So was Alice—she just had a moment of confusion about the how and when. Now you tell me, has she made the same mistake ever again?"

Reluctantly, I answered, "No. At least, if she did, nobody told me that, either."

"She didn't. She's a warm, caring person who's grown up very nicely as far as I can tell. People can make mistakes, but they can also learn from them." She refilled my mug of hot chocolate and poured her own. Sitting next to me at the table, she patted my arm. "There's an old-fashioned saying: when you point a finger at someone else, you have three fingers still pointing back at yourself."

I didn't understand. Mrs. Toussaint lifted a hand and pointed at me and I saw what she meant—that three fingers of her hand, folded against her palm, were like arrows toward her own self. "But what does that mean?"

"It means that when we start pointing out other people's flaws, it's usually because we're bothered about the same flaws in ourselves. Maybe you want to be ashamed of Alice, so you won't have to think about whether you're ashamed of something you've done yourself."

Tears leaked out of my eyes and my nose began to run. "You just said I did a good job!"

"You did, Shawna, you did a very good job. But we all have things that shame and embarrass us. You might talk with your mother, with Connie, about that. It's time you did."

The door from outside slammed open, and a rush of cold air and voices hit us. I wiped my face quickly.

Mrs. Toussaint patted my arm again. "We'll talk more some other day. Here come the others." She pushed her glasses up her nose and went out into the hall to slow down the rush of returning searchers, to explain, and to tell Mrs. Warwick to calm down before going into the bathroom to see Teddy: "Take a deep breath, my dear, and pull that smile back onto your pretty face. Your little one needs to see you calm and smiling."

A tired and sad place inside me tried to make me cry again as Mrs. Warwick paused, pressed her hands against her cheeks and eyes, then moved them aside and forced a smile. It grew a bit more real, and Mrs. Toussaint let her pass toward the bathroom.

I worked to make my own face smile, too—I didn't want anyone else to know I'd been upset.

I stood up and began to fill cups with hot chocolate and coffee, and soon the kitchen and hallway were jammed with relieved people, hushing each other to keep their relief from getting loud enough to scare Teddy.

In a few minutes, Mrs. Warwick came out of the bathroom with Teddy, all clean and looking ordinary in fuzzy yellow Big Bird pajamas that had green feet at the bottom. He clung to her and buried his face in her chest, and she rubbed his back as she said quietly, "Teddy and I are so grateful that you're all here. Please do stay for a while and get warmed up. I think Mrs. Toussaint has sandwiches ready, too. I'm going to take Teddy upstairs to bed. I hope you'll stay."

People made room for Thea's mom to go upstairs with Teddy, and Thaddeus followed along. Thea slipped into the kitchen and started helping me with pouring, and Mrs. Toussaint carried plates of sandwiches to the dining-room table so that people could help themselves.

My mother arrived with the last group of searchers, the ones who had been furthest out in the woods. What a relief to see her, with all the neighbors pressed into the house and talking with each other. Thea kept explaining over and over how we searched the house and found the tunnel.

I stood at the doorway between the kitchen and the dining area, with my mom. My adopted mom. She kept reaching out to rub the back of my shoulder as Thea told the story again.

Mr. Perkins, at the far end of the room, asked, "Did you girls already know about the tunnel?"

"No," Thea assured him. "We never saw it before. I guess there was something in the way, under the shelf. I don't know how it got moved."

"Did the little boy move it?" someone else asked.

I realized, then, that I knew the answer, or at least that part of it. I raised a hand as if I were in school. Mr. Perkins saw, and nodded at me.

"I think I might know what happened. It was our cat."

"What?" Everyone, including my mother and Thea, looked bewildered. Except I saw that Mrs. Toussaint understood right away, because she gave a kind of surprised nod.

"One of our cats, Midnight, came out of the tunnel when I was going into it," I explained. "If that tunnel goes under the road, it must go someplace on our farm. Maybe the cat got into it, came through on this side, and pushed past whatever was in the way to get out of there."

"That makes sense!" "Yes!" "No kidding!" People nodded all around me. Mr. Warwick added, "Teddy loves cats. If he heard the cat crying, he might have tried to help it. That might be part of the explanation, too."

Mr. Perkins called to Mrs. Toussaint. "Jennie, tell us about the tunnel. You must have known it was there!"

My mother and I moved to one side so Mrs. Toussaint could come out of the kitchen. The room fell silent as we waited for her reply.

She began slowly, in a quiet remembering sort of voice. "As I was saying to Shawna, I thought that tunnel was long gone. And in a way, it was. The other end of it—which the cat must have discovered—is in the little barn by the road, what we used to always call the 'old barn.' Perhaps something's been moved there recently?"

Jeff Perkins spoke up. "We moved some of the wagons and hay earlier, when we searched the farm for the little boy."

"Ah! But it must have been before that, of course, for the cat to find it. Perhaps the door at that end has some sort of broken corner or something, so that the farm cat could slip beyond it. I'm sure there were mice in there."

Ick! Mice. I'd been crawling through a tunnel of mice. I would have nightmares tonight for sure. I wiped my face again. Double ick.

The librarian tipped her head to one side and pursed her lips. "We don't talk much about the nineteen twenties and thirties in this village. But no doubt some of you youngsters realize that

North Upton sheltered some high commerce during that time."

People looked at each other for answers, puzzled. Then Mr. Warwick guessed: "Rum-running? During Prohibition?"

Mrs. Toussaint nodded. "That's right. It was against the law, so when that time was over, nobody said much about it. But your home, this inn, I'm afraid, was the center of quite a bit of activity."

"Because there was a tavern here in the inn?" Mr. Warwick kept up with the revelations.

"Not really. No, we all made enough dandelion wine or birch beer or—in some cases, which I won't name just now—some people might have kept a small still up in the woods, for liquor or applejack. And everyone who cared to could have hard cider in the back shed easily enough. During the Depression, there was enough to share with the few visitors who came this far north. Mostly, though, the inn was full back then of neighbors and family who couldn't afford to keep their own homes going. Times were hard."

She paused and looked around the room. "I can speak just for my own family. I know that my older brother did a few trips to Montreal and down to Boston, with liquor in the back of the car. He needed to, to be able to get feed for the cows."

My mother spoke up. "My father did that, too. But why would anyone need a tunnel?"

"Well, I guess some of us wanted a back way in and out, you see. It's one thing to know you've got to do something that's not quite right, in order to make ends meet. It's another to feel like you'll be caught or find your name in the paper." A ripple of understanding ran around the room. "It was good to know folks could move from the farm to the inn or back again without being noticed, and without questions about what they were carrying. The women mostly took care of making sure the men didn't get themselves in trouble, you know. Don't we always want them to be happy?" She glanced quickly over at me.

"So the tunnel?" That was my mother again. Mrs. Toussaint took a breath. She had all the words lined up in front of her, I could tell, but it was like there was a layer of dust over them, like they'd been preserved untouched for years, and she had to take them out carefully, one by one.

"Simply this: When the liquor arrived here in town, most often it could be hidden someplace at the inn, because vehicles came and went and so did a lot of people. The next night, someone would bring some of it through to the farm. The girls would gather at the Lee farm for some task—donut making, or quilting—and sometimes a group would quietly head to the old barn and do a bit of bottling. I don't know quite when we stopped, but I think it went on for some years." She turned to me. "Shawna, I know you were very busy in the tunnel this evening, and we're all proud of you for working so hard to bring Teddy out of there." People nodded and agreed. Mrs. Toussaint asked, "Did you happen to see any old bottles still in there?"

I shook my head, no. "But the flashlight was really small and it didn't work for very long. Oh, Mrs. Toussaint—is that your mother's handwriting on the wall in there?"

She looked puzzled, then remembered what we'd pointed out when the video crew had been there.

"No, no, that's not my mother's. Maybe it's one of the younger Dearborns, though."

I wondered whether Thea's father would believe us now: There went another bit of evidence that could have been from the Underground Railroad but was really from another time. Mrs. Toussaint smiled at the crowd in the kitchen.

"As I said, I thought it was long since collapsed. Many a truck has rumbled over this road, and I believed the entrances were blocked years ago."

"Teddy's foot was caught in some wire fencing in there," I offered.

"That makes sense. I guess time's just shifted things around a bit. I'd say it's time to block the tunnel properly and fill it in, for everyone's safety."

"No!" Mr. Cobleigh called out from behind Mr. Warwick, who was also starting to shake his head and open his mouth.

"That tunnel is village history. If we're going to put the village on the map for the Underground Railroad, we might as well have it on there for rum-running, too. Think of all the people who'll come to see this."

The room buzzed with conversations and suggestions. Mr. Johnson raised his voice over the others. "Mrs. Toussaint? Another question, please?" Everyone, I noticed, even the adults, were acting like we were in school and Mrs. Toussaint was the teacher. No one could help it—she just did that to people.

"Yes, young man?"

"The Underground Railroad. With a hiding place on this side, at the inn, wouldn't the tunnel help people escape over to the farm back then?"

Over all the excitement and exclamations, Mrs. Toussaint had to rap her fist on the table for quiet to reply.

"In all honesty, that's a question I can't answer. I don't think the tunnel dates back that far. But it can wait until another day. I think there are children here who need some rest, after all this commotion. I know I do."

People took the hint, and passed cups and mugs toward the kitchen. Mrs. Toussaint left with most of the neighbors. My mother washed, Mr. Warwick dried, and Thea put away; I started to sweep the dining room and kitchen but Mr. Warwick said not to bother, so I sat and waited for my mother to be done. It didn't take long.

"Thank you," Mr. Warwick said in a very tired voice. "Thank you, Connie. And Shawna, thank you so very much. You and Thea are good for each other. I'm glad you're friends."

I felt my face turn red. "Um, you're welcome. I'm glad, too."

Thea added, "Me, too," and gave me a careful one-armed hug, to protect her sprained wrist and my scraped elbow. She helped me find my snowsuit so I could carry it home. At the last minute, Midnight came bounding into the kitchen. My mother carried him out the door, and he instantly ran back to the farm. So my mom—that is, my adopted mom—and I held hands as we crossed the slippery, icy road where the barn's safety light cast its soft golden glow.

We didn't speak until we were in our own kitchen, where my mother asked, "Need a bedtime snack?"

"No thanks," I told her, surprising myself. "I guess I'm not really hungry. But I sure do want a shower." And I did, to get all the spider and mouse and cellar dirt out of my hair and off the rest of me. Harry came into the kitchen, cleaned up and ready for bed himself, and said he and Carl were proud of me, too. Everyone knew already that Teddy was safe. I didn't take time to ask how they'd found out. I was so tired. A shower and pajamas, that was all I could think of.

As I crawled into bed, with my hair still wet but clean, I realized the next day would be Monday, a school day. I set my alarm and turned off the light. My head was pounding with so much new information, and my eyes ached and itched. But I fell asleep right away.

In the morning, I didn't go to school. Instead, I woke up with the flu.

WELL, IT MIGHT be more accurate to say that I didn't much wake up. When my alarm buzzed on Monday morning, I'd already been coughing and sneezing and blowing my nose half the night. I punched the "off" button on the clock and pulled up the blankets around me, shivering. "Mom!"

No answer. She was probably still in the barn with Harry. I drifted back into an achy, uncomfortable sleep, and around eight o'clock, when I should have been leaving for school, I woke to find my mother's hand on my forehead, rough from work but cool and comforting. When she said, "Fever," I nodded, and I think I asked her to tell Thea—which she probably couldn't do right away because Thea would already be headed for school herself. Anyway, I slept all morning, interrupted only by doses of Tylenol and cough syrup and a glass of ginger ale that I sipped for a moment before falling asleep again. In the afternoon, it was Harry bringing things and adjusting the blinds to keep the room dim. He piled an extra comforter on top of my bed, and I dreamed of being someplace in the South, someplace hot, sweating and panting for breath.

Then the dream went cold as winter, cold as the packed earth in the tunnel floor, cold as a fugitive slave trying to escape to the North. I dreamed I was in our little old barn by the road, holding a flashlight at the opening in the floor where a trap door lay flipped back, and brown-skinned people kept crawling out of the dark place, lines of blood down the backs of their shirts. I was crying. I felt like somebody very fierce and mean was outside the barn, trying to see inside it. I kept saying "Ssh!" to the people coming out of the tunnel, and they crept up into the barn's hayloft, one after another.

My mother came to wash my face with cool water in the evening, and she helped me to the bathroom in the hall. For a few minutes I stayed awake, long enough to hear her go down the stairs and answer the phone. Vaguely, I thought it had been ringing a lot. But everything hurt so much, my back, my legs, my head, and I slept again.

Tuesday morning no alarm woke me, but I woke up anyway just after nine o'clock. Standing up challenged my muscles, which ached and trembled. But holding onto chairs and doorknobs, I made it to the bathroom, and brushed my teeth to get the sour taste out of my mouth. A fit of shivers struck, so I wobbled back to bed and slept again until about noon, when my mother insisted that I eat some chicken noodle soup. It tasted good, and the heat eased my sore throat a bit better than the cough syrup had.

I struggled to sit up in bed. "I need to call Thea," I whispered.

"Later," my mother told me. "After school. I'll bring the phone into here, after she's home."

"Okay." I lay back down, hot face against cool pillow. Then I coughed more, each jerk of a cough striking pain into my head again. My mother left the room, coming back with a vaporizer that she plugged in next to my bed.

"Breathe slowly and gently, don't try so hard," she suggested. She rubbed a dab of Vicks onto my chest. Her hand and the ointment made a good heat; I slept again.

When I did finally talk on the phone with Thea, I could

hardly hold it to my ear. Weak as a kitten, I thought to myself. To Thea, I whispered, "How's Teddy?"

"He's good," she assured me. "He won't let Mom do anything without him, but he's okay. He says he loves you."

I laughed, which made me cough. When I could speak again, I whispered into the phone, "My first boyfriend, three years old."

Thea giggled. "Hey, Josh wrote me a letter, with a list of all his favorite music. I'm going to write back and send him my own list. You'd never know he's related to those twins, he's a lot smarter." She asked, "Did Kyle get hold of you yet? He told me he's been calling your house, but you were too sick to come to the phone."

"Not yet." I was too tired to wonder about Kyle. Besides, important things needed arranging. "The history project," I murmured. "Deadline."

"Yeah, I know. We have to write the project outline. Listen, I'll make a draft, with lists of what we'll exhibit and stuff like that, okay?"

"Just a minute." I blew my nose and picked up the phone again. "Mr. Harris. We've got to spell out how the Underground Railroad meant something here, even if we can't prove what happened in the secret room." Coughing stopped me for a minute. Thea waited for me. I continued: "We have to make a chart of evidence. Pro and con. Show we've looked at both sides."

Thea agreed right away. "Listen, as soon as you're better, I'll come over with some posterboard and we'll do it together. This weekend is fine. You know, half the school's out with the flu. People are saying somebody came to the dance who was sick and gave it to everyone else."

"Not you, though?"

"Nope! Not me. It's boring at school. There were only three other eighth graders today and all we did was read and watch movies. Maryellen Bryce threw up in the hall. You better get well soon."

"I'm trying!" I promised to call her again after school each day, until I was well enough for us to get together.

The only good thing about staying in bed for two more days was that I finished reading *Uncle Tom's Cabin* and all the other English and history reading assignments for November. Friday morning I felt well enough to sit at the kitchen table and catch up on math homework, too.

Saturday, while my mother tramped up on the mountain, checking out where "her" buck was rambling, Carl came to stay with me while Harry went to town. He made tea with honey to share, and we had sloppy joe sandwiches for lunch, my first real food for the week. Even so, I only managed to eat half a sandwich, while he ate two and a half. Plus ice cream.

"Carl?"

"What's on your mind, Shawna-Fawna?"

"I don't want to see Alice." Less than three weeks now to Thanksgiving, which meant less than three weeks until Alice came.

"Yeah. I can see how you'd feel that way. You know," he offered, "she won't be here long. Just for three days. And she'll bring you stuff, probably. You used to like it when she came home."

"But that was when I was really little, and before I knew ... I mean, I don't even know what to call her."

"How about calling her by her name, like you always have?" Carl scratched at a scab on the back of his hand, then looked sideways up at me. "You weren't planning to call her Mom, were you? Because honestly, Shawna, I don't think that's going to work for anybody."

"You mean that's not why she's coming home? I thought she was the one that made Mom tell me." Outside, the November wind blasted harder, and the porch door rattled. I was snug in a flannel shirt and sweater and sweatpants, but I could feel the cold draft across my ankles where they stuck out of my slippers. I tucked my feet up under me and repeated, "Carl?"

"Hold on. Let me try to say this my own way, kiddo." My

big brother rubbed his chin, then scratched there, too. "I guess I can't speak for Alice, and she'd be mad at me if I tried. But Mom and Harry and I were talking earlier this week, while you were so sick. And I think really that Mom meant to tell you a lot sooner. She just never found the right time, you know? What Alice did was just say, hey, it's time."

"Time for what? I mean, do I have to live with Alice now?" Even though everyone said I wasn't going with Alice, I couldn't stop worrying about it.

"No way!" Clearly the thought surprised Carl. "No, Shawna, nobody wants you to do that. Not even Alice. Hey, she's just barely getting her life together in some ways. She's doing fine, and maybe someday she'd like you to visit her in California, but she knows you belong here with us. Isn't that what you want?"

"I guess." But I just had to make sure. "You mean, she doesn't want me back?"

"Jeezum, Shawna, you're getting it all mixed up. Alice loves you like a sister, and she's never going to stop being part of you and us and all. And Mom loves you like a mother. Nobody's letting you go. Not ever." He grinned. "Probably if you ever have a boyfriend or get married, we'll all still make you stay here. How's that sound?"

I laughed and punched his shoulder, which started a very unfair wrestling match. Even if I hadn't had the flu, it would have been unfair! Carl has monster muscles.

Laughing felt good, and made me feel lighter, too. Which I was in another way, too: Not eating much for five days made my clothes all a little bit loose. The funny thing was, there didn't seem to be a rush to eat a lot more and grow back into them. With Carl's explanation, I felt more settled, more quiet inside than I ever had before.

Thea's visit that afternoon fit into the quiet mood. Just like normal, like any old afternoon, we settled on the rug in the living room, by the warm comfort of the woodstove, to make lists and draw ruler lines onto posterboard and prepare a class presentation of what our history fair project was going to cover.

All we needed for this week was the outline that could be hung on the classroom wall. Then, after Thanksgiving, we'd put together our displays.

"The Underground Railroad Years in North Upton, Vermont," Thea carefully lettered across the top of the white posterboard. Good thing she'd hurt the left wrist, not her writing hand—her handwriting was way better than mine, so she had to do the poster if we were going to have the best project.

Together, we listed our evidence: the writing from inside the hidden room that had started us looking, but turned out to be from Prohibition instead; Henry Dearborn's journal showing how the house was an inn back then; the letters of Mrs. Woodward, the doctor's wife; a page of description from the Goodwillie House in Barnet, talking about the hiding place there; the map from the state survey and another one that showed the old stage routes, including one that ran to the Canada border. We drew arrows to show how the pieces added up: not to hiding people in Thea's cellar, but to the outside world being part of things here in the village. And we'd need a copy of that old picture of the inn with the black person's face at the window.

"We have to write a bibliography, too," I reminded Thea. "We can put our history book on the list, and also the town history. And that 'Friends of Freedom' survey."

"Oh, I've got another book for us." Thea jumped up to pull a blue volume out of her backpack. "It's stories by this man, Rowland Robinson, who was a Quaker and lived on the other side of Vermont. His house was definitely a station for the Underground Railroad, but nobody had to hide there, they just worked on the farm, even though some of his stories involved blacks escaping in the woods."

"Cool!" We checked the format on Mr. Harris's handout, and starting writing the bibliography in alphabetical order by author.

I leaned back on the rug and asked, "What are we going to say about the tunnel?"

"You mean, whether it was for fugitive slaves or not?"

"Mmm-hmm. I mean, we know from Mrs. Toussaint that people used it for hiding the rum-running during the twenties and thirties. But we don't know whether it was a passageway for people before that."

Thea nodded. "I've been thinking. Mrs. Toussaint said we already know how to figure it out. She meant we've got to go into the tunnel and look for evidence, right?"

"Or maybe she meant we've got to look at more letters and stuff from people who lived here then," I offered. I didn't want to go back into the tunnel.

"Both," my friend decided. She nodded at what I hadn't said out loud. "I know, I don't want to go in there, and you don't want to go back in. But it's going to be different this time. My dad says the college will want to be involved, and they'll have lights and maybe even an archaeologist to make sure the evidence gets collected properly. We can be there and take pictures of what they find. But," she insisted, "we've got to get them to come soon, so we can use the results in our own project."

So we agreed, and finished our chart, and Carl, who'd been fixing a water line, came back into the house and insisted on making hot chocolate for us all. It was a perfect afternoon, and I slept well that night, knowing that I had the best possible friend, someone to talk with, study with, think with, plan with. If it hadn't been for Alice coming, I would have said my life was pretty great. Especially because nobody was going to get me up early for barn chores the next morning!

EVEN THOUGH IT was really winter, the weather stayed quiet—no sun, no snow, No-vember, goes the expression—and the week from Saturday the eighth to the evening of Friday the fourteenth really was nothing much as far as I was concerned. Even though I was back in school, so many kids were still out with the flu that class time stayed light, with lots of "enrichment" videos and time for reading. Half the teachers also had been sick, and although most returned by mid-week, nobody had a lot of energy to spare. Thea and I finished our outline and hung it in Mr. Harris's classroom, but he didn't comment on it, since only a few others were ready on time. He gave out an extension, the way most of the teachers were doing: final outline due date, December 1, the day after Thanksgiving weekend. By then, Thea and I figured we'd already have our display materials ready to assemble. It looked like we'd still be waiting for the archaeologist to explore the tunnel, though. Too bad.

Something a little different was that Kyle Everts talked with me on the phone twice that week. Both times, we talked about math, and basketball, and a little bit about what we'd like to do when winter's snow would really set in. I didn't stay on the phone very long either time; my mother and Harry were too likely to pick up the extension in the barn in order to call for a feed delivery, or to wander through the kitchen unexpectedly. I had a sneaking suspicion they were checking on me. But that was okay. I liked feeling safe and enclosed in the family I'd always known. Emerson came for supper with us most nights, mostly quiet and tired, but still, I was glad we could all be together. Each day, as Alice's arrival came closer, I wanted to be sure of how we all fit together, before all that supposedly "set-you-free" truth would take over.

Friday evening, the night before the start of rifle hunting season for deer, our house was in predictable confusion. Even though Friday night chores in the barn were supposed to fall to me and Harry, according to our calendar schedule, Carl came to pitch in and left me in the house. "Take the night off, Princess," he told me. "Work up some muscles for Sunday morning chores, though. I doubt that Mom will get her deer in one day."

"Don't even talk about it," my mother called across the kitchen. "Don't say anything. I don't want to think about other people and their ideas while I'm up there. Anyone seen the big yellow flashlight?"

She was stuffing a duffle bag with sweaters and a second pair of boots. I passed her the cooler, loaded with a pan of lasagna for tonight, and for tomorrow egg sandwiches and milk, and a thermos of hot sweet coffee, so she wouldn't have to cook at four in the morning before heading out to her tree stand. She wouldn't even tell us where she'd placed it this year—her scouting and tracking meant a lot to her, and if she'd chosen the right place, she'd have a deer within a few days of the season opening. And if she hadn't chosen right ... well, she didn't need her own kids teasing her about it.

Carl gave her a hug for luck and headed to the barn. Harry probably had the milking machines ready by now. It was close to five o'clock.

"Mom, what else do you need?"

She stared at the wall, going down a list in her head, and I waited. I could imagine it: hunting knife, rope, special scented buck oil to rub on her boots tonight to cover up the smell of cows and humans. Compass, just in case she had to chase a wounded animal through deep woods. If the list were in my own head, there'd be books on it, but probably the handful up at the cabin would do for Mom, as long as there was a Bible.

"Bible!" she said out loud, startling me. "Shawna, where's your Sunday School Bible? You're doing the first reading on Sunday morning."

"Mom, no! Not during deer season! You're not serious, are you? Harry and I will never get done in the barn in time."

"Start earlier," my mother said crisply. "It's Galatians 4. Go over it tonight and again tomorrow, so you won't make mistakes in the service."

Galatians 4? I blew a sigh of relief. Everyone knew that chapter, the one that said: "Rejoice in the Lord always. I will say it again: Rejoice!" And it includes the bit about "whatever is true, whatever is noble, whatever is right," you should think about such things. Everyone likes that chapter. "Okay, I will," I promised. I hugged my mother and told her, "Get a good one!"

"Right." She squeezed me snugly, then reminded me, "Don't forget to fold the clothes when the dryer stops. And get the big lasagna pan soaking right after you feed Harry his supper."

I held up a hand. "I got it. Go ahead, Mom. I hope it's a good day tomorrow."

"Thanks!"

A few minutes later, the sound of the four-wheeler engine faded into the distance and I was on my own in the house. I looked at the clock: five fifteen, plus twenty minutes to reach the cabin up there—maybe more like half an hour really, because she'd go slowly to keep the engine quieter. She'd have her supper about six thirty, I estimated. And be asleep by eight, with her alarm set.

I sort of wished I had gone along, but mostly it was a relief to stay in the village, where my friends were. Where Thea was. In the morning, we planned to visit Mrs. Toussaint again at the library. For the rest of this evening, though, I'd have to run the kitchen and all. Carl and Harry and me for supper, clothes to sort, dishes to wash. I started setting the table.

Saturday morning early, I heard Harry clump down the stairs. My bedside clock said almost six. I rolled over and luxuriated in another half hour under the covers before getting up to start some coffee for him and Emerson.

I pulled a coat on over my sweatshirt and jeans, and padded in my socks out onto the porch. Behind the mountains the sky hung pale gray, not quite light, not quite dark. In the distance I could hear shots: pop, pop, pop-pop. Then silence. Then another handful. Frost made the grass glitter. I drew in a long breath, slowly, so it wouldn't make me cough. It tasted like winter.

A truck rumbled past with two men in it, dressed in hunting clothes: green wool jackets with bright orange vests over them, so they'd be easily seen in the woods. Why were they down in the village, when deer season had just begun? You'd think they'd be out in the woods. Oh, well—as long as they didn't try to hunt from the roads. Not only was that illegal, but it was dangerous. Harry called the people who did that—who often dumped their trash and beer cans along the way—"slob hunters."

Another pair of shots echoed, but I couldn't tell from which direction. The hills and the barn buildings caught the sounds and bounced them around. I hoped it might be my mother, but I doubted it. I knew she'd get her deer with just one shot, not with the hopeful one-two banging of some less careful hunter.

Back inside the house, I stirred up pancake batter and started bacon frying. Blueberry muffins from my mother's baking sat in a basket on the table. Where was the maple syrup?

When I stood on a chair to get another jar of maple syrup from the cupboard, Alice's picture looked practically right at me. How could she do it, when she knew God wanted her to wait for marriage? And who got Alice pregnant, anyway? What did he look like? I suddenly realized he was probably alive somewhere, in the huge mess of people that was "down country," outside Vermont.

Oh! That explained why my eye color didn't match in the charts Thea and I made for science class! Thea and I had the evidence all along. I stared at Alice in the photo, her senior photo. If I could subtract her appearance from my own, the remainder would be his, wouldn't it? A math problem in subtraction should be simple. Then again, maybe it was closer to multiplication or factoring. Alice, times mysterious other person, divided by the multiplying cells, and factored for God's hand.

I climbed down, syrup in one hand, questions on my mind. At least this time they didn't hurt; they just sat inside me like a new assignment. I didn't tell Harry or Emerson about them during breakfast. We all talked about hunting camp from years past and wondered how Mom was doing up there on her own. Then the men went back out to use the tractor to move some of the monstrously big bales of hay, each the size of a small car, into stacks next to the cow barn.

At quarter to ten, Thea came across the road, notebook in hand. The Ace bandage around her sprained wrist was hidden under her fluffy white wool mittens, and with her matching beret and sweater, she looked like a magazine picture. I told her so, and she laughed. "I feel like somebody's kitten," she admitted. "Me-oww! If I saw Josh, I bet he'd want to touch it!" She giggled and asked with a lifted eyebrow, "Kyle call lately?"

"Yesterday," I admitted. "But just to check on an assignment."

"Yeah, sure!"

Really, that was true. Still, it seemed nice that when Thea was getting phone calls from Josh, I had some from Kyle. So I didn't mind if Thea teased me.

"Let's go. Aren't you bringing your notebook, too?"

I rummaged under some blankets that Mom had decided not to take with her and found my backpack. "Ready."

At the school building, in the library, Mrs. Toussaint was on the phone when we arrived. She waved us toward a table where three old photos lay, plus three enormous black notebooks and a red one.

We picked up the photos. One showed three young women with serious faces, just the tops of their dresses or blouses showing, white lace against black fabric, each with some sort of brooch or pin at the throat. Two wore glasses with thin metal rims and looked smart. The third had a big bow pinned onto her stacked-up hair. Thea turned the photo over. "The Dearborn Girls: Ruthie, Anna, and Katherine." She made a guess: "Maybe around 1900? The outfits look better than the Civil War ones, but from what I can see, I'd guess those are handmade outfits, not store-bought."

The librarian hung up the phone and came over to us. "Yes, that's about right. They were my mother's age more or less, and only Katherine ever married. The others lived at the inn, and when Katherine's husband died in a mill accident, she moved back home, too." She lifted the second photo, holding it by the very edges in her small blunt hands. "This is their mother, Mrs. Henry Dearborn. I don't know who marked the back, but it says eighteen sixty. So it's a very early daguerreotype photo, and—it would be during the last year of the Underground Railroad, not counting the war years."

In the photo, Mrs. Dearborn also wore a dark blouse, but you could see the style was different. I peered at the neckline. "What's that?"

"Most likely a hair locket," Mrs. Toussaint told us. "It would hang from a necklace or be pinned to the collar, and the front of it would open up to a small space that could hold a very short lock of hair. Maybe her husband's, or a dead child's, or a son gone away."

"Into the army, maybe," Thea speculated.

"Perhaps. Although that would be more likely a year later, when so many young men from this village enlisted to fight for the Union. Stay with the date, my dear. This photo is from just before the Civil War started. And this," she touched the first one again, "this is a generation later, but these young ladies were grown women during Prohibition. And living at the inn, no doubt they helped with the village business at the time." She peered at us sharply: "Do you girls understand yet why the village doesn't talk about the Prohibition years and the rum-running?"

Thea shook her head. "Why not? Why aren't people excited about it? It's like a movie, an adventure!"

I shook my head. "It was against the law, and I bet a lot of them were embarrassed. Did anyone get arrested?"

Mrs. Toussaint pursed her lips. "Not that I know of. But you're right: The village people knew they were breaking the law, even though it was a law that only a few people supported. The minister, for instance, had a group of Temperance ladies who made sure anyone known to be a drunk got tossed out of church. They had good reason, too—think of the families destroyed by 'Demon Rum,' as some folks called it."

Now she tipped the third photo toward us. I gasped. It was a photo at a hunting camp! But instead of a wooden cabin, a group of men, all wearing hats and jackets, stood next to a large canvas tent. In front of them, hung by its back legs from a tripod of three tree trunks, was an enormous deer, a buck, with his antlers so large they nearly reached the ground. The librarian pointed with the eraser end of her pencil toward a man in the center of the front row.

"That, I believe, Shawna, would be your mother's father—Connie Allen Lee Quinn's father," she clarified. "Horace Allen. And I believe this was his deer, although most likely all the men were out together, hunting as a group."

Thea's face creased in puzzlement. "A group?"

I explained: "It's when they all work together on a length of woods, one group spreading out like a half circle and pressing the wildlife slowly toward the other group. You're most likely to be able to get a deer that way, when it's a team."

"Oh. But isn't that unfair? I mean, the poor deer, with a whole group of people and guns?" Thea moved back from the photo, distressed.

I was glad Mrs. Toussaint answered. "It depends on how

hungry people have become, I'm afraid. Remember, during the Great Depression, most of this village couldn't even afford to have meat more than once a month, except for chickens if they did well. Hunting together made sure there was meat to go around."

Thea murmured, "I'd rather just not eat meat."

"Not if you had farm work to do, you wouldn't. It takes meat and potatoes to keep you warm and strong in winter, when you're working hard."

I nodded in agreement. Being strong was important.

"So the men had to eat meat," Thea argued. "But the women didn't have to, did they? I mean, they wouldn't be plowing and all that, right?"

"Most wouldn't," Mrs. Toussaint admitted. "But making butter and baking bread and doing the wash in a big tub of water you've hauled after pumping it yourself, that takes strength and stamina."

"Hmm." Thea still looked doubtful. "I wouldn't want to have to kill the animals. Not even a chicken. I don't eat meat anymore, not since I turned twelve, and I'm still strong."

"Well, I'm afraid we've wandered from why I wanted you to see these photographs," the librarian went on. "I thought you girls might like to photocopy the women's pictures, for your history project. They more or less outline the time period you're working on, don't they?"

True. Thea gathered them into a small stack again. "But what are these books?" she asked.

"Early village records, called the Grand List. The town office has its own copies, but these are duplicates. Each household is recorded each year with its assets, for taxes."

We scrambled to open the books. The writing in them was small and faded, and edges of the pages had split, which slowed us down and made us careful, right away. Together, Thea and I bent our heads close to the faint pages and searched for the eighteen fifties and Henry Dearborn's inn. More evidence!

There it was: Dearborn, Henry, Jr. House and four acres.

Village. I traced the line across to the opposite page, where the assets of the inn were listed: "Two horses. Wagon. Six sheep. Furnishings. Oh, two dogs. Wait, what's this?"

Using Mrs. Toussaint's magnifying glass, we studied the spidery handwriting and its cryptic abbreviations. Something had been crossed out and rewritten. "Polls," Thea said suddenly. "What's that?"

"Number of people," said Mrs. Toussaint. "Go on."

I said, "It looks like six men, two women. Crossed out, and changed to two men, two women. Could that be right?"

"And? What could that mean?"

I blurted in sudden inspiration, "What if some of the men who lived there left town, to go help out with the Underground Railroad? Could that be?"

"Good guess. In fact, our own Thaddeus Stevens was in Congress then. If you look at this book from my personal library, you'll find evidence that he helped the Underground Railroad himself. I've always wondered whether he reached back north to his roots in Upton Center." With a nod, Mrs. Toussaint stood up and said, "I'll let you explore the books and copy down what you need to. And I'll photocopy those pictures while you girls are working. Be gentle with the pages."

But even after we'd copied everything that seemed to hint at people living at the inn and then leaving, we had little definite evidence that any of them had been working for the Underground Railroad, no matter how much we wanted it. Pushing back in our chairs, Thea and I shared our discouragement.

The librarian was talking on the phone again. We gathered up our copies and our notes, stacked the books and photos neatly, and whispered our thanks with a wave as we left. Mrs. Toussaint waved back to us with a half smile, still talking.

We scuffed down the road, dragging our feet through ruffled brown leaves, the frost burnt off them from the bit of sun creeping through the overhanging clouds. A wind from the west came slicing at our faces. Thea was okay in her white mittens and hat, but I'd skipped wearing any, and my fingers ached from cold as I clutched my notebook.

"We'll go to my house and add these to our chart," Thea announced. "Come on. Teddy wants to see you, anyway."

The aroma of vegetable soup and the steam from cooking made the Warwick kitchen a friendly place to be. After getting hugged by Mrs. Warwick and Teddy—who I practically had to peel off me, he was so excited—I settled next to Thea at the dining-room table so we could spread out all our papers and the big chart. Carefully, we lettered the new evidence, and the new exhibit objects, the women's photos, onto the chart. The hunting photo wasn't for our project— I'd take that copy home with me instead.

A commotion outside caught our attention, just about two o'clock. Harry and Emerson, talking with some men in a pickup truck, stood outside our small machinery barn, the one where the other end of the tunnel must be. I realized we hadn't even explored it yet. "Hey," I suggested to Thea. "Let's go see what the other opening to the tunnel looks like!"

Harry and Emerson noticed us as we crossed the road, but just nodded and kept listening to the visitors. I didn't recognize the men or the truck; it had a Massachusetts license plate. The raw November wind cut so sharply that I was glad to get into the barn, where at least the three and a half walls offered some shelter. Turning on the lights, I looked around as Thea picked up a piece of plastic pipe and began to probe the floor. "I don't want to go sliding down some hole like Alice in Wonderland," she called to me.

So I picked up a length of pipe too, and in the same kind of partnership we'd used for searching her house for Teddy, we carefully worked our way back from the open doorway, toward the shadowy corners where lumber, burlap bags, and buckets of tools and parts sat.

Thea found it. "Over here!" She knelt on the wooden plank floor and moved old hay aside. I could see the cat-size opening broken in the floor as I hurried across to her.

"Is there a trapdoor?"

"Yes, look—here's a hinge. Uh-oh, this is stuck, and I bet it's heavy. Is there something stronger that we can pry with? A big screwdriver maybe?"

I shook my head and backtracked to where I'd seen what we needed. "There's an old iron pry bar here that we use when we're putting up fencing. Hold on."

Together we wedged the bar under the edge of the hole at the trapdoor corner. We leaned on it, combining our weight. I felt my shirt untuck from my jeans, and the cold air made me yelp. But we kept bouncing onto the pry bar, our lever, and with a shriek of wood separating from where it had stuck against wood, the door popped loose.

From the doorway, Emerson called out, "What are you girls up to in there?"

"We found the other end of the tunnel! Emerson, we need a flashlight!"

He came to see it first, the man-size bulk of him in his coveralls and big booted feet crowding us aside. He peered into the damp darkness below, where a half-rotted scrap of wooden ladder rested. "Whoa—you don't just need a flashlight, you need a decent ladder, too. Wait here."

While my brother went for the light and ladder, Thea and I cleared more things away from the tunnel opening. I stacked some buckets, and she kicked old hay aside.

"Hey, Shawna?"

"Yeah?"

"Listen, things have been so busy. I just wanted to tell you—about your mother, I mean, the adoption and everything?"

My stomach cramped. I tried not to show it. "Yeah?"

"Well, I mean, I wanted to say I'm really glad you and your family let me stay with you that evening, when you found out about it. I mean, in Connecticut I knew a couple of kids who'd been adopted, and there was a boy older than me who lived with his grandparents. But I never was right there when someone first found out. It was pretty cool."

Amazing. The worst evening of my life, and my best friend

thought it had been cool. Carefully I asked, "You don't think it's really weird?"

"Not really." Thea's face always showed when she was concentrating on a math problem, and she had the same look now. "Don't you think families come in all kinds of shapes? I mean, like, some kids have parents who are gay. That can seem like it's going to be really complicated, too, but it kind of just ends up working out and being pretty normal, you know? And your family, well, I think it shows how much you all care about each other, and I think it's a good thing."

Tears jumped to my eyes and I brushed them off and cracked a smile. "Thanks, Thea. I like your family, too."

Thea asked, "When your—I mean, when Alice comes to visit you, can I meet her, too?"

"Sure. Sure, why not? Hey, you know what—last night I was thinking about when we were doing the eye and hair charts for science class, and how I couldn't make my eyes come out right, remember?"

"Wow! That's why—because you had a different father! Whoa. Hey—I wonder where he is now?"

Thank goodness, just then, Emerson came back, an aluminum ladder over one shoulder and a coil of cord with a dangling lightbulb in his other hand. "Better than a flashlight," he announced, plugging the long cord in behind us and flicking the light on. It was bright and could go into the tunnel with us for—well, at least twenty feet or more.

"Emerson, that's great!" I helped Thea pull out the old wooden ladder, which came apart the rest of the way as we tugged it up over the edge of the wooden frame in the floor. It smelled like moss and mold and wet, and it left brown slime on my pants.

With Emerson to help, it was easy to get the new ladder into position down in the hole, and he insisted on being the first one to go down, to make sure it was safe. We could hear him scraping his head on the ceiling and sliding his feet along the floor of the tunnel.

"Okay, you girls can come on down!"

Thea first, easily, then me, a little slower as I fumbled with my feet on the slippery narrow aluminum rungs, we made our way down under the barn. A yellow glow from the extension light lit the dirt floor brightly, although the splintery wooden walls stood dark still. I tried not to touch them.

As we got closer to him, Emerson tipped the light in the other direction. "See?"

A heap of rocks and dirt nearly blocked the way under the road. A bit of chicken wire fence stuck out at one side, and I pointed: "That's the wiring that Teddy's foot was caught in, on the other side." When Emerson angled the light just right, you could see a space at the top of the pile where Midnight must have squeezed through. I looked down uncertainly, not wanting to have anything scurry past me. But I didn't see any movement.

As I looked up at the lit part of the tunnel again, something metal caught my eye, and I asked Emerson to tilt the light toward the wall.

A short nail stuck out, with a small old-fashioned pail hanging on it. Thea reached up and lifted it off the nail. "Hey, there's something inside!"

She tipped the pail sideways and I reached in, separating the objects inside. "A key. An old-fashioned coin, I think, but it's so tarnished I can't tell what it is, maybe an old silver dollar. And, oh gosh!" Gently I teased the fragile chain of a necklace free from the dirt-encrusted tangle. A square shape hung from it. "Thea," I said, my voice sounding funny even to my own ears, "Thea, I think it's a locket, a hair locket, just like the one in that old photograph!"

"What on earth is a hair locket?" Emerson asked from behind the light.

I started to explain, when a rumbling over our heads made us all jump. "Move back!" Emerson ordered, pushing us away from the part of the tunnel under the road. Dirt fell from the ceiling into my hair, and some got in my eyes. Thea ducked past me, headed for the ladder, holding the old pail. I followed her, the necklace loosely held but secure in my hands. I used my elbows on the ladder rungs to help climb, so I wouldn't damage the necklace by squeezing it too tightly.

Emerson climbed out last, drawing the extension cord with him. "Well, for sure, nobody should be down there. It's not safe. I don't want you girls exploring on your own down there, you hear me?"

I nodded. "At least, we won't until Mr. Warwick's professor from the college comes after Thanksgiving with the archaeologist, right? I bet they know how to make it safer."

"Yeah, well, so do I, but I don't have time just now, and I don't want to have to worry about you two girls. Promise you won't go down there alone?"

We promised.

Outside, people's voices called out and I heard the small engine of the four-wheeler. Emerson did, too: "Mom's here. Wonder whether she's got her deer already?" He clicked off the light, curled the cord deftly into a bundle, and set it down, so he could hurry outside and find out.

I looked at Thea. She whispered, "It might be the same one that's in the picture. Let's take it to your kitchen and try to clean it off a bit." Nodding, I carefully put the necklace into the front pocket of my jacket where it could rest safely until we got inside.

Out in the yard, sure enough, my mother had arrived with her deer. It was a gorgeous buck, a six-pointer—that is, its antlers were so large and it was so mature that it had three sharp points on each antler, six all together. Emerson, Harry, Mom, and the two men from Massachusetts stood admiring it. Some smoke from the turned-off engine hung in the air, and I caught the faint scent of deer, like deerhide has, the real animal scent rising from the gap in its belly where my mother had taken out the guts before hauling the animal out of the woods. A trickle of blood stained the rear end of the animal.

I turned to Thea. "Isn't it a beauty?"

"Oh," she said. "Oh, no. Oh, I didn't know it would be like

this. It's dead!"

Puzzled, I asked her, "You didn't know it would be dead? From hunting?"

She stepped closer to the buck, close enough to see its face. The black eyes still shone with moisture, although the nostrils were clearly stiff and the mouth hung slightly open, side teeth visible. My mother stopped talking with the men and came over to us. She put a hand on Thea's shoulder.

"It's hard when you see one the first time, honey," she told my friend. "I know. You see such a beautiful creature and your heart lifts up in wonder, but when you see one that's been killed, you can't help but be sad, can you?"

"You killed it." Thea wasn't asking. She looked right up into my mother's face like she couldn't believe she was seeing the same person from yesterday. "You shot it, and then you, what did you do, did you have to cut it with a knife?"

My mother nodded. "I did. That's not how it's always done, but I had to carry it on my back for about a half mile, so I needed to take out the extra weight from most of its organs." She paused and looked over at me, then said to Thea, "You can touch it if you want to."

Slowly, Thea pulled off one red, dirt-smudged glove and stepped close to the deer. The men were silent, watching. I stepped up next to Thea and as she reached out to stroke the deer's long neck, I did, too. I looked at my friend.

"There isn't really a word for it," I told her. "For the mix of sad and not sad. For feeling like the most beautiful animal's dead, and for feeling like Mom worked hard to get her deer, worked for weeks really," I confirmed. The men nodded.

Emerson said quietly, "I've never seen one like this without feeling sad, too, Thea. God's creatures are here for us to take care of, and it's hard to understand about killing them for meat. But we won't waste a bit of it, and we'll praise the Lord for the life of this wild creature."

"But it's dead," Thea repeated. "And it used to be alive." She shook her head. "I guess I might not like hunting season," she said quietly. "Hey, Shawna, I'll see you later, okay?" She turned and headed across the street.

My mother rested a hand on my arm, stopping me from following. So I called out, "I'll call you later, okay?"

"I guess. After supper, maybe."

I thought my own heart was breaking, watching my best friend walk away from me, across the road. My mother said quietly from behind me, "Give her time, Shawna. Wait a bit. It's all right for her to feel that way."

Emerson and Harry went to get some rope to hang the deer from the beam that stuck out of the back of the machinery barn, so the blood could drain out the rest of the way before cutting up the meat. The two men from Massachusetts drove away in their truck. I looked at my mother and tried to feel happy for her, for her big deer and her first-day success. "Way to go, Mom," I croaked out. "What a gorgeous buck, and right away, too. Your dad would have been proud of you."

"Thanks, Shawna." She rubbed her nose against mine, snuggling a moment. "And thanks for thinking of my father. He was quite a hunter."

"Oh—I forgot to tell you—Mrs. Toussaint had a photograph of Gramps, with his deer, and she gave us a copy! It's over at Thea's house." I turned to head across to get the picture, but my mother stopped me again.

"I can wait until later to see it, honey. Let Thea have some time to herself first. Come one, we're going to need your help to haul this big fella up in the air."

After that, with Emerson and Harry back, the deer to tie and lift, and lots of comments on how heavy and big the buck was, everyone started teasing and congratulating again, and things felt better. But still, I knew that my friend's reaction had popped the balloon of excitement for the day. And I knew that she needed me to say something that would let her feel okay about how the dead deer seemed to her. If she could tell me my family wasn't weird, I needed to tell her she wasn't weird, either.

But how could I say that, when she was so obviously acting

like a girl from down country, a flatlander? I didn't have the words or the feeling ready. I was scared that I might not be able to find them in time for this evening's phone call. If I couldn't find the right words, would I still have my best friend?

I CALLED THEA THREE times on Saturday evening, but the first time her mother said she was still eating supper, the second time her father said she was watching a movie with the family and would call back later, and the third time, when her father answered again, I just said, "Would you please tell her I'll call after church tomorrow?" And he said he would, without putting her onto the phone.

Barn chores passed in a blur. So did breakfast. All I could think of was trying to figure out how Thea must feel, and what to say to her. At church, I couldn't pay attention to the sermon or the hymns. I waited for the part when the pastor asks everyone to think of people they want to lift up to God in prayer, and all the way through the pastor's own prayer, I kept thinking with my head and my heart, "God, please help me make it okay. Please bless Thea. Please help me find the words to fix things. Please, please, please. In Jesus's name. Amen."

My mother and Harry let me walk home from church on my own. As I passed Mrs. Toussaint's house, I saw that her nephews must have taken their two dead deer back home. Most likely somebody else in the village would get a deer in the week ahead of us. It was always that way in hunting season. This was the first time I'd felt upset like this about it, though. My stomach lurched.

I started toward the house. It was snowing again, soft and slow and silent. I reached the far end of the little barn by the road, and stepped behind it to look at Mom's deer. No more blood dripped from it; the new snow had almost covered the drips on the ground. Flakes hung in small clusters on the stiff hairs of the deer hide. The eyes were dull; no snow clung to the sharply pointed antlers. I thought about how much tracking and planning it took for my mother to get her deer. It was a good thing, not a bad thing, to get a deer in hunting season, and to share the meat with your neighbors. But I could see Thea's point: Going from a beautiful majestic buck to a dead deer waiting to be cut up was a hard change to witness.

I turned and walked back down the driveway and across the road. I knocked, and Thea answered.

"I'm sorry," I said right away.

Thea cut me off. "For what? You didn't kill that deer. Your mother did." Her face was swollen and she looked tired. "It's just Vermont. I don't really fit in here, I guess. Nobody else gets it. Look, Shawna—I'll see you tomorrow at school, okay?" And she shut the door firmly.

I stared at the closed door. After a moment, I turned around and scuffed back across the road. I stood by the deer again and started to cry. Up until yesterday, I'd been so proud of how my mom went out to the woods and tracked her own buck each year. Heck, I'd been proud of my whole family, going to church, doing things right. Being part of a place where we'd always lived, where we fit in. And now it was all wrong after all.

I listed the problems in my head: (1) My family is a bunch of liars. (2) My (used-to-be?) best friend gets upset about dead animals. (3) Alice is coming home and she's going to mess everything up even more. It was the worst list in the world.

Squeezed in with my list felt like being trapped in a tunnel in the dark. Didn't Thea know I'd done that for her sake? And for Teddy's. And because I knew Emerson and Carl would do it for me.

Snow was settling on my jacket, and the things Emerson and Carl had said over the past few days began to sprinkle down slowly over my list. I remembered what I'd told them I'd try to do. To forgive my mother—Mom. To try to believe that Alice cared about me. To feel loved, like Shawna-Fawna always had. I thought about how brave my "real" Mom had always been: finally telling me the truth—a zillion years late, sure, but a truth that hurt her and shamed her. Why should she get hurt and shamed now for getting her deer? Why did Thea have to mess it all up for her?

I balled up my hands. But then my fingers pressing tight against each other reminded me what Mrs. Toussaint had said. I was pointing a finger at Thea for being upset with my mother's deer and for not fitting in—but three fingers were pointing back at me. Maybe all Thea wanted was what any of us wanted—to fit in, to feel like you're in the right place.

An idea flashed into my head suddenly, like looking at a set of points on a graph and seeing the equation that makes the relationship between them make sense. Maybe it wouldn't work, but it was worth a try.

So for the second time, I walked from the dead deer to the front door of the Warwick house. This time, though, I was a lot colder, with my nose stuffed up and my fingers numb and my mind in a different place.

Thea opened the door. She still looked upset and tired. She said, "What?"

"I've just decided to be a vegetarian. Except you'll have to tell me how it works because I don't know." I hesitated a little. Choosing all my words was hard, like algebra without graph paper and an eraser. I wanted to do it right. "But I do know I'm proud of my mother for getting her deer. You don't have to look at it, and if you do look at it, I can totally agree that it's sad that animals die. But I love my mom and I want to be your friend, both at once, and I think we can figure out how to do it."

A hint of a smile crept onto Thea's face. I took that as a good sign.

"We're the two smartest girls in the eighth grade," I added. "And you do so fit in. If you need more than me saying so, I bet Josh says so, too." Thea laughed, and it gave me courage.

"So—this vegetarian thing—I can still eat oatmeal cookies if I'm a vegetarian, right? And can I choose to have a brownie sometimes?" My friend nodded.

I took a deep breath, which, I couldn't help notice, sounded just the ones Alice kept taking on the phone. "But Thea—I'm sorry I didn't warn you what hunting season would be like. You're right, it's hard to see a dead deer. You don't have to like hunting season. And you're not weird if you don't like it. You're smart and brave and the best friend I could ever have imagined."

"Back atcha," Thea told me, and grinned at my confusion. "That's what people say in Connecticut when they mean, 'The same thing back to you.' You better come in. Lunch is on the table, and my mother won't mind at all."

Lunch at Thea's? White sauce on lettuce, or some other strange food, when my own mother probably had ready a good Sunday dinner of country-fried chicken with baked potatoes and green beans and fresh rolls, and pie for dessert? My stomach rumbled.

"Thanks," I said out loud. "Sounds good to me! Can I use your phone to check with my mother, first?"

"Of course!"

We headed into the Warwick kitchen together, and I reached for the phone. Oddly, my mother didn't sound surprised at all.

LUNCH WAS NOT cheese or chicken on top of lettuce. The best I can say to describe it was a kind of cross between a sandwich, a salad, and a Chinese eggroll. Mrs. Warwick's own recipe of shredded carrots and avocado and a kind of peanut butter spread called hummus came rolled up in something called a "wrap," like a cold thin pancake. It was pretty good. I watched the Warwicks and ate the way they did, but I was still hungry after three of the little cut sections of salad-sandwich, so when cookies came for dessert, I took two. Thea took two also, and gave me a nod. I might have wished for more to eat, but I could do it her way for now. The only real problem the whole time turned out to be getting Teddy to sit in his own chair, because he kept climbing onto my lap and saying, "I love you, Shawna," with wet sloppy kisses on my cheek!

After lunch with the Warwicks, I sped home to get my backpack, grab an energy bar for some protein, and tell my mother we'd be doing homework all afternoon. She was just headed up to the camp to pack up some of her things and enjoy a restful afternoon in the woods. She said she'd be back to help

Harry in the barn around five.

"Mom, do you mind if I stay at Thea's until late this time? The television special with her house in it comes on at seven. I'll be home right after eight, and my homework will be all finished. Please?"

"Is your bed made?"

I ran upstairs and pulled up the covers, then dashed back down. "Now it is. And there's no laundry on the floor, either."

"Good. All right, I'll expect you home right after eight tonight. Mind your manners."

"I will!"

Back at Thea's, the two of us retreated to her room to do homework and talk. Thaddeus tried to come in, but we told him it was "girl time," which made him sulky, so Thea gave him a jigsaw puzzle from her shelves to get him to go away. Teddy, thank goodness, was taking his nap.

We tackled our math assignment first, graphing parabolas and hyperbolas, which I like because they are opposites of each other—sort of cup-shaped lines that either open wide to the top of the page, or arrive in pairs like wings. Thea's electric pencil sharpener made it easy to get a really good point on the pencil, and I liked the way the graphs turned into artwork that way.

When we pulled out our history books to answer a set of questions on how railroads affected the economy and the Westward expansion of the new country in the eighteen hundreds, I suddenly remembered the necklace. I guess the whole deer thing had pushed it out of our minds, but now, I couldn't wait one more minute to go examine it. I ran down to the coat rack by the kitchen door to dig it out of my jacket pocket and bring it up to Thea's room.

We placed the little knot of chain and locket on a clean sheet of paper. "Hold on, I'll get an old toothbrush," Thea offered. With that, and the points of our pencils, the chain gradually came clear of dirt and tangles. It was the locket, though, that I really wanted to see—especially inside. Thea brushed it gently until we could see the edges of the front flap. Since it came from my side of the tunnel, she handed it to me to open. In my imagination, it would hold a soft blond curl from someone who'd become a soldier, or maybe from Henry Dearborn himself, given to his girlfriend who became his wife. Gently, I pried the front of the little box open, careful not to spill the contents.

There it was, a curl so thick that it filled the tiny space completely, wedged securely inside. Thea touched it and looked puzzled. "Feel this," she urged.

The hair, black and curling, lacked the smooth luster I'd expected. "It's thick," I said, groping for what it reminded me of. Sheep? Almost. I lifted the locket and sniffed the hair within, but could only smell the damp tunnel smell. I handed it back to Thea. Carefully, using two pencils like tweezers or chopsticks, she pulled the curl out of the locket and set it onto the sheet of paper.

"It could almost be a black person's hair," she finally said.

We looked at the tiny token of some person more than a hundred and fifty years ago that Mrs. Henry Dearborn must have valued. Could it be from some escaped slave who stayed with the Dearborns long enough to become a friend? There just wasn't enough evidence. But one thing was practically certain, I knew: This locket had to be the one from the 1860s photograph that Mrs. Toussaint had shown to us. It was almost enough to prove the tunnel was older than the 1930s. Almost—but not quite. We'd have to wait for the archaeologist after Thanksgiving, to be sure.

Thea said, "I bet Mrs. Toussaint knows more about it than she's saying. Don't you feel like she knows almost everything that ever happened here?"

"Sort of," I agreed. My mind flashed back to that night at the Warwicks' kitchen table, when I'd blurted out about Alice but she wasn't surprised at all. A small seed of an idea floated into my head, something I hadn't even known I'd still be thinking about until I said it. "Hey, I bet she knows who got Alice pregnant."

"Yes!" Thea exclaimed, but then her face quickly reddened. "Oh, wait a minute—this is way too complicated. You don't really want to know that part, do you, Shawna?" Thea paused, then said with a strange look on her face, "But if you did want to know, I bet you could just ask Alice. On the phone, even."

I shook my head. "I could, I guess, but I'd want to see her face when I ask her. You know what I mean?"

"What if she won't tell you?"

"Then we'll have something else to investigate," I decided, remembering the science worksheets. "You'd help me figure it out, wouldn't you?"

Thea grinned at me. "Sure! Clues for something only fourteen years ago should be a lot easier to find than the ones for our project, anyway. Hey, that reminds me." Thea scrabbled in a handful of pages printed from her father's computer. "I've got some more numbers here." She pulled out a report from the state government and read aloud: "'The model involves 47 fugitives (33 males, 5 females, and 9 children).' Wow, that's a really, really small number. I mean, look at all the towns and Underground Railroad places in Vermont. That would mean nobody helped more than one or two people."

I looked over her shoulder. "But that number is just the people with 'detailed accounts' in letters and newspapers and all. Keep looking." I scanned the next few pages with her. "There! 'Numbers of Fugitives'—the National Park Service ... the information from Joseph Poland ... here, Thea, I've got it. It says one to four thousand fugitives between eighteen thirty and eighteen sixty is a 'credible working estimate.'"

"Great! Let's use three thousand, because it's easy to divide it by the thirty years between eighteen thirty and eighteen sixty." Her voice fell, discouraged. "Only a hundred fugitives a year for the whole state. And with North Upton not being very close to the border, and not very close to the route to Montreal," she sighed, "I guess one person per year would be the most."

Glumly, we looked at each other. This wasn't the news we wanted. Still, we had Mrs. Woodward's letter, and the locket that matched the one in the 1860 photograph, and the hiding place and tunnel, which could still be older than what Mrs. Toussaint remembered. And on our outline were also the real hiding place at the Goodwillie House only fifteen miles away, and all the local Vermonters who were against slavery in those days, including North Upton's Dr. Woodward.

At last, Thea said, "If this were a science experiment, this wouldn't be enough evidence. But I do think we have enough for a local history theory. That's what we can call it—a hypothesis being tested."

I tried the phrase. "A hypothesis being tested. Okay, I like it. Fingers crossed, maybe Mr. Harris will like it too, and we'll get to the state contest."

Someone knocked on Thea's bedroom door. It was Thaddeus. "Mom says you need to set the table for supper. She says we're eating early because the television show is at seven."

Outside, it was almost dark already. We pulled our papers back together and bounced down the stairs. Mr. Warwick came out of his office to help us lay out silverware and to ask about our project. He liked our description of a "hypothesis," and said that even in computers, a lot of the time his work involved guesses that could be tested but never completely proved. "You young ladies should be congratulated for not insisting that you know more than the evidence can support," he commented. I noticed he didn't say anything about changing his web site and the town's tourism plan, though.

Supper, thank goodness, was something I recognized: pizza. It had chunks of eggplant and spinach on it, instead of pepperoni, but it was still good. Some of the slices had chicken on them, but Thea avoided those, and I followed her example. If it made my best friend feel like there were two of us in this together, I had to try my best at this vegetarian thing. I watched how much salad Thea scooped onto her plate, and I did the same. I was almost full after we all had bowls of fruit salad for dessert.

"Girls, help me clear the dishes, while Bill turns on the TV," Thea's mother told us. "Thaddeus and Teddy, pajamas please, if you want to stay up and watch TV with everyone!"

For people who didn't watch much television, the Warwicks

had a lot of channels. Mr. Warwick seemed to know the Burlington news station, though. I lay on the floor next to Thea, big pillows under our elbows.

"Where's our house?" Thaddeus asked as he flopped down next to us.

"Ssh. It's coming."

We had to wait until almost the end of the news program. A blond woman in a low-cut blue blouse announced, "Thanks to the Lyndon State College news team, we'll take a detour to two locations in Vermont's Northeast Kingdom this evening. First is Lyndon Corner, where a young moose walked through the center of the village yesterday, followed by a curious crowd of onlookers."

"That's not our house," Teddy complained.

"Hush, just wait." His mother scooped him up in her lap. "Our house comes next."

Then the part about the Underground Railroad began.

"The college team on the road, Karyn Thomas and Evan Converse, have a lot to tell us about the importance of the Northeast Kingdom during a mysterious and romantic period of history: the years of the Underground Railroad, before the Civil War. Karyn, what role did our region play in helping fugitive slaves escape to freedom in those years?"

"Well, Bonnie, as you can see from our map here, the Northeast Kingdom was the final stage of moving fugitive slaves along the Underground Railroad to freedom in Canada. Nearly every historic house in this region has a hiding place to keep the desperate fugitives secret and safe. Imagine the women and older men doing this heroic work, while Vermont's young men enlisted to fight in the Civil War to free those slaves all across our country. Evan and I took the News Eleven cameras on the road in northeastern Vermont this month to see some of those locations."

I looked at Thea in horror. "They've got it wrong! They're saying it all wrong! They've mixed up even the years—the Underground Railroad years came before the war, not during it!"

Thea said, "This is so screwed up!"

"Hush," her father said, "let's see it all first, then we'll talk."

Shots of Barnet and Peacham and the Goodwillie House followed. The one of the hiding place at the Goodwillie House included a lit candle inside the cellar cubbyhole, casting flickering light on the rock walls. "Corny," I whispered.

The guy, Evan, spoke next. "Here in North Upton, our news team captured footage of a newly discovered secret hiding place in the historic two-hundred-year-old home of William and Barbara Warwick. The couple's young daughter, Thea Warwick, found the hiding place while playing in the cellar with a friend."

"Playing!" Thea pounded a fist on the floor. "It makes me sound five years old. And we weren't playing, we were measuring and mapping!"

The camera panned quickly over Thea's face down in the cellar and then focused on the professor, who was pointing to the places on the wall where the shelves had rested. Back to Karyn talking, although her face didn't show this time. "Professor Thomas, who chairs the American history group here at the college, shared his excitement about the discovery. Professor Thomas, what can you tell us about this significant historical find?"

Now the program showed the professor being filmed in his office, books stacked on his desk. "Well, of course, Karyn, we take this discovery very seriously. A great deal of research and study will focus on this site. I'm sure historians throughout New England will be glad to have another location to add to the maps of the Underground Railroad routes and conductors. We've only begun to scratch the surface of the material surrounding New England's heroic role in the abolition of slavery and in the Civil War."

And that was all! I couldn't believe it. And almost every word either wrong or confused or exaggerated. Thea and I already knew more facts and reality about what happened in Vermont in the eighteen hundreds than that news team—and even that college professor—did!

Behind us, the phone rang. Mr. Warwick went to answer it. "Yes, this is William Warwick. Excuse me? No, I don't think so. No, I'll have to call you back later in the week. I'm sorry, this isn't a good time. Give me your number and I'll get back to you during business hours."

He hung up and said bitterly, "The newspaper from Montpelier. They saw the news and they want to come do a story. This is crazy."

The phone rang again. "Hello? Who's calling? Oh, hello, Jennie. Yes, we saw it. Pretty amateur, wasn't it? Yes, I suppose you're right. I'll get to work on the web site right away. Thanks. Goodbye now."

Thea's father turned to us, saying, "Mrs. Toussaint just pointed out that all publicity is good in the long run, if the village wants more tourism in the spring."

Again the phone rang. "No, I'm sorry, there are no tours at this time. But there's a web site where you can look at photos and serious documents about the site. Well, perhaps in the spring. You can check the web site for details. I'm sorry, I need to go now. Thank you."

Rubbing his face, Mr. Warwick said to his wife, "I think I'll switch it over to the answering machine for the rest of the evening. Good with you?"

"Good with me," Mrs. Warwick confirmed. She stood up, lifting Teddy awkwardly to her waist. "I've got some boys to tuck into bed. I'll be down later. Come on, Thaddeus, you can read in bed."

I stood up too. "Good night, Mrs. Warwick. Thank you very much for lunch and supper."

"Oh, you're welcome, Shawna. Say hi to your mother for me."

"I will, thanks."

I ran upstairs to get my backpack from Thea's bedroom, then back down say goodbye to Thea.

"Starting tomorrow, we're on a crusade to get the truth out

there," she told me at the doorway. "Or else Mr. Harris is going to fail us both for history after all!" We laughed together, which was a good thing.

"He might do that," I agreed. "Tell you what, let's ask him to help us get a different kind of publicity. He ought to see this wasn't our fault!"

"Deal," Thea agreed.

I slipped out the door and into the cold night. It wasn't snowing yet, but the air tasted like winter. I stuffed my hand into my pockets—no necklace in there now, since I'd left it on Thea's desk—and headed home.

It was a huge relief to get into our own familiar kitchen and see a pan of gingerbread with chocolate frosting, already cut into chunks for serving. I scooped two into a dish, but then, remembering about Thea, I put one back. The blue glow of the TV and the laughter of a game show told me that Mom and Harry were still up. I went to say goodnight to them in the living room.

"How was the news program?" Harry asked me. "Were you on TV?"

"Nope, just Thea, and only for a second. And they screwed up half the things they said about her house. We couldn't believe it."

"Hey, it's just students, right?" Harry rumbled. "Give 'em a break."

I could see it would take too long to explain it all, so I shrugged and said, "Thea and I are going to write some stuff to correct what they did."

"Good, that's good."

My mother asked, "What did you have for supper?"

"Pizza. Hey, how were things up at camp?"

"Oh, I didn't stay all that long. Too many fools up in the woods still. It's safer down here! The Bryce boys got a deer, but so far, my buck is the largest."

"That's awesome, Mom." I headed back to the kitchen with my dish.

"Oh, Shawna? Alice called and asked what size you wear. I guess she's getting you some California clothes. She sounded excited about coming."

I didn't turn around, just called back to the living room, "Hey, that's what Thanksgiving is for, right? Family." I knew I was copying Harry's phrasing. The thing was, I just didn't have the energy to worry about Alice tonight. It had been a long, long weekend, and I wanted time alone in my own room, to think about things. Or not to think. I headed up the stairs.

NINE DAYS LEFT. Monday morning was November fourteenth; Alice would arrive at the Burlington airport on Wednesday of next week, November twenty-third. I felt like I had only nine days left of normal life.

The weather forecast had been on target: All Sunday night, snow fell, and Monday morning was definitely winter. Each tree branch held a long pillow of sparkling snow. Where there were brown leaves that hadn't fallen to the ground, they dangled from twigs, glittering. Most magical of all were the evergreens, caped in layers of white and dark, their fronds and clusters of needles turned to lace.

Under my sweatshirt, I wore a fuzzy turtleneck that curled up against my chin and made my arms seem long and smooth. It felt good to pull on winter boots—the ones with thick wool felt liners in them, and fake fur at the top edges. But it was hard bending over in the thick down-stuffed jacket. Unzipping it helped. I heard Thea calling from the porch and grabbed my backpack, eager to get outside.

She said there was a new message on the answering machine

at her house, a message that told people to leave a message but that there would be no tours of the house until spring. "Why are people so crazy about the Underground Railroad?" she asked as we kicked up snow in the driveway and took long sliding steps in the slush along the road. "It's, like, everyone wants to say something about it and come and touch it. Our phone never rang like this before."

"I guess it's exciting," I said. "You know, that people around here helped save other people, and kept them secret and all. It really worked, didn't it? That's cool all by itself."

"I guess." Thea unbuttoned her jacket, showing a matching fleece vest underneath. "Whew, I'm hot! It's not as cold outside as it looked."

"Not if you're moving around. So, who's coming to visit your family next week for Thanksgiving?"

"Nobody! We're going to Connecticut. We're leaving Wednesday morning, so I'll miss the half day of school. But we're coming back Friday afternoon. My dad said he wants the rest of the long weekend for working on stuff at home."

"So," I tried to sound casual, "so, on Friday evening, maybe you'd like to come meet my sister Alice?"

"Definitely! Hey, maybe we can take in a picture of you and her for extra credit in science class, showing how your eyes don't match and all. Oh—oh, we don't have to, if you don't want to," she added quickly. "I mean, maybe you don't want to do the family tree thing, with Alice making it so, um, complicated."

"Yeah, well." I stopped for a moment and stamped my feet, shaking the snow off my boots. I didn't want to get within earshot of the other kids yet. "Mrs. Toussaint said the older grownups all know about Alice anyway. Do you think the kids do, too?"

I don't know why I asked Thea. How was she going to know what the kids in North Upton did or didn't know?

She had an answer, though. "I bet they don't. Plus, everyone can see that your mom is your mom, now, and it works, so it's not a big deal. Not like the Underground Railroad," she said with a burst of frustration. "God, I wish people would stop calling our house!" Her voice softened. "Anyway, if you just say it straight out, that Alice had you when she was a teenager, with the father gone—if you say it without apologizing or acting funny about it, people will accept it. Hey, they accept me being a flatlander who doesn't like hunting season, right?"

I laughed with her. "Everybody likes you, Thea. You don't have to like hunting."

"And you don't have to pretend about your family."

We walked closer to the school. I changed the subject: "So, what will you do in Connecticut? Are there lots of cousins and all?"

"Nope. Our family is the only part that has children. But my grandmother is a great cook, and my grandfather always lets us make s'mores at the fireplace after dinner, and there are tons of books. You'd like it!"

A snowball whizzed past us, and we ducked. The next one splattered my jacket, and Thea bent swiftly to scoop up a handful and toss it back at the Willson twins. She got Marsha on the shoulder. She whispered to me, "I forgot to tell you. Josh sent me a CD from his band! Betcha Marsha and Merry don't even have one."

A whistle blew from up at the top of the school steps. Mr. Harris called out, "No snowball fights on school grounds. You all know that." Above him, the bell started ringing for homeroom. We tramped inside, into the steamy warmth of the overheated hallway and then into the noise of our homeroom.

All day, everyone goofed around. The first real snow made it a happy day, and hardly any of it melted, so at lunchtime, the boys made three snowmen, decorating each one with bits of lunch: cookies for eyes, carrot noses, and slices of apple for mouths. Maryellen Bryce's red scarf went around one snowman neck, and the other two wore hats—a couple of kids' heads would be cold this afternoon!

After school, since there was hardly any homework, I got permission from my mother to ride into town with Thea's family to go grocery shopping. I had an energy bar in my pocket just in case, but it turned out that the grocery store was giving free samples of crescent rolls and cranberry sauce and even cupcakes. Thea watched me taking "just one" of each sample, and then we hurried to pick out the things that Mrs. Warwick kept asking us to find while she ordered at the deli counter and managed Teddy.

When I got home, I pulled on barn clothes and gave Harry and Mom a hand. The kittens were big enough now to run around all over the side of the barn where the youngest calves stood. After I got the floors scraped and the sawdust spread, I filled the calf bottles with formula and fed the three clumsy babies, which stepped all over my feet and dribbled milk on the floor, but smelled good and felt like oversized puppies as I hugged their necks and guided each to the nipple. I'd forgotten how good the cow barn could be.

The whole week went that way, easy, uncomplicated. Carl held a coaching meeting with the basketball team, and Kyle called me the day after, even though he didn't need to. I wished Alice weren't coming. Why spoil things?

The last two full days of school before Thanksgiving turned out to be stormy, dumping more snow on us, and, on Tuesday night, freezing rain that caked the trees and buildings with a quarter-inch layer of ice. The power went out Tuesday evening for three hours, and I wondered whether Thea and her family would still go to Connecticut for the holiday. But when I got up on Wednesday morning, I could see the Warwicks' car out in their driveway, steam and exhaust puffing from the tailpipe. Mr. Warwick was spreading sand on the driveway to stop it being slippery. I ran out of our house, in boots but without a coat, to wave goodbye. "See you Friday night!" Thea called, over the chaos of her younger brothers and all the bags being loaded in the car.

As they drove away, the cold and an uncomfortable loneliness swept over me. I hugged my sweatshirt close around me and hurried back inside, careful not to slip on the icy porch steps. My mother stood at the stove, flipping pancakes.

"Harry and I are headed to the airport in about twenty minutes," my mother reminded me. "Are you sure you don't want to come with us? I'm sure your teachers wouldn't mind if you missed the half day."

"No, thanks. I need to go to the library, anyway."

"Okay. But would you wash the dishes before you leave for school, Shawna? I'd like to come home to a clean kitchen."

"Yeah, sure."

At seven thirty, in the empty house, I finished rinsing the plates and turned off the hot water. A line of pies was on the countertop—my mother's signal that this Thanksgiving had to be good. Alice's photo up on the wall looked sad and serious. My stomach churned. I didn't want to see her or talk to her and know she'd given birth to me. Every time I started to think about it, I felt hungry and sick at the same time.

Half the kids weren't even at school that morning. After I checked in with Miss Calkins, I asked if I could go to the library, instead of reading in class. She nodded, and I scooped up a notebook and pen and headed down the hall.

The stuffy room was empty at first, but a few minutes later, Mrs. Toussaint came in, and when she saw me, she smiled.

"Shawna," she said. "Good. I was afraid I wouldn't be able to catch you until after the holidays. Look—I was able to order these copies from the Census papers in Burlington. I thought you and your friend might be able to use them in your history project."

I spread the pages out on the nearby table. "Eighteen fifty," I noted with pleasure. "And these aren't at the town clerk's office, or on the Internet?

"Not yet," Mrs. Toussaint said. "Things take time. Sometimes research means putting on your walking shoes and going someplace else."

My attention on the tiny columns of hand-written information blurred what she was saying. I murmured, "Mmm-hm," and kept looking. There: the numbers for "white" people and "free colored." If black people were hiding during 1850, using the

Underground Railroad system, they wouldn't be listed in the public records under "free colored" at all, right? Of course there would be no slaves listed; Vermont's state constitution banned slavery from the start.

I ran my finger carefully along the numbers. White people in the state, 313,402. "How many people live in Vermont now?"

"About six hundred thousand," came the librarian's reply.

"So we've doubled in total people," I calculated quickly. "And in eighteen-fifty—wow, seven hundred and eighteen free colored people in the state. That seems like a lot more than I would have guessed!"

"Keep looking."

I examined Caledonia County, looking for Upton, which would include Upton Center and North Upton as well. For the county, there were 23,584 white people—and only eleven people were free colored.

There was Upton: oh! Out loud, I told Mrs. Toussaint what she'd probably already seen herself: "Six of the eleven free colored people in the county lived in Upton. More than half! But Mrs. Toussaint—if they're on this list and everything, they weren't hiding here at all, were they?"

"It's all in the evidence," she replied. "You've got the numbers in your own hands, haven't you?"

I needed to tell Thea about this, to show her the papers. I glanced at my watch. Fifty-six hours until she'd be back.

Mrs. Toussaint looked at me, and her smile told me she guessed how much this would mean to our project, even if it did erase the chances of the secret room being a hiding place for fugitive slaves. "It's always better in the long run to have the truth," she added, cocking her head to one side and waiting for me to admit it.

"Some truths aren't very nice," I said.

"But they taste better in the long run, if you're grown up enough to swallow them," the librarian said with a nod. She peered into my face, then looked at the big clock up on the wall. "It's almost noon. You can take those copies with you, Shawna.

Check back with me on Monday, please, in case there are more by then. Have a good Thanksgiving."

I heaped the pages back into their folder, put it on top of my notebook, and said a quick thanks. A splash of sunshine from outside suddenly lit the little room. "You have a good holiday, too," I said, and headed back to my homeroom.

I knew the time to drive to Burlington and back, and the likely waiting time at the airport. Mom and Harry and Alice could already be at the house. Everyone in homeroom was hurrying, packing their bags and pulling on jackets and calling out "Have a happy Turkey Day" or "See you after Thanksgiving" or even "See you tomorrow" if they were cousins. I grabbed my things.

A hand on my wrist interrupted me as I stuffed the library folder in with my books. I looked up.

"Hey," said Kyle Everts. "Hey, I'll walk with you, okay? I'm not taking the bus today, and I've got time."

His reddish-brown hair stuck out at the edges of an orange wool cap, and he had a green wool jacket and big orange mittens on, made of orange leathery plastic except for where the thumb stuck out, knitted in orange wool, and the first two fingers, likewise. "Are those for shooting?" I asked him. He flushed. "Yeah, but I didn't get a deer at all last weekend. Maybe tomorrow."

"You're going hunting on Thanksgiving?" I picked up my backpack and slung it over my shoulder. A couple of kids looked over at us. We merged into the line pressing out of the classroom.

"Yeah, in the morning. I mean, the morning's the best, anyway. I'll be home for dinner by two, I guess. Unless I have to carry a buck or something, and then I'd go get my dad anyway."

Really curious now, I asked, "Where's your family's camp?"

Kyle flushed even redder. "We don't have one. I just kind of hunt up on the hill beyond the Sleepers River. I'm pretty good at tracking."

"Decent." I felt like I'd embarrassed him. "Hunting without a camp is cool. I mean, you have to have more skills, to carry your stuff and the rifle and everything. And still be really quiet.

And get in front of the deer." I rambled on, sounding like some dumb kid. He didn't seem to mind.

"Yeah, but it's hard," he shrugged. "Hey, I hear your mother already got her deer. How many points?"

"Six. She doesn't always get one that big, though." Was I apologizing for my mother's big buck?

"Awesome." He changed the subject, and I realized we were already halfway to my house. "You got company coming for Thanksgiving?"

It was my turn to blush. "Just my sister Alice, from California. And my brothers will be there, of course."

"Hey, tell Carl I said hey? I can't wait for practice. It's gonna be wicked."

"Maybe I could tell him you're around for the holiday," I offered. "Maybe he could get the gym key over the weekend."

"That would be great!" He stopped and so did I, at the foot of our driveway, by the tractor barn. "I'd like to hear more about the tunnel that you found, too. Could I—maybe I'll call you later on?"

"Thea found the tunnel with me," I added quickly. "Yeah, sure, call me after supper."

"Thanks! Talk to you later." He brushed a mittened hand against my shoulder, smiled, and strode quickly along the roadside, headed out of the village.

I watched for a moment, not sure why I felt so happy and uncertain at once. Then I finally looked down at the driveway. Fresh tracks from the truck. Mom and Harry were home.

Along with Alice.

I WALKED SLOWLY UP the driveway, watching my boots make deep prints along the edge. The truck tires had bitten deep through the snow, all the way down to the dirt under it, and some sun-melt dripped along the ridges of the tire tracks, sparkling. I squinted against the sunlight. The closer I got to our front porch, the slower I walked.

Easing the lightweight porch door open, I slipped in and stepped out of my boots. Three other pairs stood there, almost dry in the sun: Harry's old black pair, my mother's Canadian green ones, and a fancy, clean pair in black leather with high heels, side zippers open, letting the sides flop loosely onto the floor.

I eased out of my down jacket—I knew it made me look fat, so I left it on the bench, with my dark blue mittens stuffed in the pockets. The backpack needed to come in with me; I slid the straps up my arm onto my shoulders. With one hand I tucked my turtlenecked shirt into my jeans, and then tugged the sweatshirt down to be smooth and snug over it. I reached up to comb my fingers through my hair, wishing I had a hairbrush.

My chest felt tight. I forced myself to take a breath, then held it to be more quiet, and eased open the wooden door into the kitchen.

Harry sat at the table, and as I came in, he nodded and raised his eyebrows at me. Behind him my mother was standing at the sink, running the water and talking loudly over it. "I'd like to paint it again," she was saying, "maybe in two tones of pink, walls sort of a shell pink and the woodwork just a bit darker and glossy. I've got a wallpaper border of shells to go along the top of the walls."

From the bathroom down the hall, a voice replied, "Better to strip the woodwork and have it be natural wood, Mom. Natural wood's always better looking. I can send you a picture of what I did in my apartment so you'll see what I mean."

The toilet flushed, the sink in the bathroom splashed, and a moment later the door opened. I stared.

Alice looked nothing like the photo up on our wall. I could see that it was her, but her face, so round and serious in the photo, was tan and slender with dramatic cheekbones now, and her eyes, lined with some dark stuff, stood out amazingly. Blond highlights framed her face. A row of three sparkling earrings traced one ear lobe; I couldn't see the other. Instead of a shirt or turtleneck and sweater, she wore a clingy, soft blouse that wrapped across her flat midriff, and instead of slacks or jeans, she had on something stretchy that I realized looked like the yoga pants from Thea's closet.

She stared at me for a second, then squealed my name. "Shawna! Oh my gosh—you're all grown up!"

I was rooted in place, but she leapt across the kitchen and tugged my backpack off my shoulders until it thudded onto the floor. Alice threw her arms around me. Her hair bounced against my face, fragrant like coconut and flowers, and her warm cheek pressed against my chilled one as she whispered in my ear, "You're beautiful, you know that?" She was taller than I was, but not by much. I felt my arms go up on their own, to give a half-hearted hug back to her.

Harry said, "You two girls make quite a picture. City mouse and country mouse, I would say. Come sit down, your mother's got lunch on the table."

Lots of big serving dishes, the company china dishes looking wildly out of place—I saw how much work my mother had done already. I wanted to be really nice, and I wanted to stamp my feet and cry.

I eased out of Alice's hug. "Hey," I croaked. "You look great. Welcome back to the frozen north."

Alice pulled out a chair and turned it partway around, about to sit down, then suddenly turned and walked off into the TV room, saying, "I just need to breathe for a minute, I'll be right back."

Breathe? Didn't everyone breathe anyway? I guess it was like that thing she did on the phone. And yoga pants. Wow.

Alice came back into the room, not quite looking at any of us. "Sorry about that. It's just jet lag, probably. Come sit, Shawna. Let's eat, I'm starving, can you believe it's only nine in the morning, California time? Eat, and then we can do presents. I brought you stuff you won't believe." She tossed her hair and gave a crooked grin. "I remember how bad the clothing stores are back here. Do you still order pajamas from the Sears catalogue?"

"J. C. Penney's now," my mother said with a smile. "And there's a store, not just the catalogue. Maybe we'll all go shopping on Saturday."

"Mmm." My sister—my mother—the person who'd given birth to me—unfolded a napkin and spread it over her lap, and bowed her head for grace, reaching out to take my hand and Harry's. We didn't usually hold hands for grace at home, just at church, and we definitely didn't do grace at lunchtime, but I saw Harry and Mom going along with it, so I figured I should as well. It felt so strange to hold Alice's hand. We all kind of sat there, waiting for her to start or something, but she kept her eyes closed and didn't say anything. My hand started to get sweaty. Finally, Harry cleared his throat.

"Lord God, we ask your blessing on this meal we share, and on the hands that prepared it," Harry began, "and we thank you with full hearts for this time to be together. We thank you, Lord, for the beauty and liveliness of these two girls, these two young women, and we ask your protection for all the people traveling home this weekend. In Jesus's name and for his sake, Amen."

"Amen," came the quiet echo from my mother and sister. Grandmother and mother. No, I couldn't see it that way. No way.

"I can't," I said out loud. "I can't change who you are to me."

"Good," said my mother, almost prayerfully.

"Works for me," added Alice, too cheerful. "Don't change who you are to us, either. You're the cutest little sister in the world."

"I'm not," I retorted. "I'm fat, and I'm boring, and I live in the boonies." And the stuff that I'd told myself I was going to keep buttoned up started spilling out—I already regretted saying it, even before I'd said it, but I couldn't stop. "And I don't want you to be my mother and I'm not sure about being sisters, either. Everybody in this room lied to me for years."

Harry pulled his chair closer to my mother's but didn't say anything. Neither did my mother—or Alice's mother. My head ached with how stupid this all was.

Alice took a deep breath, and I thought she was going to do her whole breathing thing again, but she started to talk, slower, her voice a little lower pitched.

"I've been trying to decide whether I ran away from here, or got pushed away," she began. "And on the airplane, I figured out there was a third explanation. I didn't really fit in here. That's not a good thing or a bad thing," she said directly to Mom and Harry. "It is what it is. I love where I am today, and who I am. I love sunlight and avocadoes and the ocean, and a church full of new people who haven't always lived someplace. And I love my job."

I interrupted. "You have a job?"

Alice gave a crooked grin. "Yep. I work in a veterinarian's office. In about a zillion years, I'll have the working equivalent of a vet's assistant and get my certification. Half the dogs and cats and parrots and cockatiels of Marin County depend on me and my bosses." She stopped abruptly, like a faucet turning off, and turned to Mom. "I keep forgetting—she's not a little kid!"

Nobody said anything. I looked at my plate. I hadn't even noticed what was on it. Now I saw there was a scoop of potato salad and another of pasta salad, with a bowl of some kind of green soup getting cold next to it. I looked up at Mom.

"Vegetarian," Mom confirmed. "Alice is a vegetarian, Shawna. When your brothers come tonight, we'll have ham, but this lunch is for Alice."

"Thanks, Mom," Alice said, but she looked at me instead.

"I'm a vegetarian, too," I said. Mom raised her eyebrows but said nothing. "Since Sunday. Thea's teaching me how to do it."

Harry nodded. "She's a nice girl, that Thea. How's her little brother doing?"

"Good."

Things stalled again. I thought about my best friend, and it made me say something to Alice after all. "Thea—that's my best friend. You'll get to see her Friday. She wants to meet you."

"Does she, umm, does she know about me?" The California sunshine was a little shakier, hesitant.

Now I looked right into her eyes. "*Everybody* knows about you," I said. "Except me, I guess. Nobody told me."

My mother broke in. "We've told you now," she reminded me. "We all need your help in this, Shawna. We can't make this work without you. We did it for you in the first place, and each one of us wants it to turn out right. What do you want this to be?"

I looked away from everyone's eyes, fastening my gaze outside the window, where the driveway led toward the main road and the empty Warwick house. After a moment, I said, "I want us to be as normal a family as possible. I don't want any more lies, for any reason. And ... I think Carl and Emerson just pulled in."

The truck outside gave a loud blast of the horn, and my brothers stamped up onto the porch, kicking off their boots.

Mom and Harry jumped up to set more places at the table. Alice leaned toward me, an urgency in her voice as she grabbed my hand.

"And that goes for me, too," she said, and her voice was different, a little shaky again, but more serious. "Because I also need to know about you, Shawna. Who you are, what you do, what you want. I need to know how to send you the right stuff, not dumb old Halloween costumes. So—what do you like?"

The door whipped open and cold air and loud happy voices flew into the house. The amount of noise that my brothers made always seemed disproportionate to just two people, like an exponent or something.

"Math," I said, the first thing that popped into my head. I could feel myself blush. It sounded so childish that way. But I couldn't help it; it was true, and I knew it was true. "Yeah, and that was how my friend Thea and I became friends, because we were the only girls in the eighth grade who knew about numbers."

Alice stared at me and snorted, but kind of in a friendly way. "Math? Are you kidding? I'm hopeless with numbers and stuff." She wrinkled her nose, thinking. "But," she added brightly, "I'm awesome at organizing! Which—um, is kind of like math?" She pulled out a fancy cell phone and thumbed it on as she handed it to me. "Check it out."

Emerson and Carl came into the room, and she bounced out of her chair and across to them, giving each of them the same shoulder punch they always gave to me.

I looked at the photo that jumped onto the lit-up phone screen and realized it was me. Alice's phone showed a photo of me, every time she turned it on.

It shook me, because it was evidence. It was evidence that Alice wanted me in her life, or at least she wanted to look at me, even though she lived in California. Maybe she even showed my picture to her yoga friends out there.

Just then, our house phone rang, and Mom answered it. "Just a minute."

She waved the receiver at me and put it down, returning to pouring mugs of coffee. I went over, still holding Alice's phone too, and said, "Hello?"

"Shawna? It's Kyle. I—yeah. I just wanted to say, some of us are going sliding tonight on the big hill behind the school. There's supposed to be a full moon for it. I've got a wicked good sled. Think you could come?"

"I think so." I looked at the others, tangled across the table in talk and laughter. "I should have some things straightened out by then. What time?"

"Seven," Kyle told me. "I'll be at your place at five of. Dress warm!"

"I will," I agreed. "See you later."

People were so busy talking that nobody asked me who I had just talked to. At least that was almost private for now! Alice asked for her phone back, and started showing other pictures around the table. I sat back in my chair and listened as everyone talked about the snapshots of Alice's apartment, the beach nearby, and even her new boyfriend, as well as the church in California. Then Mom started laying out a stack of old photos on the kitchen table, photos I was pretty positive I'd never even seen before: of Alice as a kid, chunky, almost like me. One of the photos caught my eye, and I quietly slid it off the table and into my lap, to look at in private—a picture of Alice from before she left home, with a tall blond boy with dark brown eyes. It had to be him.

I kept the picture in my lap, under my napkin. When we all cleared the table, in order to wash the china to have it ready again for tomorrow's holiday feast, I tucked the photo into my backpack, inside the folder from Mrs. Toussaint with the lists of people who'd lived in North Upton in 1850 and who their relatives had been.

And when everyone else went to the barn to rush through the milking chores together, and Alice and I finally sat alone over mugs of California tea, I pulled out the photo and set it on the table.

"Is that ... him?" My throat cramped up.

Alice bit her lip and stared at the picture. "Yeah," she finally said. "But he didn't know about you. I never thought about you wanting to know about him instead. Do you?"

"Sort of," I admitted. "Maybe. Maybe not right away, after all, though. It's not what I expected."

"That's for sure," Alice said. She folded her hands on top of her stomach. I guessed at what she was thinking.

"Alice," I asked at last, "do you miss me in California?"

"I do, Shawna," my big sister said, putting down the old photo and smiling at me, a real smile. "And I'm going to take some good photos of you while I'm here. I want to take pictures of you and your friends, and the cats, and of course your secret room thing, and all that. With you and Thea in the room."

I thought about pictures of me and Thea getting shown to people in California. Then I thought about sliding in the moonlight behind the school, with Kyle. Having a family home for Thanksgiving, and four kinds of pie. Vegetarian pie. And seeing Thea again on Friday, and finding out what her Thanksgiving was like, and introducing her to Alice.

"Sure," I answered. "She's my best friend, you know."

"I've always wanted a best friend," Alice agreed. "And to find a secret room."

In the quiet kitchen, I almost said my theory out loud, but decided at the last moment to keep it inside and look at it a little longer.

Even a little kid knows when something doesn't quite fit, so probably I'd known all along that my family had a secret, but I didn't have the words before, or even the right questions.

Take one family, any family, and imagine they have a secret room. How can you tell what's in there, and why?

I could almost feel the doorknob turn in my hand.

AUTHOR'S NOTE

Almost everyone I've met admits they've looked for a secret room or a hidden compartment someplace. In Vermont, where I live, and in New Jersey, where I grew up, people often expect those cleverly concealed places to connect with the heroic stories of the Underground Railroad.

The Underground Railroad wasn't a train, of course (although lots of younger kids think it might be, and go looking for it); it was a network of dedicated Americans who believed every human being had the right to live free, "in pursuit of happiness," and tried to help African Americans reach places where that would be possible. Although there are wonderful records of some of the work done by these helpful allies, both black and white, many well-meaning people have confused the historical records. The 1996 (real) report "Friends of Freedom: The Vermont Underground Railroad Survey Report," explained kindly that "The Vermont Underground Railroad was not an organized movement." It didn't have "stations" at people's houses, or definite routes from one safety zone to another. But it did have anti-slavery activists who acted as guides for fugitive slaves, many of whom may have reached the state through "vigilance committees" in Philadelphia, New York City, and Boston.

Is the (real) hidden room at the Goodwillie House in Barnet a former hiding place for fugitives? When abolitionist leader Willam Lloyd Garrison visited nearby Peacham, was he meeting with people who sheltered runaways? Many of the "secret rooms" in northeastern Vermont were used instead to hide whiskey during the years when it wasn't legal to make, transport, or consume it—and in Vermont, those years extended from 1850 to 1902, then with the rest of the nation from 1920 to 1933. Sorting out this tangled braid of places and causes is an endless detective story.

The Secret Room is placed in a village more or less like North Danville, Vermont, which gave me the pattern of houses and family histories. But it is entirely fiction. The stage route ran nearby but not directly here, and the tunnel grew from my imagination. Part of the magic of writing these details, though, was finding out later that there is a water tub on a nearby farm that has always been talked about as "for the stage horses," and one neighbor even recalled a tunnel in another part of the village. The Census details, on the other hand, are both real and accurate: More than seven hundred "free colored" people lived in Vermont before the Civil War, including in the "real" Danville. For me, that number reshapes the common picture of Vermont's past.

I appreciate Gerald LaMothe's history of North Danville village (*One Village, Two Centuries, Several Families*) but didn't base the characters in this novel on the actual families that he described. My thanks go to Alice Lee and Steve Cobb, each of whom agreed to lend a name within the story, and each of whom exhibits some of the kinds of courage that I hope are captured here.

When I write a book, I lean on a team of chapter-by-chapter readers who keep me going and watch the details, and another team of careful historians to help sort out different kinds of truth. This time, special support came from Lois, Katherine, Ruth, Cheryl, Josette, Hilary, and the ladies at the Danville Inn, who remember many kinds of family adventures. In addition to Gerald LaMothe's work and the town histories of St. Johnsbury, Barnet, Peacham, and Danville, I received great insight from Peggy Pearl, Mary Prior, Dave Warden, Lynn Bonfield, and the research and writings of Jane Williamson of Rokeby. My husband Dave and my sons Kiril and Alexis kept me balanced during the long writing process.

Finally, my thanks go to Adrienne Raphel, editor extraordinaire, who saw the secret rooms hidden within this book, and helped me to find the entrances.